RUNE MAGIC

THEA ATKINSON

Have you got your free ebook yet?

Be sure to visit http://theaatkinson.com to get your freebie.

CHAPTER ONE

I EXPECTED A DEATH mask to be more frightening, to be honest. As it was, the life-sized mask just looked like a plaster cast of a mannequin's face with about as much vitality as a plant pot. There was no life in it. Nothing to fear in the least as far as I could tell.

And yet it terrified the woman standing in front of me. She had brought the thing into my shop twenty minutes earlier in a fabric bag that she probably got at a boutique store since the handles were gold satin ribbon. The bag sat on my counter a hand span away. The mask resting in my palms did not feel boutique. It felt rough and homemade.

"You say your grandfather made it of your mother when she died?"

The blank expression molded forever into the plaster effigy I held looked fairly serene. I turned it over as I waited for the woman to say more. The faint markings of skin texture captured during the molding faded away at the edges. I thought I could detect a few hairs stuck in the plaster.

I was considering running my finger over what looked like a red strand until she spoke, distracting me.

"He was old when my mother died," she said. "Probably seventy."

A sharp glance up at her proved she had to be at least seventy herself. The well-coiffed hair cut into a neat bob was completely white, but it had a youthful curl on the ends that curved around her earlobe where she'd tucked it back. Snappy black eyes peered back at me with a girlish vigor. I was willing to bet she was a fire cracker in her day.

She must have caught some expression of surprise on my face because she sighed with resignation.

"I know what you're thinking," she said and shifted her handbag to her elbow from her wrist. "The mask is very old. My mother died in childbirth. Teenage pregnancy. I never knew my father." A small flicker of humor played in her eyes. "I never knew my grandfather either, really. I was ten when he passed away."

The mental math on that one made me wonder if she had lived with the old man until that time or if she'd been passed off to the care of another relative. Then my mind went to all sorts of possibilities. That was the trouble with a traumatic childhood; you saw bogeymen everywhere.

I placed the benign looking object on my counter with incredible care. Knowing it was a relic with a fair amount of age, no matter how scared she was of it, added the need for an extra layer of caution. I'd hate to break the thing when all she'd asked me for was a good old fashioned exorcism.

My gaze studied it instead, inspecting curves of features from a few inches away as I leaned over and panned across it with a practiced air. I wasn't averse to performing an exorcism, it was just that I'd decided to try to go the straight and narrow, and exorcisms definitely weren't on my newfound high road to goodness.

She waited patiently while I noted the grime around the edges of the facade, oiled from too much handling. The patina matched certain colors in my burled wood counter top. The surface had cost me a pretty penny, but I didn't regret one coin because I loved it. It reminded me of a short time in my life when things felt normal.

Now, catching sight of it, I inhaled sharply at the sight of a huge gouge in the surface, a leftover gift from the man who had tried to kill me two months earlier by swiping at me with a scythe and digging it into the top. A grim reminder that my present was anything but normal anymore.

I straightened up a little too quickly at the memory, and blackness swam around the edges of my vision.

I kept my gaze away from the gash in the center that ruined the shellac and the river of blue paint that had been artistically poured into the crevices left behind by bugs and decay when the wood was a living tree.

Reminders of the psycho who tried to end my life, and who left that huge dig marring the surface were about as wanted as a seven year itch. I tried to keep a desk blotter over it so I wouldn't end up spoiling the whole counter.

The blotter usually did its trick but sometimes, like today when a client ran their hands over the surface, it got pushed aside and the memories came flooding back. I still had no idea what the man had wanted or why he was killing psychics and witches, and neither had the police.

That mystery looked like it was going to go unsolved. The newspapers mentioned it now and again, but people seemed to have breathed a sigh of relief and went on to worrying about crimes that affected them and not a caste of society they thought of as charlatans anyway. Seems we were as disposable as prostitutes.

I was of the mind that if it never got solved but never fell at my doorstep again, I could be OK with the mystery going cold too.

I settled my gaze on the mask. "He must have loved her very much," I said to the woman, swaying a bit as my blood pressure normalized.

"I would assume so," she said. "Although I haven't seen the thing in decades. I thought it had got tossed when he died, but I found it in a box of things in the attic when I had to clean everything out."

She eyed me as though she expected me to ask for more information, and then added in the answer I didn't ask for. "I'm not getting any younger and his house is far too big to stay in alone anymore. I'm moving to a nice senior's apartment."

I didn't want to judge, but I thought it odd that a man would memorialize his daughter that way; evidently, she did too because she made a sound deep in her throat that caught my attention. When I looked at her, her face was pinched, as though she wanted to be done with the transaction and flee back into the street.

"When you phoned, you told me it was cursed," I said, trying to segue back to the issue at hand.

She nodded and I noticed she wouldn't look at the mask as it sat between us.

"Do you think you can neutralize it?" she said. "I don't really want to get rid of the mask but..."

I sighed heavily. I never really did anything magical no matter what my shop sign declared. Everything I managed came from the practiced art of misdirection and character study blended with a host of skills and knowledge that lent me the air of a true spiritualist.

I'd got good at that sort of thing over the last three years. And I wasn't ashamed to admit to myself that much of the skill had come from my mother. She'd claimed to be a witch and kept a trove of relics and books that would put a horror movie to shame. It was only lately, after her death that I began to think there was more to her claims than I'd realized.

Even so, I'd worked at cultivating a reputation as a woman of power because even if my mother might have had some magical abilities, I did not. I'd duped a good deal of people in the name of paying my mortgage. I'd even recently managed to pick up a little work through the police, lending them insights into cases that I touted as magical but that were just plain old psychology. Things they could have figured out for themselves if they'd taken a step back from the evidence.

But some things had changed. After discovering my mother's amulet and grimoire possessed real magic, after the police officer who had requested my insights into a series of murders turned out to be a wolf shifter, I didn't take things at face value anymore.

As incredible as it was, I'd had to face the fact that magic existed. That didn't mean I had to face what I thought about my mother or the things she'd done to me as a kid that sent me on the run and then into the foster care system. I didn't think I owed her any more than a passing interest in the things she'd left me that allowed me to pretend to be the kind of woman my clients needed.

Admittedly, I'd used more than just my good instincts with my clients. Recently, I'd used a bit of psyche-delics to aid me in my 'magic', offering those who were resistant to believing but who desperately wanted to believe, some way to get there.

I didn't use the psychedelics anymore. It had never felt right anyway, and nearly getting caught and convicted of the offense had set me on the good and righteous path. But I did still practice the art of the con when I had to in order to keep my shop running, and I tried to keep the majority of my revenue to innocent sales of candles and potions and paraphernalia.

I couldn't afford to be picky, and I would rather put my talents to use helping people instead of duping them, but the bank didn't care about my druthers whatsoever.

What this elderly lady was asking of me was something I would have charged a fair bit for in my previous life. Anything that required research and spiritualistic connections brought in a pretty penny. Add in a bit of mystique and danger and you had the makings of a full months' mortgage.

This woman was exactly the kind of client I preferred. Namely, a woman who needed help healing when she thought she needed something else. I might not have true magic, but I did know a thing or two about human nature, and while I was far from a therapist, one thing I was good at was helping them come to terms with their past.

I didn't want to admit to myself that some of that might have come from the psychedelics, but I supposed it didn't matter in the end. So long as they went away more at peace than they'd come, I didn't feel bad taking their money and they always left feeling better than when they'd come. Win win in my book.

So when she'd phoned, I'd agreed. In the past, I'd have tried to eke out as much service revenue as I could. Now I gave her what truth I knew and let her decide what direction this would go.

"I don't specialize in that sort of thing," I said as I ran my finger down along the inside of the mask's cheekbone. Yes, definitely a hair. I had to fight the urge to scrape it out of the plaster cast. "Exorcisms are difficult and unreliable."

"I'm willing to try if you will," she said. "I'd like to keep the mask since it's the only thing I have of my mother's." She gave me a wry smile. "You must think it's creepy to want to keep a death mask, but..." she trailed off with a shrug.

"I don't think it's creepy at all." I pulled my hands back across the counter to shove in my pockets. It was the only way I could keep from digging into the plaster to extract that hair. "I just don't know if I can do anything about the— what did you say it was doing again?"

Her gaze dropped to the mask sheepishly. "It watches me," she said. "There are times when I look at it that I can swear the eyes are moving."

"Painters study how to create that effect," I said, remembering a visual artist who once told me it was easy to make a painting's eyes follow you through the room once you knew the trick.

She tapped the counter in the direction of the mask. "But this one isn't painted," she said countering my rationale. My fingers curled and uncurled in my pockets as I resisted the urge to pick it up again and scratch at the hairs on the edge.

"You can leave it here with me if you like. Pick it up in a week."

I gave it a thoughtful glance, assessing the amount of time it would take to figure out how to dissuade the woman of the trauma that no doubt fostered her suspicion of the thing without faking some mojo to make her believe I'd exorcised it.

"Happy to," she said with a shudder that made her necklace move against the lily white of her chest. "I'll pay in advance."

She started digging through her purse, a name brand that I knew was being knocked off and sold in the tourist section, and yet this one was the real thing. The suppleness of the leather was the first giveaway, and when she ran her fingers over the clasp, it drew my eye to the logo stamped into the metal. The stitches were even and the label on the inside was crisp and clear.

The woman had money.

She pulled out a wallet equally as authentic as her bag and rifled through it. I wanted to tell her she shouldn't be carrying around such a wad of cash so close to the docks, but she pulled out the entire wad instead of selecting a few bills.

She held them over the top of her purse with a flourish. The bills smelled of spearmint and old fabric. A flash of memory made my cheeks water as I tasted again the cloistered taste of gum harbored in the depths of a purse for months on end.

I squeezed out the image of the mother who'd passed a stick to me from her side of the car as she pushed me out into a hostile schoolyard with the comment that if I went to school like a good girl, she'd put a hex on the bullies for me.

"I want to keep this memento," the woman in front of me said, pulling my attention back to the present. "I don't care if you can or can't exorcise it, but I'm happy to pay for the attempt. If you can actually clear it of its bad energy, there will be another five thousand when I take it home with me."

I blinked. This woman hadn't just wandered into the area with a stash of money; she had decided before she'd even left the house what the service was worth and probably slipped exactly that much into her wallet before leaving.

I hesitated over the fold of bills. Five thousand was a lot of money to pay without expecting a result. I stole a glance up at her and wondered, not for the first time, if she had some sort of mental issue that was seeding the haunting. She could be schizophrenic, or suffer from dementia.

I thought of the bad trip a former client, Sherry, had taken while on my mushroom tea and did not relish a repeat. If I merely suggested to a woman with mental illness that I'd performed the exorcism successfully and I hadn't done a thing, it might backfire later.

"Are you sure all the mask does is watch you?" I said, testing the limits of her story just in case.

She laid the bills on the counter and closed her wallet with a snap. After she had tucked it back into her purse, she pinned me just as effectively with her black eyes.

"Isn't that enough?"

I let slip a thoughtful murmur that it might be more than enough and she chuckled.

"I'd destroy it but there are also times when I feel as though it comforts me. I know it's weird, but it's not all bad."

She gave a sad little smile that looked as though she might be thinking of those moments. "Let's see where things go," she said. "And if you need more information, you can phone me."

At that, she dug back into her purse and extracted an elegant looking black business card with gold lettering. No business name, just a lovely monogrammed A and a phone number. I took it with a reverent air I didn't expect I could muster and tucked it beneath the mask.

"It's Maureen," she said. "Maureen Attenburg. Text me if you make any progress; otherwise, I'll just check in this time next week." Her gaze flicked to the mask again and she shuddered. "Be careful," she said and turned on her heel.

Her palm ran over my custom counter as she spun around and she let her fingers trail along the surface the entire way to the end. She knew quality when she saw it, and I bet she couldn't help the admiring touch.

She headed out of my shop with a staccato clicking of heels and turned to stride up the street. I watched her go, the sun catching the crown of her hair and lighting it like platinum, and then I heaved a sigh.

Five thousand dollars. Just to try. I pulled the stack of bills from the counter as my foot tapped thoughtfully. I couldn't just leave this much money in the register. My Buddha urn was home, relegated to the dark confines of my closet until I could prove to myself that I didn't need the psilocybin as a crutch to help my clients make the leap to belief and then to healing.

Pity. It might be just what I needed to help her. Most folks who sought magic in the first place had a special sort of desperation that traditional therapy couldn't touch. Psilocybin possessed more therapeutic properties than the suggestion of magic did, and recent research had borne me out on that score.

I stepped out from behind my counter and headed through the shop to my apothecary galley. There were a few pottery jars with cork tops that were empty and labeled with impossible ingredients that no self-proclaimed witch or norm would be interested in. I kept them for their aesthetic quality, never planning to sell them to anyone who came in. And no one ever asked to buy them.

One of them, neatly labeled DEAD MAN'S SWEAT would do just nicely as a hiding place for a few hours.

I shoved the money inside, figuring I'd extract it at the end of the day, then for good measure, I moved the jar to the top shelf behind one that said ZOMBIE VOMIT.

I almost laughed at my own ridiculous caution, but growing up in foster homes, you knew to take precautions with valuables no matter how ridiculous. Once, I'd even had a foster brother steal the five dollars I'd hidden in the nook above the inside lintel of my closet.

After that, I got more particular about where I hid things, and sometimes in plain sight was the best. The ten dollar bill I taped to the top of a potato bin stayed there till I retrieved it weeks later.

I had just shoved the jars back into place when the door to my shop opened. I leaned around the corner of the apothecary galley, ready to shout that I'd be right with whoever had come in.

I almost expected it to be Maureen coming back for her money, but when I turned, I saw it was a police officer.

And my mouth went dry with remembered fear.

Chapter Two

The last time a policeman stood in my shop, three psychics had been murdered. The police had stormed my shop on the hunt for a killer, worried that whoever had taken the lives of the three women and hung them like gutted tuna on the wharf might have found their way to my shop.

My heart went to my throat when I saw this one just inside the door. He was panning left to right with his gaze as though he was scoping the place out.

When he caught sight of me and my defensive posture, he immediately headed in my direction.

"Can I help you?" I said, rubbing my palms together to get the plaster dust from the mask off as I exited the galley. I couldn't help a glance over my shoulder to make sure I'd pushed the jars with the money inside far back from the edge and when I looked back in his direction, I halted instinctively.

Something flashed in the depths of his gaze as he swung it on me like a torch. Like neon yellow sign that said: BACK OFF.

I squared my shoulders. I hadn't done anything remotely illegal since Layne had first stood there weeks earlier. I had nothing to be afraid of. But cell memory was the damnedest thing. It refused to listen to reason.

"Are you looking for something, officer?" I was careful not to sound too paranoid but his demeanor wasn't making it easy.

"Brie Duncan?" he said in a tone that was not a question even if it rose a little in pitch at the end.

"Guilty," I said without thinking, then flashed him a smile when his expression clouded over. I recalled Layne's comment that most policemen thought everyone was guilty until proven innocent and I hurried to close the distance between us. I stuck out my hand in welcome. "Sorry," I said. "Bad joke."

He wasn't uniformed, but he'd taken his badge out when he'd entered the shop. He held it now in front of him like a shield. He grazed my hand with his glance and his jaw went all tight and rigid. I could swear I saw a vein pop out in his neck.

His gaze ran over my shop then, lingering too long on places that shouldn't interest him.

"I'd like to ask you a few questions," he said in a deadpan tone that indicated he'd said the same thing a thousand times already and wasn't truly speaking on anything other than autopilot.

I dropped my hand when he didn't take it and shoved it into the pocket of my jumper dress.

"Ask away."

"Not here," he said. "I need you to come with me to the precinct."

Deja vu can be a very disconcerting thing when you walk a line you now realize is a hair's breadth from reality. I knew I wasn't guilty of anything, but that visceral reaction was pretty strong. I had to fight the urge to bolt out the back of the shop.

"Why do I need to go to the precinct?" I asked, planting my feet wide enough apart out of habit that he wouldn't be able to budge me easily if he decided to arrest me. Some habits and worries just don't go away easily. "What could you ask me there that you can't ask here?"

Something shifted in his posture and I knew without him saying a word that whatever it was, it was bad.

Since there were no more psychics handy and their shops were closed up and barred, I was the only self-proclaimed witch working in the area. My mouth went dry as I intuited what he wanted me for and, right or wrong, my mind went to the only thing it understood.

He didn't want me for insights from the world of psychic phenomena. Dread lodged itself at the bottom of my spine and clogged up my throat.

"It's happening again," I said.

It, being the horror that had reigned in the psychic district at summer's start, a horror that touched five women who did no more harm than tell a few fortunes. I'd helped Layne with his investigation by providing a few insights and in so doing, ended up a target myself.

If it was happening again, then I was in renewed danger and I didn't need him to say out loud that I was right. I could read the tightening of his mouth, the subtle shifting of his gaze from my face to the counter and know it was true.

I sighed heavily and went for my sweater, telling him I needed to lock up since I knew it would take longer than the time I had left in the shop day. We left the shop together, and I climbed into his cruiser. The silence between us was so tight, it made my head hurt as we drove to the precinct.

It was no secret that while I had offered some insights to the police, as a whole, they weren't overly keen on asking me for help. It was Layne who always called me in because he believed in magic. I supposed a werewolf didn't have to take a huge leap of faith in the supernatural, but I'd not seen Layne in a couple of weeks. I recalled the amulet he and I had stolen from the evidence room a few weeks earlier. My own amulet, to be fair, but I was pretty sure mucking about with evidence was a crime, and they'd not given me back my necklace yet even though they'd closed the case.

That didn't bode well.

By the time he'd led me down the hall, past security and into a small interrogation room, I was already feeling the effects of panic. After he left me to sit there for twenty minutes waiting for him, I was angry on top of it.

So when he finally deigned to sit opposite me at a sticky table that served as a sort of desk, I'd had plenty of time to think. Plenty of time to brood.

I stared at him with hooded eyes. I didn't think he knew I recognized him. Time to fix that.

"You were at my shop before," I said and peered at his name tag, memorizing the shape of the letters. Farrel, they read. I decided it was an apt enough moniker.

He leaned back in his chair, a plastic thing that looked like it was a relic of the 70s.

"You were with Layne the day those three psychics were killed. You and he broke into my shop."

The thin smile did nothing to make him look like he possessed a sense of humor.

"Officer Gardner and I did not break in," he said, correcting me on Layne's name. "Your door was open. It's a shop, after all. Public space."

I knew from Layne that was the case, but I wasn't about to let him think he was completely off the hook.

"You came in without a warrant. You chased me through the streets."

"We are trained to chase someone who runs," he said. "They're usually guilty."

"But you know I'm not," I said. "You know I was asked for my insights into those murders." I laid my hands on top of each other in the cleanest space atop the table that I could find. "You know I helped to find the killer."

"I'm not sure trolling in a killer as bait can be considered help."

That wasn't how it happened and he had to know it. The killer had stalked me and broke into my shop with an axe. At least, an axe is what showed itself as the weapon once the man had died on my floor. When he'd first attacked me, it had been a large sickle but I'd kept that to myself since I doubted anyone but Layne would believe me.

The killer had intended to murder me like he had the other psychics, but my mother's grimoire and the amulet—two things that I'd reluctantly had to admit contained power when I'd thought all that witch stuff was fake—had protected me.

The amulet had discharged some sort of magic that drained the killer of whatever power he was using to become a beast of some sort. In the end, he'd died of mysterious causes. As far as I knew he was cremated and gone.

None of which this officer would know, but he should realize I'd been a victim and that I'd defended myself.

"As far as I'm concerned," I said. "If I ended up as a victim, it's because the police were reacting instead of acting. Had you guys done something with the information I was giving you, that man wouldn't have killed more people."

He shifted in his chair and had the grace to look uncomfortable. I kept up the pressure because it was all I had to keep me from shaking like a leaf in fear and anxiety.

"And what useful information was it exactly, that you gave us?"

The chair creaked as I leaned forward. "The numbers. Have you found out what they mean?" I said.

"What numbers?"

A whiff of old coffee swirled around me as he shuffled in his seat. He didn't have a mug in front of him, so I presumed he'd taken those twenty minutes he'd made me wait to enjoy a bit of Java. That fueled my pique.

"The number three at the first scene, the number thirteen at the last. Seems to me the mystery is not entirely solved if you don't know what they mean. The guy is just dead. Thanks to me." I leaned back again, not feeling smug just wanting to get away from the sour aroma of residual caffeine.

"Yes," he drawled. "Thanks to you we have no way of knowing what they mean. Very helpful."

I stared at him thinking he'd drop his gaze but he didn't. There was something different about him that I couldn't quite place. He was the same officer with the same strawberry hair and bright blue eyes who had come to my shop the first time, but he looked different now.

Maybe the lighting in the room was set to put suspects on edge. He certainly reminded me of a cornered predator. The coiled muscle I noted beneath his thin suit jacket certainly made him seem so.

"What am I here for, officer?" I said politely. "You didn't read my rights so I'm obviously not under arrest."

"Why did you say it was happening again?" he asked.

I shrugged with one shoulder. "A girl doesn't forget that kind of thing in a lifetime. I also worry about needles after a few bad blood tests as a kid."

He held my gaze for a long time, and the longer I kept it, the angrier his face grew. Rage danced in his eyes in bright yellow sparks.

I waited, and each second that passed, I felt less and less confident, but I remained silent because it was the only weapon I had. He finally blinked and shifted in his chair. He bent to retrieve the stack of folders and papers he'd presumably grabbed from his desk on the way into the room.

These he tossed onto the table between us.

"Would you mind looking at a few pictures?" he said. "We have a new crime scene, the abandoned flophouse in the old part of town."

It was almost nonchalant, the way he said it, but he leaned back in his chair again with an air that indicated his tone and his actions were deliberate. The plastic cracked as though his weight had renewed a splintered seam in the seat. With arms folded over his chest, he waited for me to pick up the top folder.

"You'd think the precinct would get you better chairs." I wiggled into mine, noting that there was a bit of padding on my seat. Why he'd offered me the more comfortable one, I couldn't know, but eventually I sighed in resignation. It seemed this wouldn't end until I looked at his stupid folders.

"You want my insights, I'm guessing?" I said, a nervous clot settling into my belly. I wasn't in the mood for more murder scene pictures. "Something nasty went down there?"

I knew the flophouse he meant. There was only one building the locals called the flophouse. At one time, it had been a hostel for sailors. Now abandoned, it offered perfect cover for all sorts of nefarious activities, but to my knowledge, most of that was a bit of partying and prostitution.

"Something nasty," he intoned. "You could say being the scene of a grisly triple homicide something nasty."

I balked for a moment. Hearing about a triple homicide was bad enough, but the word grisly put my hackles up.

"Why isn't detective Garder here?"

"Detective Garder is out of town on family business. He told me I should check with you for things like this."

He flashed a predatory grin that did nothing to ease the knot in my stomach. My fingers touched down on the corner of the manila folder and I tugged it in my direction.

"A little warning first, maybe?" I said, peering across the table at him.

"You're the psychic," he said. "You should know what's in there already."

I pressed my lips into a tight line, refusing to take the bait. My shop sign said something similar so his comment didn't have to be a dig. Maybe he was trying his hand at humor.

"The only person who would know what's in there would be the killer and you," I said because even if he was joking, it wasn't prudent to make it seem like I had any foreknowledge about murder. He had to know I wasn't that stupid.

Still, he made a thoughtful sound deep in his throat at my comment.

I'd helped on two crimes since the psychic murders. Both had been cold cases that opened up again. I knew they were tests. I didn't do more than give them a fresh eye and found a couple of details they'd missed.

But this didn't seem like that. It seemed as ominous as that first homicide.

In the same way I would pull away a bandage from a deep cut, I flipped open the folder.

The first picture was no more than a black and white cheap printout someone had downloaded from their digital SLR and hastily sent to the office printer. Relief washed over me that it wasn't some awful mess of blood and tissue. But I knew it for what it was. A toss away, a warm up kind of photo to get me feeling safe and comfortable.

If I squinted at it, I could make out cracks on the plaster of the wall it had captured. Swirls of paint traced a circular pattern that dribbled and drooled its fluid through the shape.

Whoever had taken the picture had taken it too close to see the entirety of the wall and had focused instead on the pattern.

"Do you recognize it?" he said.

I peered at him over the folder. "It's an awful mess," I said. "Is it supposed to be something I should recognize?"

He shrugged. "Maybe I see something that's not there." He shook his finger at the folder. "You should keep looking."

I tried not to show my exasperation but lifted the bottom corner of the photo and flipped it over, laying it face down on the left side of the folder.

The next picture was a blowup of the same area. Gone, was the clarity of wall stucco, replaced by careful focusing of the top half of the circular pattern. It was still black and white and the close proximity offered me a better look at the drawing itself.

"Are those finger prints?" I asked the officer.

"Certainly looks like it to me," he said in a voice that held so much smug he could have bottled the overrun like fine whiskey.

I pulled the printed photo closer, holding it in both hands. I tilted it to the right, hoping to catch enough light off the ceiling fixture in just the right way to reduce the glare. My reward was the smudged appearance of three fingerprints.

"Seems to me you wouldn't need me at all," I said. "Looks like you have pretty good evidence right there."

"It might be," he said. "If they weren't so ruined." He leaned over the table, crossing his arms on the surface so that his elbows took most of his weight. "I think the next picture is a little bit better."

I nodded silently and flipped the second picture over onto the first. What waited for me as the next offering was in full color, panned back by the photographer to show the entire wall.

I heard my own sharp intake of breath as I realized that the edges of the pattern had already begun to turn rust colored and in places where the fluid was extra thick, it was crimson and clotted.

"That's blood," I said.

CHAPTER THREE

I GRAZED THE PHOTO with an anxious eye. An internal mantra cycled through my mind that begged the photo to not be showing me blood. But the more I looked at it and studied the long drools of viscous fluid that marred the clarity of the drawing and traced the main figures, the more certain I grew that I knew exactly what it was.

I felt nauseous. "It's blood," I said in a deadpan voice that disguised my anxiety pretty well.

I dropped the picture back onto the desk. I didn't want to look at it any longer. Instead, I eyed him across the desk. His jaw slipped ever so slightly sideways as though he expected me to react differently. When I didn't, he reached over the table and pulled the photo back toward his side.

"Good call," he said and gave the photo a little shake, as though he were snapping wrinkles out of a towel. Then, he laid the picture between us again. It made a scraping sound as it slid across the grain of the table. He spun it around to face me, tapped the circular pattern on the paper.

"Don't you recognize this?" he asked in a voice dripping with accusation.

I dropped my gaze to the picture again but for the life of me couldn't figure out what he was inferring with his tone. Whatever he thought I knew, I didn't. No matter how long he glared at me, I'd not get the point.

When he cleared his throat, I looked up at him again reluctantly, and held his gaze with a determination that I knew I'd regret later. He wasn't the sort of man to take resistance well.

He sniffed into his fingers, clearing his sinuses before swiping his hand across his pants.

"I seem to remember you being pretty involved in a nasty serial murder a couple months ago," he said.

"Involved isn't how I'd describe it," I said, feeling distinctly like he wanted to make me feel guilty for something. "Your partner involved me and you know it. We've been here before. The murderer hunted me down in my shop. You arrested him."

He tapped the desk. "Be that as it may, you seemed to have a lot of helpful information back then."

I shrugged. "It's what Layne asked me for." I narrowed my gaze at him. "Why don't you ask your partner all this?" I said. "I'm sure he can clear your muddy memory."

The fingers that had lighted on the table moved to his thigh, where he tapped his leg. "Perhaps my partner trusts you, Ms. Duncan, but I've never found it useful to date the suspects."

I nearly choked on my fury.

"I was never a suspect. And I don't even know where Layne is," I said, feeling the sting of his comment in my cheeks. "Surely, if we were dating, I'd have seen him over the last few weeks."

"Officer Garder didn't tell you he was leaving town?" he said with a smirk as he insinuated with the official title that my using his given name indicated I knew Layne better than I was confessing to. And that if I wouldn't cop to that, what else was I refusing to confess.

"Maybe it's Officer Garder you should be speaking to," I said.

"I'll be doing that when he returns," the officer said. "But for now, I could use your...help."

That last said with a derogatory tone that made my neck tingle. It wasn't help he was after and he had to know he wasn't fooling me.

"Why don't you look at the other folder?" he said and laid his palm flat on the stack and pulled that back toward him too. Without turning it around the way he had the photo, he flipped open the second folder.

It had been cunningly arranged so that the photos inside were perfect portrait orientation for me. I might have made a sound or I might not. Things went sort of hazy in those seconds.

There, staring back at me was the face of a man whose eyes had been gouged out of his sockets. The symbol from the wall had been cut into his forehead as well. The blood from the wound leaked over the edges of the thin lines carved into his skin but not enough to mar the clarity of the symbol.

"Do you recognize it now?" he asked and I knew he was staring at me, watching me for the minutest flicker of muscle in my face.

"It's a Hecate's wheel," I said without taking my eyes off the picture because the poor man captured in death deserved some respect. What had been done to him deserved a witness and it felt wrong to look away, no matter how horrific the picture was. No matter how badly it made my stomach clench into knots.

"Some call it a stropholos, I went on, reciting the research I'd done when I'd opened my shop and investigated the symbol on my mother's amulet. The recitation was more to calm my nerves than anything else. "It's not uncommon in witchcraft practice and crunchy granola types love the way it looks."

He made a hemming sound deep in his throat that managed to be both noncommittal and accusatory.

I folded my hands over the top of the table and looked away from the photo finally. I watched him as he leaned back in his chair again. The creaking of the plastic made me nervous he'd split right through the seat.

Strangely enough, he wasn't a heavy set man. He seemed pretty fit beneath his cheap suit and tie but a rough sort of hard muscle bulged beneath the sleeves of the jacket, and I had the feeling he was far more fit than I'd given him credit for. Muscle weighed a lot.

Judging by the creaking of the chair, he had more muscle beneath his clothes than the seat could hold.

I held my breath, expecting it to give way, but when it didn't, and he tossed his feet up onto the table on his side, I cringed.

"It's also the same symbol as on your business logo," he said.

I shrugged and leaned back too, aiming for the same casual air as his except I had the feeling my heart was hammering. His nostrils twitched as though he could smell my blood racing.

"You'll find that symbol everywhere," I responded.

He hummed again. "And what do you know of it?"

I was running low on patience but tried hard not to show it as I answered.

"It's meant to show the labyrinth of life and death. It represents rebirth and renewal," I said, explaining it in the simplest terms I could.

I doubted he'd care that most practitioners of Wicca used it for everything from inviting love to divining prosperity. As a runic sign it was fairly benevolent. But the one on the man's forehead and on the wall wasn't the typical common wheel, and the blood was anything but benevolent.

I had the feeling Farrel had done a bit of searching on the Internet and had probably come up with a few theories of his own. The symbol carved and painted on the crime scene was more traditional than the one most retailers sold to feminists and wiccans. If he'd done any research at all, he'd know there were different versions, but he probably didn't know they were the same representation.

I pointed to the picture of the wall because I didn't want to look at the murdered man and his face again. I'd paid him his due. I didn't need to seal his image into my psyche.

"That symbol is older," I said of the wheel. "You can tell because it shows the Y in the center instead of the star."

"Interesting," he said but his tone wasn't impressed in the least. "Why the difference, do you think?"

I sighed. "It could be anything, really. But typically, Hecate is a three aspect goddess. You can look it up on the Internet and get all sorts of information. You don't need me for that."

I didn't say I thought he'd already done just that. In truth, I'd done the same at first so I could offer the same Wiccan practitioners gobs of merchandise to fawn over and buy. The symbol on my mother's amulet had seemed plenty mystical to me and lent just the right sense of mystique for the shop. I made a point of remembering the things other witches or norms seeking magical truths might want to hear.

But after the murders, I'd done much more research. I learned a lot about Hecate the goddess of witchcraft.

"And just what is a three aspect goddess, pray tell?" he asked with a look of distaste crinkling his mouth.

"You ever hear of the holy trinity?" I asked, getting a bit annoyed with it all by then, and getting less capable of hiding it. "She is maiden, mother, crone." I shifted in my seat, arching my back to ease the kinks out. "I mean, there's a lot of lore on her. She helped get Persephone out of Hades, so she is considered to have power of death and can raise the dead. She has power over the earth, land, and sky. The moon, the sun, the stars. All threes of a sort. She even has an affinity for three part crossroads."

He still didn't look impressed. Mostly just suspicious. I supposed it was part of the act. Layne had been very similar at first. He'd admitted that most cops don't trust most people. Now, thinking about Layne, I pushed to the edge of my seat. I'd had enough and it was time to go home. I didn't like Layne's partner one bit.

Like a consummate pro, he let me stand before he spoke again.

"I have one more picture for you," he said and pulled out yet another folder from beneath the stack on his side of the table and slid it toward me.

I looked down at it but didn't pick it up. He didn't fool me. Whatever he wanted me to look at, this was the coup DE gras, the one he'd been waiting to show me. The climax. The finale.

Well I wasn't interested.

"I think I'm done for the day," I said. "If you aren't specifically asking for my help, then I'd rather not look at any more murdered souls."

He grinned, a feral smile that didn't reach his eyes. "That one isn't a person. Just a picture. So no nightmares waiting to jump into your sleepy head."

I sighed and thumbed the corner of the folder, flipping it open. My mouth went dry when I saw a close up shot of an amulet with the Hecate symbol on it. The cord was made of leather and it was draped artfully over the stone it encircled. There was a familiar bit of wear on the leather very close to the stone.

I flicked my gaze at him over the folder, but I said nothing. I didn't need to. He knew the amulet was mine and he was waiting in silence for me to lose my cool and say something. But I knew the game as well as he did. I stood perfectly still and pressed my lips together firmly.

He tired before I did.

"It's yours," he said simply and I nodded.

"Look at the next photo."

Dread climbed my spine, but I tried not to let my hand shake as I turned the picture over to reveal the next one. This time, the photo was panned out, and the amulet in it was captured perfectly as it lay across the man's chest. He clutched the end of the cord in his dead hand.

I felt my vision tunneling.

I recognized the stone and the leather cord the man held, and I knew it was the same as in the first picture. Except this necklace had blood on the leather string.

"My amulet is in your evidence room," I said without looking up.

The crime scene photo went gently out of focus, the way an artfully blurred studio portrait might look. I felt as though my chest was getting tight.

"You all have my amulet," I said louder as though he hadn't caught my inference. "If it's at a crime scene, then one of you put it there."

He chuckled softly and when I looked up at him he was holding my necklace by a bit of leather. It dangled in the air, swaying back and forth. I was busy trying to figure out why he would be tainting evidence by handling it when he tossed it at me.

Out of reflex, I grabbed for it.

And it burned me.

Chapter Four

It took a full two seconds to feel the pain. Even as the stone snuggled into my palm, even as I curved my fingers around it, I felt very much like I'd laid my hand flat on a hot griddle. I was sure if I opened my palm, I'd see blisters rising to the surface.

The stone dropped with a thwack to the floor. It lay at my feet between the officer and me. Both of us stared down at it. No doubt he thought he'd tossed it so hard it hurt my hand and I'd dropped it out of reflex.

The truth was, it had hurt me, but not the way he might think.

But that wasn't the worst of it. In those seconds the stone had touched me, I had a very clear, very prickling sense that I was in danger.

Most women know danger when it prickles their neck like mine was doing right then. It doesn't take a witch to use intuition. If my mind was shrieking at me that I was being threatened, I'd listen.

I clenched my fist tight and held it against my thigh as I stared at the chunk of stone and leather resting next to my ankle-boot.

"Seems it found its way out of the evidence locker and onto our murder scene," he drawled. "Care to explain that?"

He didn't move to retrieve it and I certainly didn't want to touch it. The bubbles of skin on my palm were already rising to meet the ones on my fingers. I felt them the way you'd feel pebbles in your grip. I ached to dunk my whole hand in some ice water.

I lifted my gaze to his, and even though his face swam in front of me, blackening out at the edges, I thought I managed to speak coherently.

"I'm afraid I can't give you any insights into how my amulet found its way out of your police evidence room and into a crime scene, Detective," I said. "And I don't think your superiors would be interested in having any-one speculate, but if you'd really like me to do so, I'll stop by their offices on my way out."

I put my fingers to my temple, and not just in a feigned act of exhaustion. My head hurt. The dizziness made everything off kilter in a way that knotted up my stomach.

"I think I'd like to go home now. That is, if you've finished with me."

He pushed himself to his feet. The chair scraped against the floor in a grating sound that made me wince.

"You're free to leave any time, Ms. Duncan," he said. "But please don't leave town."

My head snapped up at that. I felt as though my eyebrows had knit together into one straight line.

"Are you saying I'm a suspect?"

He shrugged. "I'm saying there are too many coinci-dences to ignore. All that stuff from a couple months back. You were pretty involved in all that. And now—"

"I was involved at your partner's behest," I countered. "And that 'stuff' had nothing to do with me except that some maniac had decided to murder women like me."

His fingers touched down on the table right at the corner. "Your amulet was found at a murder scene. And that means that despite your professed innocence and seeming alibis, I'll consider you a suspect until you prove otherwise."

It's not every day a woman gets accused of murder. But if he was dead serious, he'd have arrested me. Instead, he was letting me go. It didn't stop me from sending him a look that might have been deadly if I had that sort of power. He was abusing his position and we both knew it.

I sidestepped the amulet neatly, aiming for the door as I turned to speak at him over my shoulder.

"I'd think you'd spend your time more wisely working on finding the real killer, detective. Because blood will be on your hands when it happens again. Not mine." With that, I fled, trying not to slam the door on its hinges as I swept through to the other side.

An exhausted sigh escaped me when the door closed. With heaviness to my shoulders that hadn't been there when I'd entered, I leaned my back against the wall.

The precinct was a bustle of activity. A few female officers sat at their desks typing on old fashioned type-writers even though the computers on their desks were perfectly capable of accomplishing whatever documents they needed to process. Two male officers stood next to an archaic photocopier drinking coffee and ignoring everyone else over whatever had them so engaged in discussion.

This cop shop was a relic of a time gone by, and it was obvious not just by the setting but by the ridiculously lazy policing being done by the man inside the room I'd just left. I suppose I shouldn't have expected any sort of enlightenment from the man who had done nothing but glower at me from the time he'd met me.

I was still wondering whether or not Layne's partner knew he was a werewolf when I hailed a cab. Layne kept it fairly hush hush as far as I knew. I hadn't lied when I said I hadn't seen him for two weeks.

It had bothered me at first, that after we'd hit it off so well, he'd not bothered to call or contact me. I half-expected after all the hubbub of the murders died down—no pun intended—that we might pick up a date or two, see where things went. We'd worked together on some cases at first, but he'd not initiated much beyond a few questions. No potential dates.

After a while, I gave up waiting and went about my regular routine. Now, I felt that same desperate bloom of hope open up in my chest. If he was out of town, it would explain why I hadn't heard from him.

While I had an explanation for Layne's silence, I was still unsure about what was going on with his partner. There was something off about Farrel that I couldn't place. He was different somehow than the first time I'd met him. And it wasn't just that he'd been the quieter one before. I had a good sense of people. He hadn't liked me, but he wasn't the type to be aggressive about it.

Granted, I'd not given him much attention, and it was entirely possible he'd lost weight or gained it or even grown a mustache. Those sorts of things always put you into a can't-quite-put-my-finger-on-it mentality, so I was willing to believe it was something easy like that.

I settled into the back seat of a cab with my sore hand cradled in my lap, I mulled over the entire encounter because while I could pass off the man's strange sense of change, something else niggled at the back of my neck, something that told me I should sit up and take notice.

I decided it would come to me when I least expected it, so I watched the city go by in silence, never quite managing to grasp the thread of what bothered me about the whole thing. It wasn't just the prejudice of the officer; it was the entire conversation. The pictures had been brutal, and despite wanting to turn my gaze away, I'd only seen enough to know that the police would not stop until they'd found who'd done it. These were no toss away hookers or drug addicts dying in an unfortunate shootout.

The victims had been well-dressed and well fed. Business class, just a hair above middle class. Someone would be barking at the department and into media microphones if the killer wasn't caught and fast.

But that didn't explain why Farrel had insisted on making me think I was to blame for it. He had to know from Layne that I'd been cleared when the scythe man had attacked me in my shop. It was true that Layne indicated there had been nothing to really tie him to all the violent murders of my colleagues, despite him attacking me right in my store.

But something being true didn't necessarily preclude the notion that he hadn't committed the crimes. Just that they couldn't tie him to them. And it seemed far more plausible in my mind that the attacker was the more likely perpetrator than the frail female psychic terrorized in her own shop.

If Farrel was trying to infer that I was not only the murderess from this impossible crime but the ones before, I had to presume he planned to find a scape goat to quiet those barking voices and the rabid media before they got too loud.

I sighed as the buildings became less business-like and more residential. My apartment squatted in a cheaper area of the city, in a neighborhood with decent folk and a school that had been abandoned for newer quarters. I saw the gaping maw of its playground and knew as soon as we turned the corner that I'd be home in a few moments, and I'd still not managed to figure out what really bothered me about the encounter with Farrel.

The driver pulled over a block away from where I'd asked him to deliver me, but I didn't mind. While the interrogation had taken the rest of my work day, the sun was out, and with the end of summer approaching, a gal took what good weather she could.

I paid him and slipped out the back seat, perfectly content to take the last block by foot so I could clear my head. Maybe a little air and a brief walk would help loosen the cogs. The burning in my palm had lost a lot of its sting while I'd sat in the cab and I shook it out now and again to test it. Twice, I peeked at it, expecting blisters to show against the skin but found nothing but normal flesh. I began to wonder if the amulet had truly hurt me at all.

Lost in thought, I was several yards away before I realized someone was sitting on my stoop of my apartment building.

At first, a jolt of cautious surprise ricocheted through me. I didn't get many visitors, and after all the trouble with the man who'd tried to kill me, I was even more cautious than before. But then I caught sight of the halo of red hair as the person unfolded from the steps and stood. The tension in my shoulders eased.

I knew exactly who it was.

"Parrish," I said, knowing the smile on my face probably was a bit of overkill, but I couldn't help it. I'd met her a few times during the earlier investigation, and I liked her. She was brash and over the top and had a charisma that I was glad to get distracted by all things considered.

She jammed her hands into the front of her jeans shorts and rocked back on her heels as I closed the difference between us. I half-expected her to show the same pleasure at seeing me as I had her, but the expression she gave me was a blank canvas.

"Brie," she said and leaned heavily against the railing of the stairwell. "I'm glad you're home."

I swung my purse over my shoulder. "So I am I, to be honest."

I eyed her, taking in the combat boots she wore with the shorts she wore as the last of summer clung to autumn's fingers. "You want to come in? I'm starved and I've had a hell of a day."

She sucked at the back of her teeth in sympathetic agreement.

"You think yours was bad; I'm not sure I'll be able to eat ever again, but I'd love to come in." She shot a furtive glance over her shoulder at the apartment's door. "You might find a bit of blood on your door handle."

"Blood?" I said carefully.

She looked sheepish as she pulled her hands from her pockets. "I didn't realize I had some on me still." She splayed her hands in front of me to show a smear across one palm. "I washed up and all, but..."

"Doesn't matter," I said. "It'll wash off. Come on in."

I headed up the stairs, expecting her to follow, and when I went for the doorknob with my uninjured hand, I saw it did indeed have blood on it.

"I guess I can be thankful it's not worse, knowing what you do for a living." I twisted the key in the lock with the hand that wasn't blistered from the amulet and it clicked open.

She sighed heavily. "It's not from work," she said hastily. "I wear gloves and am suited up then."

I looked over my shoulder at her and for the first time realized she was bleeding. A cut somewhere along her jawline had trickled a line down her neck. "Good God," I said. "What happened?"

She reached past me to the door to open it because my good hand was shoving the key back into my purse and I was babying the other.

"It's nothing really," she said, pushing the door open. "Just a scratch. It's already healed." She grinned, showing me very white teeth and snapped them together. "Got caught on a bit of barbed wire."

"I'm not sure I want to know," I said as she pushed the door open for me.

"I'm not sure I want you to know either, since it involves a dog and a beautiful woman with a pocket full of hotdogs."

She followed me in and heeled off her boots. I let her close the door behind us and headed for the sink to run my hand under cool water. While I didn't have any blisters the pain still made my skin ache.

I didn't have to prod her further to come in. She tossed the light jacket she wore onto the hall tree and in three steps had thrown herself onto the sofa with one leg slung over the arm. She caught my eye and adjusted herself, pulling the leg down to a respectable position, her back straight and shoulders squared.

"Sorry," she said with a note of chagrin. "I forget my manners sometimes." She ran a hand through her hair in a masculine gesture that reminded me of Layne. "Especially when I'm preoccupied."

I shrugged and headed for the espresso machine. "It's not a problem for me. Make yourself at home."

I pulled open a kitchen cupboard to hunt for the cocoa. I only had decaf coffee grinds and after the day I'd had, I thought both of us could use a jolt with a bit of chocolate for comfort.

I lifted the coffee canister and tilted it in her direction.

She nodded. "If it's going to be a latte, then hell yeah."

I grinned. "My kind of gal," I said.

"I hear that a lot," she said with a chuckle then sobered immediately and sank back down into the sofa. She pulled my throw blanket onto her lap and fiddled with the fringe. I kept silent, waiting for her to decide if she wanted to spill why she was there and what had her so antsy, but I kept an eye on her as I worked.

It took a while for me to prep the drinks with one hand and by the time I had the coffee pressed and dribbling into a cappuccino mug she had started watching me with a suspicious gaze at the machinations I had to go through to prep the Java while babying one hand. I smiled casually and shook out my fingers.

"Burned it," I said. "But it's getting better." Even as I said it, I realized it was in fact getting better. Enough that I was beginning to think it had been psychosomatic and not an actual burn.

"Have you heard from Layne?" she said a little too carefully.

I faced her, leaning the back of my hip against the counter as the machine spit and burped behind me. "Should I have?"

I noted the way she held my gaze and decided she was still working through telling me everything and wasn't sure. Best thing I could do for her was to make her feel safe to do so. I pointed to the bathroom.

"I'm sure that scratch is itching by now," I said. "And if you think you'll feel better washing that dried blood off your neck, you're welcome to use the sink." I mimed pulling open a drawer. "Face cloths are in the second drawer. Most of them are black so I can wash my mascara off without ruining my linen, so you should be fine to take anything you see in there without worry." I smiled to encourage her.

She heaved a sigh and pushed herself to her feet. "Ya," she said. "It wouldn't hurt."

After she'd closed the door to the bathroom and I heard water running, I poured the frothed milk into the coffee and chocolate and sprinkled on a bit of cinnamon. I was holding it out for her when she returned and she took it and raised it to her lips as she held my gaze over the rim.

"I haven't talked to him in nearly ten days," she said, "and I'm scared."

CHAPTER FIVE

IF PARRISH WAS SCARED, then I decided there had to be something going on that was worth being afraid for. My heart squeezed at the thought she'd not seen Layne, but I chose not to panic over her comment. It wasn't like she was his family or anything. He wouldn't have to check in with her to let her know what he was doing. Even if she was a close friend, a small spate of time without communication wasn't abnormal. Was it?

"Maybe he's just busy," I suggested, telling myself I'd tried to convince myself of the same thing.

She took another sip from the edge of her mug, gathering courage, I thought.

"I don't think that's the case," she said and when she caught my eye, I could see a struggle within her gaze. Secrets she didn't want to divulge, maybe. I waited for her to decide.

"Packs have a sort of bond that gives us a sense of each other," she said as she turned on her heel, more to avoid my eye, it seemed than anything else. "Ours have been weird lately, admittedly. Alphas have the strongest connection to the pack, but I should at least know if he's OK."

I peered at her over my mug. "Are you trying to say you're the alpha or that Layne is?" It was tough trying to sort through the waft of emotions she was throwing into the air along with concepts I didn't understand. I had no idea what being an alpha meant, or what magics they might possess, but if a werewolf could change, it made sense that the same magic that allowed for seemingly impossible transformation would also let them sense one another.

She sucked at the back of her teeth and let loose a weak chuckle. With one hand, the one not holding the mug of latte, she gestured at her chest and said, "Not alpha material over here."

So Layne then. Layne was the alpha. That made perfect sense to me.

I remembered her reaction to an order he'd given her weeks earlier, and her reluctant, but grudging submission. If being an alpha meant he could order submission from other wolves in the pack, then her acquiescence made sense. I made a mental note to try to research what it all meant, but that was a task for another time. Right then, I still had to unravel why she was so worried.

"When was the last time you felt as though he was OK?"

She sighed. "Too long." She slurped at the edge again but held my gaze. "I'd ask his father but he doesn't exactly like me. And since a she-wolf has no real rank, I doubt the alpha would even talk to me."

I hitched myself up onto the counter next to the sink, realizing what she was telling me. "So Layne is not your alpha?"

She canted her head at me. "Not exactly. He's *an* alpha but not *our* alpha. It's complicated, but basically there can be several dominant wolves in the pack. They all have a rank after the true alpha. Alpha as a term is more of a tendency to lead, a strength of will, and an ability to control the magic of the bond. Layne has all of that. He'd be alpha if not for his father."

This was more than I'd heard from Layne about what he was, and I found it fascinating. In light of the awful afternoon I'd had, I was greedy for more information that warmed my blood instead of chilling it and news of Layne was very much like a quick bolt of warming alcohol.

So I waited, not quite patiently, for her to fill the silence with more details that could keep that fire going.

She strode over to the counter and set her cup, empty and upside down, onto it. I stared at the rim of the thing as it leaked out vestiges of creamy coffee onto the counter, amazed she'd pretty much drank the entirety of a steaming mug without so much as wincing at the burn. She either had a high tolerance for pain or she was really worried.

Her hands were still on the sides of it as she spoke, face toward the wall, back to me.

I put the cup into the sink and wiped up the counter with a dishrag, all the while watching her struggle with the decision of how much to tell me drawn onto every muscle of her back and shoulders.

I wasn't surprised when her concern for Layne won out.

The sigh she let escape was as much a pressure release as the words.

"I hoped maybe you'd heard from him. I really need to talk to him."

I couldn't help myself from dropping from the counter onto the floor again, letting my feet touch down gently. I inched the few steps toward her that could have me within touching distance. She must have heard me, but she didn't move until I laid a comforting hand on her shoulder.

It was then that she spun around, wild-eyed and fierce looking. It was such a shock and so unexpected that I yanked my hand back. A flare of yellow surged in her gaze and went out again.

My hand went to my throat instinctively, feeling at once that I was in the presence of a predator and not a friend. It was a confusing muddle that pushed me back a step.

"I'm sorry," she said as the light tampered down. She nudged my foot with the toe of her shoe. "My wolf is in a right state."

"I understand," I murmured but I backed up another foot just the same. "He's a friend. You're worried."

She examined the space I'd put between us and her shoulders sagged.

"He's not just a friend," she said. "I owe him my life. I don't know if Layne told you anything about me." She paused a moment, gathering either the thoughts or the courage to continue, and while she did, I cupped my elbows, staying very still so not to distract her. Or freak her out.

"Layne brought me into the pack when I was newly changed," she said in a voice that held more than a modicum of self-loathing. "I was a wreck, doing things I shouldn't." She shook her head as though the memories were very fresh and unwanted. "I needed a pack to rein me in, but no pack wanted me. His father, the alpha, didn't want me either, but Layne stuck his neck out for me. He could have been killed for that transgression."

She leaned backward, propping her elbows on the counter behind her as she stared at me.

"Like I said: they're both alphas, but since Layne is younger and hasn't challenged his dad, he's second. He makes decisions for the company if his father is busy or out of town. That was how I got in. His father was away and Layne made the decision without consulting his father."

The way she said it made me think Layne had arranged for his father to be out of town so that he could make the move to bring Parrish in.

Her hands tightened into fists as they hung off the edge. I had the sense it was a difficult memory but nothing except her hands revealed what she thought of it.

"They fought like the blazes over it. No pack wants a lesbian wolf. It's a misogynistic, archaic, and totally ridiculous patriarchy." This last with a bitterness that revealed itself in the curled back lip. "Female shifters are rare enough, you'd think they'd cut off a paw to have one in the ring."

She looked like she was going to spit on my floor and I put my cup down on the sideboard to remind her where she was. Her jaw clenched, whitening around the ears but she swallowed visibly enough that I knew I'd been right.

"I'm sure they were a bit discombobulated with you," I said in sympathy. She wasn't exactly the fawning type.

She brought her fist down on the counter, pumping it twice against the surface.

"Layne brought me in despite his father, who rules like it's the dark ages. Most of his pack had already started to get more woke, which is how he was able to do it. But Layne's dad? He don't budge so well. Things have been strained ever since, but his father doesn't doubt Layne's loyalty. You shouldn't either." She eyed me like she was trying to see through me. "I know how he feels about you."

The sudden shift in topic made me flinch.

"If he felt anything for me, I'd have heard from him," I said. Though I tried to keep the whining out of my voice, she must have caught it because she patted me on the shoulder.

"That he hasn't makes me all the more worried."

"You think he's being intentionally incommunicado?" I said, purposely ignoring the way my heart sped up at the comment because until I heard it from Layne, I couldn't trust it. We'd had the one date and it had ended in a man murdered outside the fancy dinner he'd taken me to. Maybe he thought I was bad luck.

Now, he was unreachable, even to his best friend. I didn't want to think that the only thing that added up was that he was either hurt or didn't want to be found. That was too macabre, and I wasn't macabre. Not anymore. I was a positive force, dammit.

She splayed her fingers out against the cream colored counter and my own hand ached to open and lay flat but the stinging deep in the skin kept my fist curled as she spoke. "To be fair," she said. "I always worry about him when he goes like this."

She looked very earnest and I was willing to bet that she actually cared what I thought. For all her tough exterior, she was probably soft as caramel beneath the hard shell of candy.

I noticed the comment that indicated Layne went away often. If he went on family business as much as that offhand comment indicated, then even if she was worried, it wasn't out of the ordinary.

"He probably just doesn't want you to know what he's doing," I said.

She pursed her lips at me, indicating she didn't like the suggestion. "Bastard better have a good reason for scaring the shit out of me."

But the tension in her shoulders eased. "Occam's razor, right?" she said and I nodded.

"I'd like to believe it's the most likely thing that's the truth right now," I said. "Rather than the possibility that he's hurt." I narrowed my gaze at her because things weren't adding up. Not at all. She surely didn't need me, a near stranger, to tell her Layne was probably fine.

"You didn't just come here to talk about Layne," I guessed because she wasn't giving up the vibe that she thought he was hurt. If she was, she wouldn't have taken up time describing her past or Layne's part in it.

"You know he's safe or at least not in danger. Your bonds would tell you that. Isn't that what you said?"

She hung her head, avoiding my gaze for a moment, and I knew I was right. She'd used Layne's absence to get into my apartment. Whatever she'd come for, she felt odd about doing it and she felt like I would refuse to let her in unless I thought she was upset.

"You got me," she said as she lifted her gaze to mine. One hand rose over her head in surrender. A squarish crystal ring glinted in the light of the overhead light.

"Layne told me before he left that if something odd happened I should talk to you. Well, something odd is most definitely fucking happening."

I inhaled to brace myself for what she was about to say, because I knew what was coming even if she didn't realize I knew. The math on it was just too close to one plus one for it to add up to anything other than the bodies in the flophouse.

"My boss is on vacation," she said. "I'm left in that stinking basement with three bodies that creep me the fuck out, and Layne is MIA." She straightened up off the counter and hugged herself. She looked so vulnerable I found myself taking a step toward her again, enough that she gave me a fleeting, shy grin that said she expected me to do just that.

It had been the right thing to do, I realized when she didn't stiffen up again.

"You're dealing with the murder victims from this morning," I said, putting the events of my morning together with hers.

She nodded. "You know about them?"

I sighed and spun on my heel and aimed my feet for the fridge. "You might say I got a good interview with the detective investigating the scene."

"Farrel," she said, spitting the name out. "Fucking' piece of work that guy. He ask you to do his dirty work?"

I laughed. "Right. If pinning the job on the easiest target is getting me to do the work, then yeah."

"He suggested you were the killer?"

I gave her a long look and she shook her head. "That's just ridiculous, and I think every detective in the place would know better." She went silent for a moment, with hands clenched at her sides then she shoved them into her pockets and rocked back on her heels. "He'll recant soon enough," she said. "Once his boss realizes what he's doing. Lazy bastard."

She drew in a long breath. "So you got a good look at the pictures?"

"I did."

She twisted her lips back and forth, thinking. "Then you know how bad it is. I don't usually talk about it but man, I need someone. Regular death I can take," she said. "But this. This is not normal."

I got the feeling she was fishing for me to ask what was so abnormal about the bodies, and I knew I already had a pretty good image of what it was. The thought of going through it again but from her viewpoint, where she'd seen everything up close and glistening made me queasy.

I turned away from her with a resigned sigh and swept past her.

"Where are you going?" she asked in a voice filled with suspicion. She really was spooked if she thought I'd threaten her.

"If you're going to force me to listen to your horrible day after the horrible day I had," I said. "Then I want a drink. Coffee just isn't going to do it."

"You and me both," she said. "What do you have?"

I flipped open the freezer door where I kept the good stuff.

"Canadian rum mostly," I said and plucked a couple tumblers from the shelf next to the fridge. "Unless you want a bottle of red wine." I pointed at the cupboards where I knew I'd stashed a nice bottle of cab sav.

She was behind me in a moment.

"Fuck the wine," she said. "That's for soccer moms who love to complain about the headaches it gives 'em. Give me the rum."

I poured a shot over a few ice cubes from the freezer tray next to the bottle and topped it with a few ounces of cola. I pointed the tumblers at the living room, indicating she follow me there. The coolness of the glass eased the pain in my palm.

She took the glass I offered and headed for the chair where she'd left my reading blanket and dropped down onto it, holding the glass high over her head to avoid sloshing as she dumped herself into the chair.

"You only put in one shot," she said.

"Did you drive here?" I asked.

She nodded.

"Then one shot is all you get." I sat in my reading chair that I lined with overstuffed cushions and pillows positioned opposite the sofa and raised my glass toward her. "Long may your big jib draw," I said.

A flash of humor came and went in her eye before she said, "I don't even want to know what that means but I'll drink to it." Then she upended her glass.

I watched her swallow down the whole thing and then belch loudly before I leaned back in my chair and curled my feet up under me. My own deep swallow of the drink burned just the right amount in my chest. I waited for it to spread to my belly and soften the hard edges of anxiety. I hated to admit that in the few moments it took for the burn to subside that I was already feeling less frantic.

Neither of us spoke for a few minutes, and she was the one to break the silence. When she did, it had nothing to do with bodies in morgues or the murder scenes in old buildings. That was how I knew how badly she'd been affected by what she'd seen.

The glimpses I'd had of the crime were bad enough, but they were from the sterile distance of a photographer's eye. She'd had to get close up and personal with the after effects. Her hesitation to delve into the issue right away was enough for me to offer the rum in the first place. Not because I thought she needed it but to give her the distraction and space to process how she was going to approach it.

Some things are best gone at sideways.

"You didn't ask much about Layne," she said with a raised eyebrow. "Why he's on the force instead of working the business." She waited a brief moment before saying, "Why he's off doing family business now instead of doing force work."

It took a fair amount of will not to beg to hear more, to remain nonchalant when I was dying to ask a dozen questions.

I'd liked Layne and our brief relationship had been intimate in ways sex couldn't touch. Nearly dying has a way of bonding you with someone.

"I figure it's none of my business." Was my careful reply.

She laughed with a huff. "You spent too much time in Canada," she said. "You're not nearly nosey enough."

"Oh, trust me," I said. "They are nosey. You get into one of those small towns and they don't just know everyone's business, they know the color of the underwear you wore yesterday. Drove me crazy."

She set her empty tumbler down on the floor between her feet.

"Must have been nice too, though," she said. "Having someone watch out for you."

She quirked her eyebrow at me, probably thinking about the pack bonds she seemed so fond of. I wasn't sure I'd like 'feeling' others around me all the time, but it was nice knowing someone had my back. I thought about my stint in the Canadian Maritimes and the strange, but pleasant warmth of feeling like I was part of something.

Most neighbors did check on me if they hadn't seen me for a while. I could go out and know that the neighbors were watching over my apartment. I felt safer in Nova Scotia than I'd ever felt. The life with my mother and all the foster care homes were light years away from the kind of life I lived in Canada. There were even times I forgot to lock my front door.

"It's a different way of living," I said with some resignation that it was over and grief that those things were behind me. "They were always nice, but I always knew I was a come-from-away. Just when I thought I was fitting in, some weird cultural thing would rear its head and make me feel like I'd stepped in something I hadn't seen. I mean, our countries might speak the same language, but they don't think the same."

She seemed to accept that without needing more and I wondered if that was the clue she'd small talked enough to finally spill about her day. I decided if I was going to get any sleep tonight, I'd have to be willing to risk it.

"So," I said, shifting on my chair since one of my legs had fallen asleep. "What can I help you with?"

"Hang onto your drawers," she said. "Because it's about to get freaking horrific."

CHAPTER SIX

I DIDN'T NEED TO imagine the horror when I'd seen it through photos. She got up and fetched the tumbler from my grip, then went to the kitchenette to refill it. The cubes clinked against the glass as she passed it to me.

"I hate to do this to you," she said. "But you need to hear it."

She prodded my hand with the glass until I took it from her.

"Drink up, buttercup," she said. "Because this ain't gonna be some fairytale story. It's going to be a pretty shitty horror flick."

She didn't have to say more for my brain to flash the interrogation room back to me. I smelled Officer Farrel's cheap cologne, his sweat as he scrutinized my every reaction. I saw again the victim's forehead and the symbol carved into the skin, the painted walls and the amulet. The pictures alone had made my knees weak. I couldn't imagine poor Parrish having to see the full Technicolor version.

The room swam for a moment as something nagged me from the back of my mind. Something about the photographs Farrel had shown me didn't seem right. I eased my eyelids closed just for a second, willing the images back to mind but all I got was a blurry mess of black and white. I guessed my psyche just wasn't ready to think about them again.

She abandoned me to where I sat and crossed the room to sit on the edge of the sofa, leaning forward with her hands hanging between her knees. She might have wanted to keep them still but they clenched and unclenched as she spoke, an indication that she would rather be doing anything but reliving her work with me.

"There are three of them," she said. "Three bodies. One man and two women. All from the same murder scene. Cut up pretty badly, but it's not as if I haven't seen that sort of thing before."

I found myself staring at the milk mustache that still sat over her top lip and considered the dichotomy of the innocence of it compared to the things I knew she was about reveal.

I sank back into the chair and flung my legs out in front of me. The edges of my vision started to fade out as she described the wounds and injuries in fairly graphic detail, ending with the comment that in all her days she'd never seen anything so horrific. And she was a werewolf.

I took that to mean werewolves saw their share of grisly things. I didn't want to imagine they were used to committing them. Because what would that say about Layne or Parrish?

"This fucking homicide shit has me spooked," she said, interrupting my musings. "It's bad enough doing this all on my own, but with Layne gone and after what happened last time..." she let that trail off as she caught sight of my face. "Sweet Jesus, you're white as a nun's ass."

She got up and pressed the tumbler of rum I held in my tight grip to my lips with two fingers. I took a good swallow. She stood back and watched me drain another ounce or so before she said, "Better?"

"Who knows?" I said but I took another drink, this time slower, drawing time out as long as I could. She wasn't fooled, I didn't think.

She kept watching me, tapping her foot. When I finally finished, she flung herself onto the chair, with her legs sprawled out in a wide V. The backs of her heels dug into the carpet. I imagined she was a bit impatient with my human frailty but was putting up with it because she needed me in that moment.

"So," she said, obviously figuring we'd waited long enough. "I get weird shit all the time, but not like this. This is a special kind of weird."

I set my glass down on the table next to me. Then I faced her with a deep breath.

"I know all about it," I admitted. "I've seen the pictures."

She gave me a thoughtful look then shrugged. "That explains your heebie jeebies when I haven't told you any of the best bits. I'm sorry you had to see all that, but really? The pictures ain't got nothing on the real thing."

She blew out a long gust. "Whoever killed them cut them open and stuffed the cavities with various things. Herbs. Flowers."

"You mean like the last time." It wasn't a question. I'd be damned if the two weren't connected. Even Farrel had thought so. On the surface, one could say that both involved magic in some way. The first had involved killings of psychics and while there was certainly magic in the deployment of power from my mother's grimoire that took down the man who had attacked me in my shop, the police did not see it that way.

Plus, that suspect had died in custody. While Layne and I both agreed he'd been the killer, it wasn't plausible that he'd returned from the grave to start killing again. That had to mean there was a different killer on the loose. And if there was another killer with the same intentions, then the first murders had involved more than one person.

We'd not caught the killer at all.

I was sure that the detective felt the same despite his rancor over bringing in a psychic. Like it or not, that was exactly the reason he'd half-accused me. He knew as well that the air that hung over both cases smelled equally foul.

And like me, he just couldn't figure out where the thread was buried that tied one to the other. A duck and a chicken are alike in that they both have feathers and beaks, but get past that and they are not the same bird at all.

My instincts were very good. I'd learned long ago to trust them. They had been what allowed me to see past the obvious to pick out realistic details that I could offer clients to help them believe I had real magic.

Looking at Parrish, I didn't need an answer to whether or not she thought the crimes were connected. Her body language was doing all the talking for her. Even so, she answered me, and I wasn't surprised when she confessed what I already knew.

"Ya," she said. "Pretty much like last time."

She waffled her hand in front of her chest, see-sawing it back and forth in a so-so motion.

"This shit can't keep happening to me," I said, pinching the bridge of my nose until it hurt.

"You think you got it bad," she said with resignation in her voice. "You should be the one who has to examine all that shit. The killer must have thought he was packing a box for shipping or something. Used wads of foliage like bedding."

"Bedding?" I said.

Bedding inferred that something was nestled inside all those herbs and flowers. I was starting to regret the quick intake of milky coffee and booze so close together. A low ache started in the core of my belly. I started to swallow more often.

"Funny thing is," she went on, seemingly oblivious to the way I was already fidgeting. "Only one of them had his belly stuffed even though they all had tiny little carved statues of three headed women nestled inside."

"Three heads?" I murmured so low I could barely hear it, and in the moment it escaped me, I had a flash of raw tissues and viscera and blood. The rum and the latte battled each other to get out first.

I barely made it to the bathroom before the first dribbles crested over my tongue.

I fell next to the toilet bowl and hung over the rim until the last of it squeezed out from my stomach.

I rammed my hand down on the handle to flush as I stared down into the swirling water, perfectly aware that Parrish stood in the doorway, tapping her foot.

"You really do have a weak stomach, don't you?" she said from beside me.

I looked up to see her standing in the doorway, both hands over her head, clutching the lintel.

I swiped at my mouth and grimaced. She moved toward the sink and turned on the faucet. In the next moment, a cold wet cloth dropped onto my head from above. A dribble of cold liquid ran into my eye.

I plucked the cloth off and wiped my face, savoring the cool feel of the wet fabric against my cheeks.

"I've always had a weak stomach," I said as I pushed away from the bowl and used the edge to leverage myself onto my feet. "You should see the day after a real bender."

"No thanks," she said. "I'm not the hold your hair back kinda gal."

Her comment made me think of Layne. He'd held my hair back and got splashed for his charity. Thinking of him put a longing in my stomach. I lied about not caring where he was, but I couldn't say that to Parrish. She was too close to him and if he didn't feel the way she thought he did about me, then I didn't want her to feel uncomfortable.

She waited a few moments, but when I didn't say more, she turned on her heel as she ordered me to clean up and return to the living room. She had more to say apparently.

I wasn't quite ready, though. I clung to the bowl with the tenacity of a fly to a pile of dung. It took her calling out to me from the living room for me to heave myself to my feet to sit opposite her in my chair. She paced the living room, gesticulating as she explained the procedures that she kept as part of her job, and that helped her aid the police in their investigations.

She took a sort of glee in explaining it all. I supposed she was proud of her work, of the gutsiness it took for a woman to be doing the sort of work that many men couldn't stomach.

I managed to keep control of my stomach as she detailed the things I'd not been able to pick out from photos Farrel had shown me. She seemed to perk up when I didn't run for the bathroom when she explained how she'd had to pluck out flower blossoms one by one and lay them in a tray for examination.

I was exhausted by the time she was finished and a quick glance at the clock told me we'd gone past midnight. I had to work in the morning, and I know she did, but at least I didn't feel alone. It was perversely comforting to know someone else had to deal with the horror of the murders.

She saluted me when we reached the front door after I'd yawned pretty widely.

"I'm glad I came," she said almost shyly. "You're a good listener."

I shrugged and leaned against the door frame as she yanked on the boots she'd toed off on the way in.

"It's what a good psychic does, right?" I said in a jovial tone because the night had done wonders for me too. "You know, can't dupe the marks unless I pay attention."

She chuckled, enjoying the joke. "You slay me," she said and skipped down the first of the stairs.

"It means I hope you have good luck and good fortune for a long time to come," I called out to her before she'd reached the bottom.

She turned, her face getting caught by the streetlights on one side and my porch light on the other. She was quite beautiful, though I knew she'd resist that description. The tangle of red hair was a perfect shade for her skin tone.

"What's that?" she said.

"The toast," I jerked my thumb over my shoulder toward the inside of the apartment. "It's a Newfoundland saying. Means I wish you well."

Her expression softened and for a moment she lost that worried look that had haunted her posture since she'd arrived.

"You too," she said and turned to step out of the light and into the darkness of the sidewalk.

I watched her go, striding down the sidewalk toward the corner, where I knew she'd parked her car because I saw the hood of it sticking out from a bad parking job at the end of the street where it intersected one of the main arteries toward the docks.

I squinted into the shadows as I thought of intersections and crossroads and for a second, I thought a breeze moved through my hair the way it does in the movies when something fortuitous happens to our befuddled hero.

"Where did it happen?" I yelled out to her as she yanked open her car door.

She paused and looked at me, holding the door open. The interior light bathed her in a yellow glow. I held up my hand and ducked back into the house so I could shove on a pair of hard-soled slippers, then I jogged down the steps and along the sidewalk. I was huffing by the time I reached her and she gave me a pitying look as I caught my breath.

"The city just doesn't have that much violent crime," I rasped out around the burning of my chest. "There has to be something we're overlooking. Something no one would think of because it's just so inconsequential to anyone but the murderer."

"No shit, Sherlock," she said and pushed the door closed. She leaned against it with her arms crossed.

I thought of the reasons my amulet could be at the crime scene when it had been locked up as evidence. Only two things made sense. The more obvious one was that someone had retrieved it from evidence and planted it at the scene. I'd said as much to Farrel when he'd shown it to me.

But there was another, more disquieting possibility. The night the murderer had attacked me, Layne had pocketed my amulet to put back into evidence because he said it might get missed. And now Layne was MIA.

I knew Layne's family, his pack, had protected a coven of witches in their deep past. And here was a member of that pack standing in front of me. I had to tread carefully. Because what if Layne hadn't put my amulet back at all. What if he had planted it at the scene?

Would that make him the killer?

Parrish nudged my ankle with her toe, reminding me that I'd stopped her from leaving because I'd wanted to talk to her and I wasn't doing anything of the sort as I stood there.

"It's your parking job," I said as I examined the hood of the car and the way it jutted out into the street. Something about the way she was parked tweaked my memory. Just enough to get a question popping into my brain.

"Beauty, ain't it?" she said with a grin.

"It's not just the way you parked, but where you parked." I ran my gaze over the hood again, measuring the proximity to the end of the street. "Do you know where the crime scene was located?" I asked her.

"Sure," she said with a shrug that made her jacket droop off her shoulder. "On the crossroads at First Street."

"That's not a crossroads," I said, imagining the layout. "It's a three way stop."

She angled her heel onto the tire. "A three way stop gives you three choices, doesn't it?"

Traditionally, I'd thought of a crossroads as being a four way stop, one that made a full cross, but three pathways certainly fit.

Everything sort of fogged out then as I flashed back to sitting in front of Farrel at the precinct. I'd told him what I knew of Hecate. She was a goddess of threes. Her symbol was at the crime scene, both drawn on the wall and on the bodies. Small three-faced statues of women were planted somewhere at each crime scene.

I remembered telling Farrel she favored crossroads.

"I think I know who the killer is," I said.

Chapter Seven

"WITCHES," I SAID. "WITCHES are killing these people."

A regular old serial killer was scary enough, but the possibility of a coven of witches doing the killing elevated the threat. Death magic was very powerful according to my mother. If that was true, then these witches were hooking up a nuclear power plant with the sorts of things they were doing. They were sacrificing to Hecate. The mother of all witches. The god with power over death and reanimation.

I must have murmured her name without meaning to because Parrish's voice interrupted my thoughts.

"Who in the bloody blazes is Hecate?" She wrapped her arm around me the same way Layne might have and I let her, because it was comforting and sometimes a bit of comfort makes all the difference when you're scared. And I was scared. The trembling deep in my core was evidence of it even if I wanted to deny it.

I sagged against the side of her car and Parrish bumped me with her shoulder. I shivered involuntarily, hoping it was just the chill in the fall air and not the start of another sleepless, terrified night. I'd had as much magic as I could stand for the next ten years already.

"She's sort of a god," I said. "I think she was one of the original titans. I do know she's the goddess of witchcraft and she has some mighty powerful juju over

Death. I think that's why they're doing this. They're ritual sacrifices. They have to be."

She swore and I echoed it. "Why can't it just be a regular old psychopath?" she said as she aimed me toward the front of the car. "I hate witches." She eyed me with an apologetic air then said, "You're a woman of power. Not a witch."

I backhanded her playfully against the stomach and pulled away. My slippers scuffed the pavement.

"So what are they trying to do, these witches, and if they don't get what they want with these ritual sacrifices what will happen?" Parrish mused aloud.

"I'm guessing more of the same since yon bonnie witch boss seems to be ignoring them."

"Right," she said. "Death and horror."

"Death and horror and more death," I said. "You don't go to these lengths to stop before you get what you're after."

"So that means we'll have more murders like this."

"Like this and like the last ones."

I dropped my head back on my neck to look at the sky. There was so much light pollution I couldn't even see the stars. I missed that about my time in Nova Scotia. The night skies there were peppered with them.

"I can't think here," I said.

She made a sound that could have been a curse but was probably more one of agreement, and then she grabbed me by the arm and started muscling me toward the passenger side of the car. Whether it was the faint suspicion that Layne was involved somehow and had sent Parrish as some sort of assassin, or whether it was the unexpected realization that I was being muscled toward a car, my instinct kicked in.

I didn't think at first, reflex had me reacting with a weak swat at her face and then a full on fight to escape her grip.

I wasn't in my right mind for about five full seconds but then, she yanked open the door with one hand while she held me with the other, and cursed. This time, directed at me as calmly as if I'd been as effective at fighting as a moth the entire time.

"For Jesus' sake, Brie," she said. "Stop digging at my face. Werewolves might be able to heal quickly but it hurts like the devil."

It was so casual, that comment, and despite my struggles she'd held me at bay with such ease, that I knew I wasn't hurting her. For a second, I was alarmed at the ease with which she handled me, but then I felt ashamed at my reaction. I'd been the one to follow her outside, after all. If she'd planned to kill me, she'd have done so when we were in my apartment.

I went limp in her grasp.

"I'm sorry," I said.

I might have explained myself but it seemed ridiculous in light of the fact that she'd been getting ready to leave and I'd chased her. Besides, I didn't want to think the things I was thinking about Layne. It didn't just seem uncharitable. If it turned out to be true, I wasn't sure she wouldn't alert him, thinking it all a funny joke.

"I'm spooked as hell," is what I came up with. It was the truth. Simple, though it was. I rubbed my arm where she'd held it.

"Honey, Lucifer himself would be spooked at the shit I've seen." She gave me a gentle shove, just enough to urge me into the car.

"Why are we getting in the car?" I said, pulling my slippered feet in after me as I shoved into the seat. "We can go back inside to talk if you need to."

She closed the door for me and tapped the roof four times, then rounded the vehicle. After she got in and settled behind the steering wheel, she turned to me.

"You said you couldn't think, so we're going somewhere you can think," she said. "Gird your loins."

I took that to mean buckle up, so I did, but a few blocks later, with her humming to herself, some song by Gordon Lightfoot, I think, I began to think her comment wasn't just a euphemism. What she'd really meant was that I needed to prepare myself mentally and emotionally. And by the time we turned into the parking lot next to the flophouse, I knew exactly why.

My back pressed deeper into the seat as the flophouse came into view, all bedecked with yellow tape that stretched from one end of the block to the narrow perimeter of the small yard and several feet of empty lot just beside it.

Looking beyond the yellow tape and hastily pitched security tent at the front, it was easy to see the beautiful lines of the architecture from both of the street lamps that flanked the lot.

The building was a three-story high brick townhouse from a century earlier. Each floor of the facade presented gorgeous narrow arch windows and each of them was crowned with a contrasting cement arch with finials on each end and in the center, giving them a look of arched eyebrows.

A sort of turret began on the left side of the second story, with the same windows and arches on each side so that whoever had that room on the floor would have an alcove where they could look out on the city from three sides. It rose to the third story with a similar architecture, but where the second story appeared very curved, the third seemed pointed due to the windows all having sharp dormers.

It was a witch's house if ever I did see one.

"Fucking hell," Parrish said. "Looks worse at night than the day."

"It was probably something in its time," I said, deciding that as a flophouse, it looked creepy, but as a captain's home at the turn of the century it must have been resplendent. Over the decades, it had probably been too costly to run as a single family and had been turned into apartments. When that had become too unmanageable, someone had turned it into a hostel.

Hostels never looked great. And this one hadn't been in service for years.

What had gone inside would ensure it didn't get used again.

I'd seen enough from the pictures. I wasn't overly keen on seeing any more of it up close and personal.

"We can't be here," I said.

She turned off the engine after parking in front.

"Who says we can't be here?" She tapped the wheel with the index fingers of both hands. "I'm the M.E. I have access."

My fingers dug into the leather seat on either side of my thighs. "Maybe what I meant to say is I can't go in there."

"Did I stutter," she said. "You can. I'm the M.E."

"Maybe if I stuttered," I said in a firm tone that surprised me, "you would listen to me. I won't go in." This time I stressed the won't part.

She let go a dry, humorless laugh and clutched the wheel harder. I could see the way her fingers flexed on the curve of the wheel.

"You said you needed to think. You said those fuckers would keep doing this if someone didn't stop them. You're the one who mentioned a god damned super witch."

She let go the wheel and unbuckled herself with a flourish. "You're going in."

I didn't exactly hyperventilate, but I was breathing pretty rapidly. She patted my shoulder and got out. As she reached the passenger side, she tapped the roof again four times just over my head, then leaned down to look in the window.

"Well," she said through the glass.

I looked through the windshield at the yellow tape that wavered in the breeze. Two uniforms stood in a small shelter at the front of the building, something hastily erected in case of rain. The night was clear and warmish. Both of them stood outside. They had been chatting until we pulled up. Now they watched us.

"There's security," I said and pointed at the men.

She yanked on the handle. The breeze invaded the interior, confirming how warm out it was.

"Those two bastards are scared of me," she said and flashed a toothy grin to indicate she'd probably done the same thing to them but in a more aggressive way. "They'll let us in."

I sighed and spun on the seat so I could get out. "For the record," I said in a huff. "I did not say there was a super witch."

"Whatever," she said and tugged at my elbow to hasten my exit from the car. Her gaze dropped to my feet. "Slippers?"

I tugged my sweater down over the sleeveless top. "I didn't expect to be abducted."

She chuckled and shook her head but didn't say anything more until we had walked to the tent where the men stood. Then she addressed the security officers loudly enough that I could hear the camaraderie in her tone.

I hung back, hoping they'd turn us away, so I couldn't hear what she said to them, but I did catch her waving me on. So it looked like we were good to go.

I tagged along behind her, nodding to the men as I went by. One of them elbowed the other as if I didn't have eyesight good enough to catch them. He tipped an imaginary hat to me and held my gaze until I had to pull mine away from his. Their whispers when they thought we were out of earshot made my cheeks flame.

"Don't mind them," Parrish said. "They think every woman I talk to is a lesbian, and in some riotous need of a threesome with a man to set them straight again."

"You put up with that sort of shit?" I said. It didn't fit her personality to put up with sexist remarks like that.

She looked at me over her shoulder as she lifted the yellow tape for me to duck under. "Put up with it?" she said. "Hell, I encourage it. That way, I get the chance to remind them that lesbians have zero sexual use for men."

The tape whispered along the top of my head as I slipped beneath and to the other side. The pavement outside the building was cracked and, in some places, pieces had come out in chunks that lay scattered here and there. Luckily, the streetlights lent enough illumination to see most of them, but I stubbed my toe on a huge chunk and through the slippers, the baby toe--which took the brunt--barked at me.

I must have made a sound because Parrish stopped her dogged stride forward and reached back for me.

"It gets worse closer to the door," she said. "You norms don't see too well in the dark. Best you stick close."

I didn't argue. With my toe throbbing and my stomach churning, I was happy to let her lead. She jiggled the knob once when we reached the door and then I heard a distinct snapping sound a moment before a crack showed itself in the doorframe.

"Did you just break in?" I said.

She laid her hand over her chest in mock offense.

"Perish the thought," she said. "Some inconsiderate fool locked it up when they left. I just encouraged the door to open."

She flashed another toothy grin my way and in the faint glow of the street lamp, her eyes looked yellow. I was beginning to recognize the wolf beneath the human gaze, and noted to myself that it might come handy when and if I ever got to see Layne again. That was a pretty big if.

I tried not to think about whether or not I really thought he was culpable in some way because I'm pretty good at reading people and he just didn't seem to be the sort. He'd come to my aid each time I called for him. He'd fought off a beast in the dark for me.

And he'd become a beast to do it, I reminded myself. There was violence there beneath his facade. I knew that too.

"Well," she said, interrupting my musings. "Are you ready?"

"Good question," I said, but I nodded my head anyway.

And then she opened the door.

CHAPTER EIGHT

Nothing can prepare a person to confront a murder scene. It didn't matter that I knew what I was going to see or that I'd already caught glimpses of the horror from pictures. I knew I was in the same space where people suffered and died. It was the suffering part that was the worst for me.

In my mind, all those puppies and dogs my mother had sacrificed to a god she claimed to love during a time in my life when I was just beginning to understand suffering were resurrected for me as I stood there.

I recalled the feeling of comprehension that weighed down my chest as I beheld those small furry bodies. They had suffered. They would not be alive again. Not move. Not wag their tails. That moment of finality had become a hard knob of thick gruel deep in my belly that wouldn't digest for decades until my mother passed away and I came home.

We were a mere few steps inside when Parrish pulled the door closed behind me and reached somewhere along the wall. It took me a few seconds standing awkwardly in the dark with my slippers toeing the floor to realize she was feeling for a plug. Before I could help, the area swam with a glow that had a distinct bluish cast.

She straightened up from a flood light that had been placed close to the door but that only stood about four feet high. She messed around with the angle for a few moments, and satisfied, she grunted.

Her nod toward the other wall indicated a taller flood and I ambled over, careful not to step in anything that looked like it could be evidence, then shoved the plug into the socket nearby.

We had enough light then to see the entirety of the scene, even if the lights cast harsh shadows here and there.

The area had been gutted probably years earlier. What looked like a functioning building from the outside was nothing but empty rooms and open doorways inside. This room, what must have functioned as a sort of parlor at the turn of the century, had probably become a great room where people congregated later on.

Now, it was empty of anything save the gaping maw of fireplace and the windows that were now shuttered with lopsided panels of plywood meant to board them over.

I don't know why I let go such a relieved sigh, but Parrish eyeballed me with a sort of sympathetic derision. She was shaking her head, making large shadows move across the floor and wall space with the movement.

"You thought the bodies would still be here?" she said. "What kind of monster do you think I am? They're at my morgue. Remember?"

I watched an unflattering shadow of myself elongate on the opposite wall as I closed the distance between us.

"My mind might know it," I muttered. "But my stomach wasn't so sure."

She planted her hands on her hips as she faced me.

"Is your stomach going to be alright?" she said. "Because I don't fancy trying to explain a puddle of puke to the detectives." She looked down at her expensive leather boots. "Or cleaning it from my shoes."

I winced at that comment because the first time I'd been brought to a murder scene by Layne, I'd thrown up on his shoes. But I waved a hand in front of my face to indicate I was just fine.

She didn't seem to buy my confident gesture but at least she slanted her gaze at me and waved me closer.

"Over there," she said, as she pointed at a big blotch on the wall opposite the fireplace.

I recognized the symbol from the photos in the interrogation room and nodded, making my shadow do the same.

I crunched over a bit of rubble as I made my way to the wall so I could get a better look than the sharp, angled light the floods provided. Parrish followed along behind me and when I reached out to trace the symbol, she grabbed my wrist.

"Don't touch it," she said.

"Right. Evidence." I tittered nervously because putting my own D.N.A at the crime scene right at such a critical spot would be foolish even if I could explain it away. Instead, I traced the marking from the air, running along the lines of it, in my mind comparing it to the one on my logo and amulet.

"Definitely a Hecate's wheel," I said when I felt like I could talk without having to swallow down a rush of bilious water. "Bigger than it looked in the picture."

"Took a lot of blood to do that," she said. "Whoever drew it would have had to dip into the source over again to get it so stark and dark."

She frowned as she said it and I had the feeling that like me, she was imagining the killer doing just that. I backed up a step and felt her hand on my elbow. It tightened for a second as she steered me slightly to the right.

When I looked down to see what she was guiding me away from the smell coming from the room hit me full force as though it had been cloaked before and only just decided to announce itself the moment I imagined the killer drawing the symbol.

Blood. Old, rancid, stinking blood. I gagged loudly and curled into myself, my hand flying to my mouth as the stink struck like a whip, strong and eye-watering.

"For shit's sake," Parrish said as she clamped her hand down over top of mine and peered into my eyes. "Do not--and I repeat this with as much emphasis as I can manage without bringing security in here to check on you--do not puke or I will have to kick the shit out of you."

I wasn't sure if she was being dramatic or not, but the yellow gaze that looked back into mine certainly looked serious. I held her gaze and nodded beneath her palm, doing my best to keep my eyes from bugging out as I fought the gag reflex.

She must have seen my determination in my eyes because she pulled her hand away slowly, her eyes narrowing suspiciously.

"You're going to be fine," she told me in a voice very much like the one I used when I was lulling a client into a relaxed state for a stance or medium reading. "Just tell yourself it's a pile of dirty diapers or something."

I didn't respond to the suggestion. Dirty diapers wasn't exactly a reassuring image. Instead, I concentrated on the other things I caught wind of, things that had nothing to do with blood.

"I smell sulfur," I said. "And something floral, like jasmine or lilac, maybe even rosemary or something like that."

I felt her stiffen beside me and I knew she smelled it too, probably better than me. "And garlic," she said. "But not strong like a clove."

I caught her eye. "The flower," I murmured in agreement. "Garlic is a traditional offering and if it's faint like it might be in a bud, then that fits what you said about stuffing the victims' bellies with flowers."

"So," she said. "Can you think better?"

"I'm not sure what you think I can do to help. I'm just a chick who uses my gifts to help people." It was true, wasn't it? I didn't specify which gifts.

"You know more than we do about this sort of thing," she said. "I trust Layne. If he thought you could help, then you can. Damn him for not being here." She stomped her foot in frustration, and I smiled to myself, thinking that made two of us.

I blew out a long breath and started to wander the space. I always thought better when I walked and she was right. Someone had to stop these maniacs from killing again. And there were maniacs, plural. Even a layperson would understand that with the violence, one person couldn't abduct and murder three people at once. Unless they were very strong. I tried not to let my brain interject that werewolves had to be pretty strong and that Layne and Parrish were both werewolves.

I tried not to think about werewolves at all because that just made the panic rise again. How far down the rabbit hole had I gone that I was putting werewolves at the back of the danger list.

But at least the benefit of having my mind wander to Layne and Parrish and werewolves took the pressure off the valve of murder and magic. With my mind freed of it, I calmed down enough to take in my surroundings without dealing with the full effect of the horrors it held.

Things besides dust and rubble crunched beneath my feet as I shuffled through the space. Dried herbs, I realized, when I lifted my foot to inspect what I'd been treading through.

The quiet, almost rhythmic scuffing of my slippers on the creaking floorboards created a pocket of energy around me that wasn't unlike a trance. But for the werewolf stalking my steps, I might have been able to pretend I wasn't at a murder scene. Something about the movement, the sound, maybe even the electricity of the air around me felt... off.

"I think there's magic here," I murmured, tasting the possibility of it. "A residue of it, like oil in the air."

She inhaled deeply. "If your kind of magic smells like patchouli then you're probably right."

Not patchouli, I thought. Myrrh or frankincense, probably, but I couldn't be sure.

"What do you mean my kind of magic?"

She canted her head at me, and the light caught the rim of her hair, making it halo. "Shifters have magic," she said. "You don't think science or physiology allows us to change shape? There has to be some sort of magic in us or we couldn't possibly do what we do."

I hummed in thought. "Witch magic is different, then," I said, not needing an answer. I hadn't thought about there being different kinds of magic. I'd only just reluctantly begun to concede its existence in the first place. The thought that my mother might truly have been casting spells in the basement made me shudder for the naive child I'd been.

I had her grimoire. Her amulet had possessed a magic that had transformed and harmed my attacker. I'd seen her shade in the attic, watching me. I had to believe. Even if I hadn't seen Layne shift from man to wolf, I'd eventually have had to concede that magic of some sort threaded itself through the world.

I sighed and imagined my mother casting her spells after I'd gone to bed for the night, butchering strays and dogs she'd got from the SPCA. That one night I'd woken to a strange odor wafting through the apartment and headed down to the basement to find her sitting cross legged in front of stone altar. I could easily bring back the smells of that night.

Magic, at least witch magic, smelled like death and burning fat to me.

This place here certainly smelled of death. Hecate's wheel was on the wall. There were no dead dogs but the building was on a crossroads. The facade had windows in triplicate. The trappings of Hecate were all around me.

And yet I still couldn't figure out why they would be sacrificing to a goddess at all.

I heaved a frustrated sigh because I was so far out of my depth that no amount of Internet searches were going to bring me up to speed. I was useless here and I knew it.

"Things just don't feel right." I ran my gaze along the frame of light the floods cast against the floor. "If they managed to cast some magic, I don't know how much or what it caused. Did you find any oils on the bodies?" I asked.

She furrowed her brow in thought but shook her head. "I'm not finished, actually. There was too much weird for me for one day. I'll look tomorrow."

She stepped over a pile of black earth that looked out of place in the room. There was plenty of detritus: twigs and leaves from errant breezes that blew in through the cracks in the walls and windows, but for a pile that size, that black, and that loose to be sitting there as though it had been dumped there was unusual.

I knew what it was even if later someone scoffed at me or proved me wrong. I knew because I knew that Hecate was a goddess of death and resurrection. And I knew because I'd seen a similar pile before.

"That's grave dirt."

CHAPTER NINE

GRAVE EARTH IS POWERFUL if you know how to use it. At least, that's what my mother always said. In the years I'd been aged between five and seven, she'd taken me on monthly excursions to graveyards all over the city. My father was dead by then, gone at least six months, and she'd changed during that time. The mother who laughed freely and hugged me so much I squirmed away became closed and sullen after he died.

"What makes you say it's from a grave?" Parrish asked. "It could be any old clump of dirt."

I ran my toe along the top, lightly, not enough to disturb the soil, just to feel the compactness of it.

"I don't know," I said. "But I have a good feeling it is." I dropped my slippered foot down next to the pile and scuffed the sole along the floor. Nothing scraped off. That too, made me think I was right.

Those monthly play dates started after dad died, and although I had no idea why she took me to cemeteries, the reason didn't matter to me. I was just so happy to have her back again. I would have walked across hot coals to see her smile.

She would talk to me as we strode across the lawns, and that itself was a treat because the house had grown very quiet. The things she told me had no value, no sense, to me at that age. I listened but I didn't hear.

I just watched the obituaries snap and wave like little flags in her hand as she searched for the graves of the recently deceased. When she spoke, it had the feeling of instruction, of a lecture. Of course, by then school was a chore so I happily tuned her out and contented myself with the sound of her voice.

I lifted the turf for her when we found the site. That was my job. She'd smile, a brief, sad smile that warmed my heart because it had become a rare thing and even as a kid, I understood how good it was for her to do that. I'd look up at her as I peeled away the turf that had been replaced over the brown earth and she'd scoop several shovelfuls out from beneath it with a small copper gardening shovel.

She'd always pat down the turf when she was done and she'd let me carry the copper bucket back with us to the car. We'd spread the dirt out on a muslin cloth in the sun if it was spring or summer, and on the windowsill if it was winter.

"Gets rid of the water," I murmured. "Makes the earth pure."

"What's that?" Parrish said and I realized I'd said it out loud.

I shook my head to free myself of the memory and planted my hands on my hips.

"The dirt is too dry," I said. "It hasn't been dragged in by dirty shoes. The lot sits on a sea of asphalt and the lawn is made of crab grass. The dirt came from somewhere else and it's been placed there after it's been dried out."

"Weird," she said and I murmured my agreement.

"No," she said. "Weird that you get all that from a pile of mud."

"Let's just say I have a history that helps with that stuff."

I let my head drop back and stared at the shadows on the ceiling. I wanted to go home. I wanted to back up a few weeks and never agree to help Layne. I wanted my life back. I toed the edge of the black earth and my gaze trailed along a neat line that headed to the fireplace.

I caught my breath so sharply at what I saw inside that she laid her arm across my chest in an instinctively protective gesture.

"What's wrong?" she said.

I moved her arm away and leaned down, shuffling my way to the yawning mouth above the hearth.

"Get the floodlight," I said and I heard her behind me doing just that.

Light moved across the space, throwing shadows and dispelling them as she maneuvered the fixture so it shone straight into the firebox.

"There," I said, pointing aside. "Do you see it?"

It looked like a small stone altar even if it wasn't ornate enough to be considered a formal one. Whoever had built it had used stones that were flat enough that they could be piled one on top of the other. On top of that, they'd placed a grating that might normally be used to cradle kindling and logs, but it was smaller. Long lines of congealed fat and oil dribbled down the sides and pooled at the base of stones.

Without thinking, I reached in and ran my finger along one of the grates. It was cold as I expected, but definitely covered in something greasy. I wiped the residue on my pants.

"They burned something," Parrish said from beside me.

I looked at her from my leaned over position, hands on my thighs.

"Not just something," I said. "They burned the viscera. That's where the worst of the smell is coming from."

She waved her hand back and forth in front of her nose. "I've got a pretty good sniffer," she said, "so how come I couldn't catch a whiff of this until you saw it?"

It wasn't an accusation, but I felt defensive all the same.

"You're the werewolf," I said. "You tell me."

She sucked the back of her teeth and grunted. "Maybe if there wasn't so much shit and funk all over this place I could have separated it all out."

I felt my shoulders soften at the way she was so willing to let my defensiveness slide. "Or it could be that the witches cloaked the smell so they wouldn't get traced too quickly."

I pointed to some small pieces of yellow stone pushed off to the side. "Sulfur." I traced the line of stone and oil to the grating where ashes collected in the solid parts of the grate. "Herbs and meat."

I hated to use the word meat to indicate a person's muscle tissue but I couldn't bring myself to use the correct term for heart or intestines. That was altogether too human and I needed desperately to create some distance from humanity to this horrific act.

"Do you smell it all now?" I said.

She nodded. "Rotten eggs and steak and feces."

"And herbs," I said. "Rosemary, I think."

"Good nose," she said and moved her mouth into a fleeting smile. "You'd make a good wolf."

I sighed and straightened up. I was getting dizzy and I wanted to be done. My arm hurt like the devil had kissed it and the depletion of adrenaline was making me brain fogged.

"You think we've looked enough?" I said as I moved away from the hearth. I hoped she'd say yes. I was so done.

She arched backward with her hands at the small of her back. I heard a definite cracking of vertebrae.

"I think so," she said. "You've been very helpful. Layne was right to involve you."

She canted her head back at the fireplace and said in a musing way, "I wondered why the bowels were a bit light. Now I know."

I didn't ask about bowel weight; I didn't want to know. Besides, the dizziness was starting to swim across my vision in ways that made me reach out for her, seeking a steady, solid surface to lean against.

"Hey," she said and her arm went round me. The warmth should have made me feel better. Instead, I shivered.

"Are you alright?"

Now that she asked, I was feeling worse, like all of my skin was tingling. It was almost like the sensation that comes just before you pass out but it was different somehow.

"I don't know," I said truthfully.

"Maybe we best get you back to your apartment. You probably need a good night's sleep."

At the words, a flash of memory streaked through my mind's eye. The darkness of shadow hid the worst of it and trauma cloaked the rest, but it came none the less, the way it hadn't come in years. A child's view of her mother crouched over something furry and wet and knowing, just knowing, that was she was seeing was not right.

The stink of burnt hair, the smell of wet dog and perfume, of garlic, strong and pungent tickled the recesses of memory. It was enough to make me stagger under the weight of remembered pain, and I reached out instinctively.

My palm met the wall before Parrish could grab for me and my fingers splayed over the surface of the symbol.

A jolt went through me as I touched down. My vision went dark and I gasped in fear. I couldn't see and the burning in my palm was already streaking up past my elbow.

I knew my knees were going out from under me but I couldn't stop myself from falling. The fullness of my weight pitched me sideways.

There wasn't time to cry out for help. I just went down.

Luckily, she caught me before I struck the floor, but I was in such a state of panic that I dragged in a breath to let loose a scream and found my mouth smothered by her palm again. Blind and terrified, with my lizard brain deciding I was in danger, I bit down on the fleshy part of the thumb.

Parrish's hand left my mouth and I gulped in air like it was going to get publicly traded at any second. As my vision cleared, I caught sight of her scowling at me as she shook her hand out at her side.

"Nasty," she said. "I might need a shot after that. And you mundanes think we're rabid."

I gripped my hand against my chest, cradling it in the other palm by holding my forearm in loose fingers. I didn't dare touch too much. I didn't even dare look at my hand for fear it would have bubbles of blisters already rising to the surface.

"I never inferred that I thought you might be rabid," I said, but I knew it came out distracted because of how much my hand hurt, and as a result, she wasn't fooled.

"What's wrong?" she asked.

"I'm not sure," I said, even though I was pretty sure I did know.

When the amulet had struck my palm after Farrel had tossed it at me, the searing pain was very similar to what had just happened. The only difference was that this time the pain went all the way up to my shoulder. It even started to creep across my chest. I found myself idly running my fingers over my breastbone, checking for evidence I'd been burned.

Everything in my hand still felt the way it might if I'd wrapped my fingers around the business end of a flat iron.

"You're hurt," she said, and pulled my aching arm out from its cradle of elbow and bicep.

She lifted it to the light so she could inspect it. To my relief, I didn't see a single blister.

Without injury it might be easy to fool myself into thinking nothing had happened when I'd touched the wall, but I knew better. Something had happened. I just didn't know what. And I knew that because my arm burned from fingertip to shoulder cuff. Where she held my wrist, the skin felt altogether too raw.

I tugged just enough for her to release me.

"I can smell your pain," she mused aloud. "But there's nothing there. No cut. Nothing."

"OK," I said and turned away from her because things were getting far too freaky for me. "You're creeping me out now."

She sidled up next to me when I moved away, so close, crowding me and making me feel claustrophobic.

"Stop it," I said, pushing at her shoulder with my own. "You're making me nervous."

"Tell me what happened," she demanded. "And don't lie."

I spun around, my slippers scuffing in the black earth.

"I got burned, alright?" I said. "At least, it felt like a burn."

I lifted my hand to the floodlight and turned it back and forth in the light. She was right. There were no evidence of attack or wounds but the skin still burned like a mother.

"There's nothing there," she said. "Are you sure you aren't just spooked?"

I dropped my hand to my side. "You smelled my pain, remember," I said in a deadpan tone. "So, yeah. I'm sure. Whatever it was, it burned me. It still burns."

"You said something again," she said. "Like you did when you went into that trance when the psychics were murdered." She narrowed her gaze at me, and I considered telling her that the trance had been faked. Then I remembered I had actually talked to myself when I'd protested to have that magical seizure to get away from the cops.

"Did I talk about puppies again?" I asked, putting a heavy layer of casual playfulness in my tone that I didn't feel. "Were they cute and cuddly?"

"They were dead," she said in a bald voice. "You said, and I quote, 'Don't kill the puppies, Mama!'"

She crossed her arms and toed my slippers with her foot, nudging me into a response.

I waved my hand in a motion that might indicate it was foolishness and no more but I couldn't stop the dizziness that washed over me again. Parrish's fingers squeezed into my elbow and I realized I had done it again.

"If you've got some deep dark secret that has something to do with this case, then you best spit it out," she said. "And don't spare the details."

I wavered on my feet and weighed whether or not that short but traumatic time in my life really had anything to do with what was happening now. My mother's amulet had some sort of power and the symbol she had drawn on her grimoire obviously was connected to these murders. Whatever connection there was to my mother's past and this horrible present, however tenuous, might be important.

"I think I need to sit down," I said as I scanned the area for something that could work as a seat.

Parrish pulled over a three step stool that someone had left behind when they'd examined the room. She dropped it in front of me and jerked her chin in its direction.

I sat on the top step and pulled my feet onto the first one. With a sigh, I determined to find a way to explain the things I'd buried in the dark closet of memory and all I could come up with as a start was, "She was a witch. I didn't even know what a witch was except for those things you saw in stores and books and Halloween costumes. I had no idea that witchcraft was real."

Parrish was careful not to lean against anything but she had the look of someone being supported by a strong frame.

"Who was a witch?" she asked. "Sister? Mother? Hell, do you even have a sister?"

"Mother," I said. "You wanted to know how I knew it was grave dirt, and that's how. She used it in her rituals. Spell casting. Whatever."

"So you come by it natural-like?" she said. "You call yourself a woman of power, not a witch. Is it the same thing?"

I was grateful she didn't sound as though she was judging me by the actions of those witches who had committed the heinous acts she was investigating, but I heard the curiosity behind the words. She wanted to know if being a witch meant the same things as she'd seen in her morgue.

I didn't tell her I wasn't a woman of power. I still had a reputation to keep, and a living to earn. Best she and Layne still believed I had some magic.

So I explained about the cemetery visits and the night I'd come down the stairs to find her crouched over the dead body of a puppy she'd picked up from a pet store. That I'd thought it was to be my pet right until the moment I'd smelled its fur burning and saw its poor little body crushed on an altar very much like the one in the fireplace.

"Shit," she said.

I laughed but it had no humor. "She's dead," I said without emotion. "So at least I know this isn't connected to her, and I know it's not her doing this. Three years ago, I got a call from her lawyer telling me she'd left me everything. I know it seems similar, what she did back then and what is happening now, but it's not."

"I know," she said. "I might love me some pooches but they are not people. This is far more heinous than the sacrifices she was making."

"I ran away then," I said thoughtfully. "She didn't seem motherly anymore. Not after that. I couldn't sleep. I was terrified of her. It took several times before social services finally interviewed me and determined she wasn't a fit mother."

"Ouch."

"No, not really. Not at first. I was ecstatic to leave. The family I ended up with finally was very good to me. I send them cards every Christmas and they send me money in the hopes I'll visit."

I smiled as I thought of the last card stuffed with Canadian ten dollar bills. I couldn't do much with them but saved them up so I could go back to Nova Scotia for my next vacation.

"Don't they know better than to send money through the mail?"

"They're Canadian Maritimes. They don't even lock their front doors." I shifted on the stool when my butt started to go to sleep. "

Parrish must have noticed because she held out her hand to me. I took it and let her pull me to my feet.

"Well, as traumatic as all that was, I don't think it's in the same league as our killers." She put her arm around my shoulders as though she thought I might not have the strength to walk alone. "So we'll just tack it up to stress and get you a good night's sleep."

"So I'm off the hook?" I said. "You don't think I was involved in all this?"

We had reached the door by then, and she hooked the plug from the first floodlight with her foot.

"Honey," she said. "You are involved. Why in the hell else would I drag you out here if not to hear what you thought about all of it?"

"Detective Farrel isn't being quite so casual about it," I said.

She yanked her foot and the lights went out. "Farrel is an idiot," she said. "And when Layne gets back, I'm sure he'll dissuade him of the notion that a wee girl like you could kill and disembowel three people."

She opened the door and let the night air waft over us. We stood there for a moment, letting the breeze cleanse our senses of the stink of death and magic. She waved to the security guards as we walked by and opened the car door for me like a gentleman might and drove me home without mentioning the flophouse or the case again.

It wasn't until she'd pulled up outside my apartment that she told me she believed me. In me.

"I've never been one for all that crunchy granola shit," she said. "But you I believe in. A werewolf should understand magic, but if it's outside of what we do, it's hard to comprehend. Still, I believe in you. I believe in your magic."

I caught her eye as the car's light went on overhead, the result of me cracking open my door to climb out. I wanted to tell her I was a fraud but the earnest look on her face kept me from telling her the truth. It felt nice to have someone believe in me, and that was what I wanted to tell her.

I almost did, except she pointed past my shoulder and interrupted me.

"That your dog?" she said.

CHAPTER TEN

THE DOG. I DIDN'T need to follow the direction of her gaze to know which dog she meant, but I twisted around to look at it just the same. There, haunting the hedgerow lurked the massive dog that had protected me when the scythe man had attacked me outside my apartment. Broad and deep black, it stepped into the streetlight for just an instant, but it was enough for me to confirm my suspicions.

It was back.

It had been the harbinger of some pretty awful shit the last time. I remembered she'd asked the same thing of me the day it had haunted the outside of my shop when the killer had attacked me and my mother's grimoire had blasted magic at him. If the dog was back, I wasn't sure I'd be able to sleep.

I swallowed my nervousness long enough to ask, "Are you talking about the dog lurking in the bushes. Big thing. Black as the dark?"

"You see another dog around here?" Parrish asked. "I remember seeing it at your shop. Don't you bother to tie it? It can't wander around loose. Too dangerous."

I managed to shake my head without looking too guilty. I wasn't sure how I'd be able to explain away a magical dog to her even if she was a werewolf.

"It's a stray that's been hanging around," I said.

Parrish mumbled something about strays that I didn't catch because I was already hauling myself out of the passenger side. I leaned down before I closed the door, intending to say goodbye.

"I'd like to thank you for the ride," I said, "but I would have preferred a good shot of whiskey in a dark bar somewhere quiet."

She tapped the top of the wheel four times before starting the engine again. "Maybe next week," she said. "I like to space out exciting dates like this. You know, not wanting to show all my good cards all at once sort of thing."

She gestured at me to close the door, so I did. I watched her back up and drive off down the street with my heart in my throat. I did not want to turn around. I wasn't ready to see the stray again.

I cursed myself for not asking Parrish in so I wouldn't have to enter my apartment alone. Now that the dog had turned up again, I was leery of what might be waiting for me inside. I tried to remember if it had ever turned up during a time when I wasn't about to be attacked and recalled the first time I'd seen it had been when Sherry, the girl who needed a spell to send her dead father to hell, had left my shop.

Layne and his partner, Farrel had burst into my shop that day. The next time, it had hung around the first crime scene not long before the scythe carrying man had come to my store for the first time. Later, it had tried to protect me from the creature that same man became. So no. I couldn't recall a time it had shown up that I wasn't in some sort of danger.

But I couldn't just stand outside forever. It was nearly one o'clock in the morning and a girl had to sleep.

I took a deep, bracing breath and spun on my heel, determined to be a big girl and face my fears. I'd locked my door, left a bunch of lights on. I should be able to go inside my own home without feeling like something was going to jump out at me.

I wasn't normally so spooked, but it had been a hell of a day. Catching sight of the stray again when I'd thought it was gone was just the next sharpest picker in the blackberry bush.

But the dog was gone when I turned and I wasn't sure whether to feel relief or more fear. I scolded myself for being so ridiculous and marched up the front steps with a determination strong enough to bully the fear into a little ball.

It wasn't until I went for my key in my pocket that I remembered I hadn't locked the door after all. I'd run out after Parrish in my slippers and hadn't given a thought to locking up behind me. That changed things, a bit, I had to admit. My bravery shrank.

I panned sideways, glancing to the left to see if the dog was anywhere in sight. Nothing met my gaze but a few leaves from the burning bush as they waved in the air currents. I turned my attention back to the door and gripped the knob in my hand.

It turned easily, proof that I hadn't locked it behind me. I pushed the door open the way a police officer might, throwing it open and bracing myself for whatever might come at me from within.

But nothing moved. The key still sat in its dish on the foyer table. My shoes were separated from each other on the floor by at least three feet, exactly how they'd landed when I'd kicked them off. The refrigerator hummed quietly, keeping time with the dripping of my kitchen faucet, but no other sound broke through the quiet homey music of my apartment.

I sagged against the door when I closed it behind me and let my heartbeat slow to something more normal. It was late already, and while visiting the crime scene with Parrish had battened down the hatches of my appetite, I felt like I should put a little something in my belly to help me sleep. Like a nice, warm glass of milk and a sleep aid.

I crept around the house, first, though. Quick peeks into dark corners and backs of closets revealed nothing unusual. I stood still for long moments in the middle of my living room, waiting to see if any sound whispered through the apartment in the lingering silence.

Only after I'd satisfied myself that I was alone, did I shuffle to the medicine cabinet and pull out a bottle of melatonin. I knew it would knock me out for a few hours but it would take an hour, and usually the hormone woke me up like a rooster at 4 am. I dropped it back into its basket and rifled through the back of my cabinet. The place I kept some stronger prescriptions.

I didn't take anxiety medicine often although my therapist in Nova Scotia had prescribed them for me with the comment that if I wasn't going to be honest with myself about why I couldn't sleep in the first place, then at least I could use them for the worst nights. Like a sedative, she said. But don't over use them.

She was very big on good, natural sleep, my therapist. And medicated sleep was not restorative. The body stopped being able to do what it needed to in order to unwind if it kept relying on helpers to get there.

At the moment, I didn't care much whether I went into a sleep coma from natural methods or chemical. I just wanted to die for a few hours.

I swallowed down a tablet with a large gulp of milk and stumbled to my bedroom, peeling off my clothes as I went. The trail I made along the floor left me naked by the time I got to my bed. I threw myself onto the top and rolled over, pulling the cotton bedspread with me so that I became the center of a warm roll of blankets. Exhaustion took me long before the meds kicked in.

I woke feeling like I was hungover. One quick look at the clock next to my bed told me I was late to open the shop. Not a great way to start the day.

I rolled from the bed rather than jumping out the way I would on a regular day I overslept. The meds left me groggy and slow. My mouth tasted like I'd chewed on my pillowcase while I'd slept and the ache in my back told me I'd slept twisted in an unnatural position.

All reasons why I left the bottle at the back of the medicine cabinet. I hated the after effects. I'd slept, but it wasn't a good sleep.

I yawned as I stumbled toward the bathroom, intending to wash my face and dirty bits in the sink instead of a shower. I turned on the faucets and let the water run to heat up as I dug around for a wash cloth and soap. The mirror fogged over quickly, and I decided the time it would take to deal with wiping the fog away long enough to put make up on would be a waste.

After splashing lukewarm water onto my face and chest, I grabbed the bar of soap and rubbed it over my chest and beneath my armpits. The lush washcloth wiped away the residue and in just moments more, I'd scrubbed all the parts that needed a good cleaning and was heading for my bedroom to pull on some pants and a pretty sleeveless pink top and sweater that looked great but was soft and comfortable, a favorite for days when I needed to feel flubby.

I grabbed my purse from the foyer along with my keys, shoved on a pair of flats and dashed out the door. I was all the way to the sidewalk before I saw the dog again. This time, it tagged along behind me at a respectable distance. When I sped up, it stepped up its pace. When I slowed, so did it.

But the distance never tightened or slackened. It was as though I had it on some sort of tether.

I made it to my shop with ten minutes to spare, and that gave me time to refill the dishes I left outside for the stray cats. From the open door of my shop, the dog watched me dumping kibble into plastic and stainless steel dishes. I paused and watched it sit down, all eager and hungry looking.

"You want some?" I said, lifting one of the bowls.

It wagged its tail in a sweeping motion that moved the dust on the sidewalk. So definitely not a hallucination or else the dust wouldn't have budged.

I chewed my lip, considering whether I should be encouraging it.

"You're not bringing some big bad monster to my doorstep, are you?" I asked as I crossed the storefront with bowls in each hand. "Because if you are, I'll have to call the dog catcher."

The dog backed up a step without standing. Its ears perked up. From my side of the threshold, I could smell the musk of its undercarriage.

I waited till I heard it whine before I crossed over to the outside of the shop. It gave me space while I plopped both bowls down, one on either side of the door. The rest of them would go to the back alley where the more skittish cats hung out.

"You're not exactly good for business," I said to the dog. "Bit big. Way too hairy. You'll scare off my customers." I stood with my hands on my hips.

It cocked its head at me.

"Go on, then," I said. "Eat."

As if it had been waiting for the order, it dove at the bowls and emptied them as though its mouth was a vacuum. In no time they both warbled on the pavement from the frenzied attention the stray had given them. Finished, it backed up several more feet until it was at the mouth of the alley. It watched me silently.

I sighed, and checked my watch. There was no sign of Sherry, the girl who had been in my shop the day Layne and his partner had crashed in.

"You think she's alright?" I asked the dog but it kept its counsel.

With a sense of dread, I stooped to pick up the bowls so I could refill them. There were two fluffy money cats that frequented the front of the store and gave it the general impression of authenticity as they hung around. I liked to keep the bowls full to encourage them.

The dog was gone when I returned to the sidewalk with both bowls filled. The stray cats had begun slinking around my sandwich sign, so I knew they were hungry. Their loud yowls indicated they were tired of waiting.

"Sure sure," I said to them and put both bowls at their regular spots, sentries to each side of the front door.

They leaped for the bowls, one for each side. The cat with a black smudge on its nose got to his first but even as he dropped his nose to the rim, he jerked back as though he had been burned. I toed the bowl toward him.

"Go on, you sourpuss," I said. "It's your favorite."

He looked up at me and yowled but stayed clear of the bowl.

"You'd think you wouldn't be so picky." I dropped to my haunches, thinking I'd pour the contents into the other bowl and go wash the one the smudge nose wouldn't touch, but the other cat acted the same way.

I tried tossing some of the kibble in their direction, but they scattered after that as though I'd tossed hot water on their tails. I stood there, mulling it over when I noticed the dog's snout peek out from the corner of my building.

I knew then, the cats would not be back and I had a feeling it wasn't because of a stray dog.

CHAPTER ELEVEN

SOMETHING HAD SPOOKED THE tom cat. It had lived a hard life on the streets until it found my doorstep and it was a tough little thing. The first time I'd managed to catch it watching me, it had been in a fight of sorts and it wasn't much older than a few months. It was a fighter. A scrappy feline that I'd seen take on a pit bull tied outside the coffee shop across the road.

Knowing the dog had started to show itself again and that the tom was spooked by the smell it had left on the dish made the dread weigh my shoulders down even more. I watched the cat streak across the street with his lady love hot on his tail and I hugged myself thoughtfully. I wasn't ready for more shit to go down. Too much of it had already darkened my door.

I gave the dog a glare and shooed it with a wave of both arms.

"Get the hell out of here," I growled. "If you've got some bad news for me, give it to me on a day when I'm not already feeling like a dirty rag."

The beast disappeared in a waft of smoke.

Trying not to think about the fact that the dog came and went like a bad wind, I went back inside and hoped for the best.

I checked the clock over the counter as I crossed the shop. Sherry's appointment had come and nearly gone. A quick check of my text messages indicated she canceled in favor of visiting her sister, who was down in the dumps.

I was secretly relieved I wouldn't have to face Sherry today. She had been a bit rabid when she'd been here last and I wasn't sure I wanted the reminder that I'd slipped her a bit of psilocybin. That was a different me. Moving on was much easier if a person didn't have to be reminded of mistakes.

So things were looking up, minus the dog and a murder scene that I couldn't get out of my head. All things considered, I could maybe breathe a bit easier without having to face the guilt I still felt over drugging the poor woman. Maybe the bit of mushroom had helped her after all.

The back alley bowls needed to be refilled, so I set about doing that and spared a few moments to watch the stray cats skitter over for their morning meals. The loud purring that filled the alley calmed me in ways I looked forward to every day. By the time the bowls were empty, I'd regained my equilibrium.

I was on my way back into the shop proper when the bell over my front door rang. Someone had come in and I hoped it was with a big enough wallet to make up for the hours I'd missed yesterday at the police station.

I checked the corked bottles and jars on my way by, pausing at the Zombie Vomit canister and remembered I'd stowed a good bit of cash in there that I'd had to leave the day before. I reached behind the jars in front of it and gave it a shake to make sure the money was still inside. When I heard the telltale shuffle of paper within, I breathed a sigh of relief.

With a shove that put it back in place, I spoke over the side of my shoulder, raising my voice enough for whoever had come into the shop to hear me and not leave because no one was around to help.

"I need a few days to prepare for a séance," I said and straightened the bottles before striding the rest of the way through the galley to the main shop, "but if you need a reading or something lighter like a bit of merch, I have time right now if you like."

I stopped short at the end of the galley. Layne stood there, all six foot something of him, with his brush cut a bit longer than it had been last time I'd seen him. Now, it was long enough to catch the breeze of the door closing behind him.

The overall effect of him nearly took my knees out. My throat did clog up at sight of him, and I was pretty sure that if I wasn't still a bit doped up from the sleep meds I'd feel the warmth of early morning lust climb my leg like a dog in heat.

But that's what sleep meds did to me: gave me an overall sense of stupefication. Instead sending out signals to my body that a man worthy of rolling around in hot, sweaty sheets with was in the vicinity, my brain all but shut down on me. The damn thing left me with no more than a distant pleasure he wasn't dead.

It was just as well, really since I couldn't scrape the barest of words from my throat as he strolled into the shop the way a man might if he knew every inch of the building and could walk it blindfolded.

"Good morning to you too," he said when I finally managed to get my legs moving and headed to the counter to busy myself so I didn't have to hold his gaze too long. It had been two weeks or more and I wasn't sure I could look at him without making a fool of myself.

I made a show of sorting through receipts that I'd pinned to a clipboard for filing later, but found the time to lift my gaze to his. He'd crossed all the way into the store and stood within touching distance if I were to reach across the counter and slip my hand around his neck. I could have sworn he licked his lips as his gaze momentarily dropped to my mouth.

Or maybe that was my imagination finally waking up from its medicated slumber. I had a whole host of fantasies I could start spinning if I wanted, not the least of which involved me gripping that muscled neck with both hands as I pulled him closer.

But a gal didn't give in to reckless fantasy in the middle of the morning with a dozen things to get done and a policeman standing in front of her with what looked like mild annoyance.

I shook out the image and laid both palms flat on the counter. I was all ready to give him all the welcome he deserved after going MIA for two weeks, when a movement beyond him caught my eye.

Lurking several feet behind him, scowling with great aplomb stood Farrel. The reddish tint of his hair took on a purple glow in the light of the shop.

I groaned out loud, not bothering to disguise my impatience or annoyance at seeing the detective. Maybe the meds were responsible for that too, but I doubted it. On the one hand, I'd be delighted to see the lovely picture Layne made as he leaned against my counter with one elbow propped sideways. On the other, it was too damn early to be facing down the officer who thought I might be involved in several heinous murders.

I dropped the clipboard onto the counter with a thwack. "If you've come to take me to the precinct again, I'm afraid it will have to be for resisting arrest."

Layne's eyebrow raised half an inch at my response. "I might have expected a better reception," he said.

I squared my shoulders, and rocked back on my heels. I cupped my elbows as I flicked my gaze to Farrel. "Yeah, well, I have things to do today. Like make my rent. So if you two just dropped in to intimidate a poor working girl, you can move on."

Farrel avoided my eye, and the residue of meds in my system gave me the courage to stare at him and will him to look at me as I said, "Are you here to arrest me, Officer Farrel?"

At my question, Layne looked over his shoulder, and reaching back, yanked the other officer to stand beside him. Farrel shook him off and squared his shoulders defensively. It wasn't hard to see who the top dog was in the partnership.

"Say it," Layne said.

Farrel raised his eyes to mine and there wasn't a hint of sincerity in his gaze when he said, "I'm not here to arrest you, Ms. Duncan. I'm here to apologize."

I blinked at him as I inhaled my surprise. "Apologize?"

"Yes," Layne interrupted. "My partner here is under the impression that you are a killer."

I barked out a laugh at that. "Oh, but I am a killer, Detective Garder. Make no mistake about that. Just ask the merry little band of rats that live in the back alley."

Neither detective cracked a smile. They just stood there, one looking angry and the other looking cha-grined. I didn't have time for either of them.

"Listen," I said as I scuffed the toe of my flats across the floorboards on my side of the counter. "This shop has to make money if I'm going to eat this month. So either you arrest me or you buy something. I don't have time or inclination to deal with you today."

To make the point that I wasn't interested in continuing with the conversation, I stormed over to the coat rack I kept in an alcove next to the washroom. I grabbed a sweater from one of the hooks and pushed one arm through the sleeve.

I caught Layne's eye as I was pulling the other sleeve up and settling the sweater over my shoulders. He looked bewildered. That infuriatingly gorgeous hair of his rustled as he ran both hands over the top.

"Am I speaking in tongues?" I asked with a lifted eyebrow. "I'd like you to leave."

Layne prodded Farrel again with his elbow and the junior detective plucked a candle from the nearest shelf in a motion that might be described as a hissy fit if he were a woman. And like any woman he checked the bottom for the price.

"Fifteen dollars," I said.

"It says ten ninety nine," Farrel said as he looked up at me.

I shrugged at his comment to indicate I didn't care what the price tag read. With a barely suppressed sigh, he dug into his pocket for his wallet then crossed the room to drop a twenty on the counter. He slapped it with his palm.

"I'm sorry," he said and this time, although his expression didn't look apologetic, his voice managed to sound it. "I was mistaken."

Layne grunted but said nothing more.

I shot him a look of irritation as I returned to the register behind the counter. I palmed the bill without looking at Farrel.

"I'm sure you were just doing your job." I hit the register key with my free hand. It rang as loudly as the bell over my door did when it announced a client's entrance. I loved the feeling of having an old world shop and part of that ambiance was the sounds it made. I enjoyed stuffing the officer's bill into my till almost as much.

Without another word, I slipped out his change. This I dropped onto the counter and stood back with my arms crossed. The steam was already going out of my pique, probably one more effect from the meds.

"Thanks," Farrel said.

I leaned my hip against the counter, careful not to catch sight of the huge gouge in the surface. "Don't mention it," I said, sagging now that the transaction was over and my reaction made me feel a bit too bitchy for my taste. That wasn't really my style.

"I actually feel safer somehow knowing you are suspicious of everyone," I said, and it was true enough.

It was his turn to grunt but at least he didn't argue. I waited for them both to leave with my eyebrow cocked in Layne's direction because he wasn't making the move to go anywhere. Instead, his gaze dropped to my throat and traveled my collarbone in a lingering way that made me pull the collar of the sweater tighter against my chest.

Something was up, and I knew it for sure when Layne turned to his partner.

"Can you wait for me in the cruiser?" he said to Farrel. "I need to speak to Ms. Duncan alone."

I watched something move between them, a communication that was no doubt born and fostered by hundreds of hours together. Farrel did not want to leave us alone but he wasn't sure how to refuse.

In the end, he nodded and turned to cross the shop. The bell clanged as the door shut behind him. I could see him hanging around the planters, digging his hands into his pocket and coming out with a cell phone. He tapped furiously on the screen.

I came out from behind the counter and hovered within touching distance of Layne, not sure what was going on, or why my body had decided standing next to him was the right and perfect place to be.

"What is it?" I said to Layne. "You want to explain why you and your partner keep insinuating I'm guilty of some atrocious violence?"

I knew full well that it hadn't been both of them accusing me, and I expected him to argue or defend himself, but his response was to trail his finger down my throat, fetching up at the collar of the sweater and burrowing beneath it.

The sleepy lust climbed out from behind the wool blanket of medication, finally. It took several seconds of utter shock for me to realize he was tugging the sweater off me. That I could feel his calloused fingers whispering along my bare skin.

The electricity of his touch combined with the after effects of the medications almost made me gasp. My skin felt deliciously raw.

"Aren't you afraid of a sexual harassment suit, officer?" I said in a low voice. "That kind of interrogation can't possibly be good for the department."

His brow furrowed in bewilderment as he closed the distance between us with a single step. He was close enough that when his other hand buried itself beneath the material covering the other shoulder, I had a dead certainty of the feeling I'd get if he completely undressed me.

My knees sagged.

"Your arms," he said as he pulled the sweater back off my shoulders. I felt it sag beneath my shoulder blades as it hung on my wrists. "I didn't know you had so many scars. I don't remember seeing them before."

Now it was my turn to be confused. "I don't have any scars," I said. "What in the hell are you talking about?" I stepped back, clutching at the fabric as it started to fall away. I shrugged the sleeves upward onto my shoulders again.

"I think," he said. "You better close up shop today."

"Oh hell no," I said. "Psychic. Single Woman. Needs to eat and sleep beneath a rooftop."

He dug into his pocket and extracted his wallet as he swung on his heel. With it in hand, he started lifting candles, statues, signs, pillows, and the like from shelves and chairs and piling them on the counter. I watched until the counter swelled with merchandise that threatened to fall onto the floor at a breath.

"Add it up," he said, rifling through the wallet. I thought it decidedly old fashioned that he carried cash when most people used cards. Maybe the rich were different and liked to show off their money.

"What are you waiting for?" he said, jerking his chin at the pile. "Charge what it costs and then take my money. It should be enough to pay a day's rent. And then," he said with a note of command in his voice that brooked no refusal. "Then follow me. I need you to see something."

I dutifully added up the collection and put it in bags, tying them afterward with black and purple ribbon. Twice, I looked past him to where Farrel stood outside, still texting, still looking far more bitter than he'd appeared when he'd stood next to Layne. I barely had the bags settled onto the floor for him to collect when he grabbed my hand.

We were standing on the client side of the counter and I looked up at him. His eyes had melted to that honey look again. His palm was warm and rough when he curled his fingers around mine. For a moment, I thought when he lifted it that he would put my arm around his neck. My throat squeezed tight in desire and my knees buckled just a little bit. I checked over his shoulder to see if Farrel was watching.

Then Layne laid my palm along my opposite arm and ran it down the length from shoulder to elbow. I felt my own skin against the softness of my palm as he led it up and down my arm.

My knees buckled for real then.

"Sweet Jesus," I said in a tight voice. I ran for the door. I flipped the sign to closed as Farrel furrowed his brows at me, then I turned to lay my back against the solid frame.

Because what I'd figured out in those seconds my palm whispered along my own flesh exactly what he meant. My skin was raised in spots, like smooth worms creeping along my arms.

I had scars alright, but I had not had them the night before.

CHAPTER TWELVE

WHAT I SAW IN the mirror when I ran to the bathroom horrified me.

Not just scars in patterns that looked like some sort of litany of symbols, but each raised bit of skin was traced in an outline of black. I peeled away the collar of the dress and for each inch of skin I revealed, more symbols showed. I grabbed the collar and pulled it away so I could look all the way down to my belly button.

A sound escaped me like I'd never heard myself make before, not even when I'd found the remains of the dogs my mother sacrificed to her spell casting. I bit down on the noise as I stretched the material to the left and right, inspecting my shoulders, and then I let go the fabric, dropping the sweater to the floor.

I rolled my arms back and forth one at a time and had to lean against the sink to keep from sliding down to the floor.

The symbols stretched all the way from my collarbone to my wrist, and had I not been in such a hurry that morning, I might have noticed them long before this. I might have seen them and been able to freak right the hell out in the comfort of my own home.

I felt someone creep up next to me, and in the moment, with the horror of seeing the assault to my skin that had happened sometime between the time

I'd dropped into bed and got up again, I jumped high enough that I knocked my knee on the bottom of the sink.

I stumbled backward and fell onto the toilet seat with my hand cupping my leg to contain the pain that streaked downward into the kneecap.

"Sorry," Layne said, reaching down to help me back up. "You left the door open behind you."

I let his fingers curl around mine for a moment, maybe because his touch was grounding. Maybe because I was just in shock. When he eased my hand away and rubbed my kneecap briskly, I bit down on my bottom lip because I knew if I didn't stop it from trembling, I would cry right there in front of him.

He seemed to sense it and when he was done rubbing the pain from my knee, his hand whispered up my leg beneath the dress.

I grabbed for the hem and yanked it down over my legs chastely and his hand withdrew to plant itself on the toilet seat next to me. To avoid looking at him, I peered down at my arms. I had the feeling he was smirking at me over my reaction.

"I'm alright," I said even though I wasn't.

"You didn't know they were there, did you?" he said softly.

His obvious concern in his voice made me feel ashamed that I'd even suspected him of planting the amulet to frame me. I shook my head quietly.

"I didn't think you get scarified in the two weeks I was gone," he said. "Or that someone might have turned you in my absence." This last was said in a tight voice that sounded a bit territorial, so I decided not to ask. I had my own issues to deal with right then.

I blew out a long breath, the relief magnified now that my suspicions seemed so ridiculous. He gave me his hand when he noticed I was trying to stand, and I let him pull me to my feet. If I examined the markings, I'd noticed they weren't a dark black, more a sooty looking ashen color. The weals of skin within the outlines already looked less red and puffy.

Maybe that was a good thing, a step in the right direction. I could breathe if I thought that.

In getting up, my free hand touched down on steely muscle. He flinched and I took my hand away, deciding not to feel offended that he didn't want me to touch him.

I wasn't quite tucked in close to his chest, but the proximity of him, of the tiny bathroom, allowed the heat coming off him to fill the space. I was grateful because in that moment, I felt very cold.

"What's going on, Brie?" he said in a rasping voice.

"Damned if I know," I said. "I have never gotten a tattoo in my life." I examined my skin again from wrist to shoulder, snaking the limb between us so I could give it a good look.

"Tattoos?" he said as he snagged my wrist and lifted it for inspection. "There's not a stitch of ink on you." He thumbed my skin with a whisper of touch. "Just some reddish looking scars and even those are getting a bit more silver now." He caught my eye with a suspicious cant of his head. "Maybe someone did turn you. You're healing almost as fast as a werewolf."

He laid his nose along my neck and inhaled. "You don't smell like a werewolf."

I jerked my hand from his and pulled out of his embrace. "I'd know if someone turned me." Then I realized I had no idea how a mortal got changed into a shape shifter in the first place. "At least, I think I'd know." I lifted my gaze to his. "Wouldn't I?"

He dropped his hand to my waist, where the warmth ran through me like water. "Oh, you'd know," he said as he guided me out of the bathroom into the shop where I had placed several comfortable chairs for customers. He motioned to the closest one, a royal blue wingback chair with fluffy cushions. "Sit."

I sat without question, and it wasn't just the command in his voice that made me feel compelled to do as he said. It was because my knees had lost the ability to lock into place.

I peeled the neckline of my dress away to expose a bit more flesh to my nervous eye. Sure enough, the runes went all the way across my breastbone. They met at my solar plexus and the sight of them marching across my skin made me drop the fabric and run my hand over it, smoothing it against my breastbone.

"What is going on?" I said.

"You tell me," he said. "I've been gone two weeks. You could have done anything in that time."

I felt my lip pooching up into the top one.

I was going to cry. I did not want to cry. I placed my hands on my lap and fisted the material of my dress to distract myself until I could speak without breaking down.

He must have realized what was happening to me because he ran his hand along the top of my head in a soothing motion that made me think of kids and tousled hair.

"I'll go get a nice cool wash cloth." He stroked my hair like it was the softest velvet ear of a beagle puppy. That thought alone almost made me wail out loud, but when he spoke again, it cut off the tears like a spigot.

"The last chick I made cry told me a wet facecloth helped."

I was left blinking at him as he retreated back to the shop's bathroom. I wasn't sure what infuriated me more, the thought that he'd dare bring up another woman to me under the circumstances or that he'd referred to her as a chick.

The chick thing, I decided. That was what made me the angriest. Because what else would it be?

By the time he'd made it back into the shop, carrying my nice white hand towel with the corner sopping wet all the way to the middle of the fabric, I was standing and my fists were curling up against my thighs.

He wasn't looking at me as he crossed the room, but was studying the material as though it might have directions on how to deal with a weepy woman.

"You couldn't find a face cloth?" I said.

His head jerked up and for a moment, an expression of concern swept across his face. It disappeared when he caught my eye, no doubt because I was glaring at him.

I lifted an eyebrow in indignation. "That's the only white hand towel I have and I like the customers to see it and think they're in good hands and now you've got it all wet and useless."

His chin seesawed subtly but I caught it none the less. "Subliminal signals of purity and holiness, huh?"

"Something like that."

He tossed the towel at me and I caught it with my right hand. I realized as soon as it met my fingers that he hadn't wrung it out enough and it was dripping on the floor.

"I mean..." I said, shaking my head as I made my way past him with every intention of squeezing out the last of the water into the sink. If I muttered as I went by, it was only because I knew the puddles were a slipping hazard.

He caught me as I brushed past him, hooking my elbow until I had to spin to face him. He took the towel from me with a gentle hand.

"It doesn't matter," he said.

"It does matter. It's getting water all over my floor. If someone comes in and slips, they could get hurt. Sue me. I'm already behind on my mortgage for this place, and even though I'm one of the only psychics left in the area, I'm still not getting enough work." I gestured in a way that would encompass the whole of the shop. "I don't know if folks are terrified by the murders and won't come in or if the attack on my shop is scaring them away or if—"

"Stop," he said as he cupped the back of my neck, with his thumbs curling up beneath my jaw to gently ease my mouth closed. He made a cooing sort of shushing sound. That was when I realized I was crying after all.

Dammit. I did not want to cry.

"None of it matters right now." He slipped his hand to my waist and guided me to the chair again. "I know you're pissed, but you're pissed at the wrong things. You've just had a shock and be damned if you aren't the kind of woman to strike out instead of asking for help, but what you need to do is sit down and calmly work through how and why you have scars on your arms."

"And chest," I said. "And tattoos."

"Tattoos?" His foot hooked the back of my knee so that I collapsed neatly into the wing back chair. I caught sight of Farrel outside watching us. He went back to typing into his phone and I looked up at Layne.

"Tattoos," I said and stretched my arm out so he could see. "The scars are fading but the tattoos are staying."

His voice was tight when he responded. "I don't see any tattoos."

I pointed to one with my finger. "You don't see this?" the mark had a quaint curve to it that made the neat horizontal lines appear almost like language. I wondered what it said.

He swallowed as his eye drifted along my outstretched arm until it landed on my face. I saw him pull down the policeman's mask and realized that whatever was going on, he thought it was very bad.

"You better tell me what happened," he said.

So I did. I explained about going with Parrish to the crime scene and seeing the altar and blood and the dried flowers. I told him about the stink of sulfur and the way my hand burned when I touched the wall.

"You broke into a crime scene?" he said stiffly.

"Parrish broke in," I corrected "And she said she was allowed."

He ran both hands over the top of his hair and held them there at the back, his elbows poking outward.

"Fuck, Brie. Your fingerprints will be all over that place."

I clenched the towel against my leg. The wet started to seep through to my clothing.

"But I went with Parrish," I said, searching for the only defensible thing in the whole mess. "She took me there. The security guards saw us both."

He spun around, his back to me and facing the door where Farrel was slipping his phone into his pocket.

He spoke to me, but I had the feeling he was watching his partner with interest.

"Let's hope they remember you and can identify you."

"They cracked lots of crude remarks," I said. "If that helps. I'm willing to bet they don't get out much and will remember."

He looked at me over his shoulder as he dropped his hands. "They made crude remarks to you or to Parrish?"

I thought about it. Maybe it had been Parrish they were riding. "Does it matter?"

"It does if they remember her more than you. She has a bit of a reputation and the guys give her the worst, trying to get her to blush."

"Yeah, well I have a feeling that will never be success-ful." I ran the wet part of the towel over the back of my neck. He was right. It did make me feel better. "So that means I'm in the rhubarb, huh? Out in the weeds all alone?"

He dropped his head back on his neck, either tired, spent, or annoyed. "Not necessarily. I'll feel around."

His hands went into his pockets and I waited for the familiar stick of gum to get unwrapped and popped into his mouth. A waft of mint crested over the room for a second and I took a stupid amount of pleasure from it.

"It's entirely possible no one will question your prints on the scene," he said and I cringed inwardly as I thought of the way Farrel had tossed the amulet at me. That had been found on scene when it shouldn't and its discovery had certainly raised suspicion in his partner's mind.

I thought it best not to bring it up right then. Surely Farrel would have told him about it and I didn't want that same look of bitterness to cross Layne's features again, at least not while I might have made things worse.

I might have considered telling him that it had burned me when I'd caught it, but Farrel started waving frantically at him through the door.

"I best be going," he said.

I nodded, deciding my little confession could wait a day or so. The way his partner was glaring through the glass, I didn't relish holding Layne back for one more moment.

"Go on," I said, knowing I couldn't hold him anyway. "If you're lucky he's just waving at you to get coffee."

"Fat chance," he said as he strode toward the door. He spared a look back at me and by then, I had already decided that once he left, I was going to go back to look in the mirror with a pencil and paper. I didn't have much artistic talent, but if the scars were disappearing, I wasn't sure the tattoos wouldn't too. And I wanted to record every bit of ink.

After the bell above the door chimed, announcing his departure, I spun on my heel and made a beeline for the counter where I stored pens and pads. Then I headed for the sink and the mirror in my powder room. Once I'd snapped on the light and peeled off my clothes, I realized the pen and paper might not be necessary at all.

The marks looked as dark as they had earlier. I leaned in close to get a good look at them in the looking glass. The darkest was on my clavicle and they rode the line of bone like train tracks, little specks of hen scratch that, yes, looked exactly like it was trying to spell something out.

My fingers touched down on the skin of my collarbone as I sought to trace them, to see if they had any tactile difference from the rest of my skin.

That was when shit really hit the fan.

CHAPTER THIRTEEN

I NEARLY PASSED OUT when the horrific image flashed behind my eyes. With a quick grab for the sink, I caught myself before I fell backward onto my ass. Dizziness washed over me and the stink of rotten meat, so strong I tasted it on my palate, cloyed on my tongue.

No matter how hard or how much I swallowed, the residue of rancid fat coated the roof of my mouth. I clutched the sink as I struggled to stand upright beneath the onslaught of images. In one, I sat cross legged in front of a mess of red and slimy coils of meat. The sound of whimpering came from somewhere behind me. Other, more terrifying images swept through before I realized that what lay before me was a dead man. He'd fought long and hard before he'd succumbed to his wounds. Wounds I had inflicted.

I cried out, wailing my horror and shock, and as I did so, I let go the sink. This time, I did fall onto the floor, but I had thrust myself so powerfully backward that I whacked my head against the wall. I slid the rest of the way to the floor, my legs splayed in front of me.

Blackness threatened to take me but I couldn't let it. I had no idea what would happen if I passed out. If something was coming for me, something that could fish around in a man's stomach without remorse, then I had to get out of there. I had to run.

I ended up dragging myself onto my stomach and worming my way to the toilet because I was going to be sick. I didn't make it all the way before the dry heaves spasmed through me.

I lay there on my side an inch from the bowl but I couldn't raise myself up to save my soul. I let the heaving buck through me and it wasn't until they died down and I was gasping for air that I realized I wasn't alone.

"Please don't tell me you saw all that," I said, trying to look back over my shoulder at the door where I knew Layne was standing. "Please tell me you just got here."

My efforts to see over my shoulder were rewarded with the blur of a soft grey sweater coming into view as he knelt next to me. The popping of his knees indicated he'd been standing very still for a long time.

"Shit," I said as I flopped over onto my back so I could see him better. "If you can't say you didn't watch all the pitiful display then at least lie to me. I can take it."

I tried to laugh, but the sound died in my throat as I realized it wasn't Layne squatting next to me. It was a stranger.

In a panic, I scrabbled away as fast as I could. I forgot I was in the bathroom. I whacked my head against the bowl and stars sparked behind my eyelids.

Strong hands cupped my shoulders, pinning me. Blinded by pain, I fought back, imagining the worst, remembering the man who had attacked me in my own shop just weeks before. I kicked out without caring where I aimed. I just flailed about, really, until a voice shushed me.

"You're alright," he said. "I'm not here to hurt you."

There was a note of command in the voice despite the soothing words and I immediately responded. Like it or not, I yanked my hands back against my chest and curled tighter into a ball.

I peered up at warm brown eyes and a salt and pepper short cut. The wrinkles around the corners of his gaze were subtle, as though he'd smiled a little too often. Although I'd only ever seen him once, I knew exactly who it was.

"You're Layne's dad," I said, the realization making my cheeks flame. How much had he seen and what would he think of me, I didn't want to consider. "I saw you. At the charity dinner."

"I might be Layne's dad, but I have an identity all my own." He smiled brightly. "Call me Owen. OWEN I might have introduced myself if things had gone differently," he said as his arms dipped lower onto my back and he pulled me away from the toilet. They were strong hands. He barely even grimaced with effort as he man-handled me into a decent sitting position.

"I suppose it wasn't the best of occasions to meet," I said and pulled my knees up, fully intending to curl them under me so I could stand. The charity dinner had ended abruptly when a dead man had been dropped in front of the hotel. The newspapers had a field day with it.

He laid his arms across his knees as he regarded me and the power of his gaze kept me from pushing myself to my feet. It didn't seem right to stand when he wasn't, but boy, did I feel uncomfortable.

"My son surprised me that night, I must say. It's been a long time since he's brought a girl home." He chuckled as though there was some inside joke I should have been privy to.

I scooched myself sideways so I could lean against the wall. "I wonder why that is," I said. I didn't mean for it to come out as an accusation but it did and his eyebrows climbed half an inch above that steely gaze.

"I often wonder the same thing," he said. Then he smiled. And in that one second his full mouth turned upward in the corners and I saw a flash of beautiful white teeth, I liked him. More than that. I found him intriguing. I smiled back.

"Do you think he's gay?" I asked in a conspiratorial tone. I certainly didn't believe so, but there was no telling what Layne's father might think. "Not that it matters but you know how some men are..."

The smile wavered but then he laughed. "Oh, I think it's more I'm a bastard than he has a sexual preference for men. He keeps a lot of women on pretty short leashes but he won't let me meet any of them. Scared I'll bite, I guess." This last was said with a note of gruffness that sounded feigned for my sake. A joke of sorts, I guessed.

I wondered at his somewhat Freudian usage of words like leashes and bite, but said nothing. I must have got a queer look on my face, though, because he suddenly heaved himself to his feet and reached his hand out at the same time so I could grab for it as he rose.

We stood facing each other. He towered over me by at least a foot, not quite as tall as Layne, but with a much more imposing stature. I caught a whiff of fading cologne and that pure manly pheromone that's hard to describe but is clearly irresistible even when you know what it is.

"Let's get out of here," he said. "It's hard to broach the subject I want to talk to you about with the smell of toiletries in the air and the sound of dripping faucet."

I swallowed somewhat nervously and nodded because with his assumption that he could decide what I would do, I found myself wanting to do it. That wasn't like me at all. The one longish relationship I'd had, my stubborn unwillingness to be submissive put us at odds with each other all the time.

With a motion for him to go ahead of me, I waited till he left the small room. Only after he'd stepped over the threshold into the shop proper, did I feel like I had the space for my lungs to expand again. I watched him examine my store with the sense that he was passing silent judgment and I soon saw all the flaws. The cushion from the wingback chair that I'd knocked to the floor in my race to the bathroom, the streaks on the windows, the scuffing on the floor where the traffic was the heaviest.

"Nice counter top," he said as he angled toward the cash register. He trailed his finger down the gash in the surface and I all but winced at the thought that he'd ask about it and I didn't, just didn't want to talk about it. Not to him. I didn't want to feel like a victim in front of him. Like prey.

"It's from Nova Scotia."

He nodded appreciatively as though I'd said it came from Carrara.

I waited for the inevitable question. I even saw it forming on his face as he turned to me, and was struggling to find a way to answer without making myself seem like a coward.

"I wonder," he said as he leaned against it and crossed one foot over the other.

"It's not what you think," I blurted out before he could ask how the gouge got there or why I left it to mar the perfect top.

He propped his hands on the edge of the counter behind him, framing himself against the long line of it. "I wouldn't presume to think anything of you," he said with a smile, "and certainly not that you'll come to dinner without giving you the chance to answer for yourself."

I blinked stupidly. "Dinner?"

He leaned forward and crossed his arms over his chest. "Dinner. It's what I wanted to talk to you about."

"I don't understand." I felt around for the edge of the wingback chair so I could sit down. "You want to ask me out?"

He chuckled darkly at that and I was glad I was sitting down because I'd obviously said something foolish. And of course I had. He hadn't planned to ask me out at all. There was obviously some fancy dinner in the offing like there had been with Layne. Or now that Layne was home, he just wanted to get me in the same space as his son so he could watch us together. What had Parrish said about him hating witches? Was he trying to ferret out Layne's intentions so he could dissuade him from making a mistake?

Of course that would only matter if I was a witch at all.

I looked around the shop at all the trappings that indicated I was exactly as I advertised and sighed.

"You're worried about being seen with an older man?" he said and pushed off the edge of the counter to stalk toward me the way a panther might advance on a koala. "It's perfectly fine to admit you don't find older men attractive, but I don't think that's the case here, is it?"

His nostrils flared, just a bit, not enough to be revolting, just enough to make it seem as though he was inhaling the air around me, testing for the same pheromones I knew were coming off him in waves.

"Would it help if I told you I'm younger than I look?"

"You look pretty damn young to me," I said, still struggling to make sense of what was happening. "I mean, for a man old enough to be Layne's father." It was truth. There was nothing remotely aged about him at all. He seemed as virile as his son.

He stopped a foot from the chair and regarded me as I looked up at him. Like Layne, his eyes had a honeyed color to them that I recognized as the beast within. My heart hammered out an SOS to my brain to get the hell out of there before I got caught in some invisible trap I couldn't escape.

"It's a delicate thing to ask a woman out when you know she's dated your son."

"You are asking me out." I could barely believe my own ears. I was pretty sure I remembered Parrish inferring he had an issue with witches. Something about Layne having a nerve bringing a witch to the fancy-assed charity dinner. I'd presumed he hated witches and as I found out his pack had been guardians for a coven, assumed his hatred stemmed from that.

He nodded. "Parrish tells me you had only the one date. That you haven't seen Layne for some weeks now."

Parrish had said that? I couldn't imagine her stomping up to her alpha and spilling her guts about a woman he didn't know existed.

"You're confused," he said and smoothed his hair back in the same gesture Layne used. "I should explain better. I did see you at the charity dinner. I saw you and wanted you the moment I caught your eye."

"I mean..." It was all I could do not to squirm beneath his scrutiny.

"You don't like that bald sort of honesty?" he said. "You'd rather I tiptoe around and woo you the way a teenager might? I don't work that way." He crossed his arms over his chest and something hard swept through his gaze. It was enough to make my spine tingle with delicious threat. "You don't get to be where I am by being timid."

"I know what you are," I said and he didn't look the least startled even if the finger in full view did jerk to life and tap out a short rhythm on his forearm.

"And I know what you are too," he said as he closed that final foot between us and leaned down to plant both hands on the chair, framing me this time as he peered down at me. "But I'm surprised Parrish thought it her place to enlighten you about us even though it was not her place to do so." His mouth thinned out as he frowned. "Very well. So you've somehow come to terms with the concept of werewolves and, I suppose, you know I'm the pack alpha."

I found it really hard to hold his gaze and found myself averting my eyes to the apple in his throat. It was interesting that he'd assumed Parrish had been the one to reveal the secret of the pack's existence and not Layne. I decided if he didn't know any differently, I didn't need to be the one to tell him. All I could do was stare at him.

"All you have to do is say no and I'll leave," he said. "I'm not a brute. Just straight forward. I can tell you like that about a man."

"Do you also think I have daddy issues?" I said because I did not enjoy how accurate his assessment of me was when he'd only just met me.

I expected him to draw back, offended, but he didn't. Instead his gaze roamed the skin of my shoulder to the pulse in my throat. I knew it was pounding out a feverish beat, and I knew he could see it.

"Layne's reputation with women is well known. If I thought he wanted you, I would let this be. I'm no poacher. Surely one date with my son wouldn't keep you from seeing the real potential in what could happen between us. You don't owe him anything."

I registered only one thing. That the man in front of me wouldn't have approached me if he thought Layne wanted me.

It was a blow to my ego. Layne had played me. Made me feel as though there might be something there between us. How many other women did he do that to on a regular basis, enough to gain this reputation his father spoke of? The hurt and humiliation rose like a flame in my throat and it must have ignited something in my expression because Layne's father smiled very slowly.

"I don't want to wait," he said as though he sensed I might be on the cusp of declaring I'd tear his clothes off right there just to spite Layne. "I can have my chef make anything you like or we can go anywhere you've dreamed of. Want authentic French? I'll jet us to Paris. Want fish from the Mediterranean? I'll have the pilot fly us to Cirque Terra."

"I don't need all that," is what I said and he drew back then, satisfied he'd claimed his prey.

"Then let me have my driver pick you up." He let one finger touch down on my wrist. It slipped over my pulse, testing. "You can come to me tonight."

I shook my head, managing to find some sense to refuse, as I withdrew my hand from his. "I feel like I'm being railroaded or shanghaied."

He chuckled, a dark and smoky sound that made my belly squirm despite the shock of it. "Let's make it tomorrow night, then. Gives you time to get ready, buy something nice. I'll make an account in your name at whatever shop suits you." He eyed me from top to bottom. "Not Victoria's Secret," he said. "Not for you. Gucci, maybe or Versace. I'll make accounts at both in your name. Come dressed as you like but how you think I'd like beneath that."

"You're pretty sure you're gonna see the inside of the package," I said. "Some women might feel like a prostitute."

"Some women," he said, "but not you, I take it." There was a sort of shrewd scrutiny in his glance as he shrugged.

"I might take you up on it just to get the clothes and then tell you to go to Hell."

He rocked back on his heels. "I can see why Layne was attracted to you," he said. "And why he gave up on you so fast. You're too much woman for him."

I was beginning to think this was more about his son than me—a turn of events that made the situation even more intriguing. A gal might just want to see the entire thing through. If just out of curiosity.

"There's no shame in taking advantage of someone who's obviously setting themselves up for it," he said, and the comment was so close to the mark that I had a hard time not sucking in a sharp gust of breath.

I wondered if he knew about my past business practices and decided that he was not the sort of man to proposition someone unless he had a pretty good bead on who they were and what they did. It took a good deal of willpower not to reveal anything in my body language as I studied his.

What I saw was a man in control. If he knew what effect those words had on me, he didn't show it.

He waited for a response from me but when he didn't get it, he sealed his hands into the pockets of his pants, probably realizing I was studying him as keenly as he was me.

"What you decide on at the end of the night will be entirely up to you," is what he said after a few moments, "but you might as well know in advance what it is that I want. And make no mistake. I want you and I'm willing to come right out and say so. If you end up feeling the same, then what's a little lingerie between friends?"

Friends wasn't the term he wanted to use, I was sure, but he smiled when he said it, as though he hadn't just treated me like a gold-digging escort. Maybe he was used to younger women throwing themselves at him for his money. Maybe he expected me to be excited at the prospect of bagging a wealthy lover.

I might be furious at Layne for making me feel like a fool, but I wasn't about to jump into the sack with his father just to spite him. I might, however, decide to teach his misogynistic father a lesson or two in handling women.

Plus, I was both tempted and repulsed by the offer. It wasn't every day a gal got propositioned so bluntly.

I was still searching for my response when he rounded on his heel and strode to the door.

"I'll send Parrish to you," he said over his shoulder in a cunning way that indicated he thought Parrish would most certainly inform Layne, and I wondered what he wanted more: a roll in the hay or to enrage his son.

He exited the shop to leave me staring at the door long after he'd left.

I released a heavy sigh and sank against the back of the chair, casting an eye around my shop as I mulled over just what the old man was up to.

And my gaze landed on the death mask I'd left on the counter. I'd propped it up against the cash register so I could catch sight of it now and then as I worked in the shop. The thought was that some sudden insight might strike me when I wasn't thinking about it too much.

Except it wasn't a death mask anymore. It was the very real looking face of a young girl.

CHAPTER FOURTEEN

IT WAS A SECOND and no more, but I bolted from the chair just the same. I had the time to catch her eye and watch a long tear drop from the chin of the mask to fall onto the floor in front of the counter. Then, as if by merely staring at it, the mask realized it shouldn't be showing anything but a plaster facade and it went back to being an inanimate thing again.

"Oh sweet fuck," I said and took five wooden steps toward the counter. Everything in me wanted to run screeching from the shop, but after battling a psycho and seeing the ghost of my mother and everything in between, I guess my spine had grown a bit of steel.

Righteous anger fueled me as I faced it down. How dare it blink out at me with real eyes and then disappear as though it presumed to make me think I'd gone mad.

"Better than you have tried to take me out," I said to it.

It laid there, staring back up at me with those vacant eyes.

I leaned on the counter with one elbow, bracing myself against the edge and hovered eye to gaping eye-hole.

"Do that again, I dare you." I pulled off the sweater I'd worn that morning over a pretty pink sleeveless top. Show the thing I meant business.

When it did nothing but sit there, I craned over it, trying to look at the back from my top-side angle. Maureen had attached a leather string to it on each side so she could hang it on the wall, presumably.

The webbing of pores and flesh was barely discernible in the plaster unless the light hit it just right, which it did right then. The young woman whose face had imprinted into the cast had several pock marks or moles in her chin at the time she'd died. Whoever had cast her had caught some of her hair in the plaster. Red. Such a golden shade of it that the girl must have had a fiery temper to go along with the auburn locks.

I lifted it from the counter so I could turn it over in my hands. I'd not truly believed the thing had been possessed. Now, I wasn't so sure.

But something even stranger happened as my palms met the plaster. The marks all across my chest tingled one after the other like Christmas tree lights tracking along one after the other, making a trail all the way from the center of my chest down both arms to my wrists.

It felt like they were singing to my skin.

I set the mask down with a hasty movement and backed away from the counter. One by one, the tattoos blinked off and went to sleep.

"Fuck," I said because there wasn't a better word, adjective, pronoun, or verb to sufficiently contain all I felt right then.

To test, I stepped toward the mask again, my gaze pinned warily to it. If it was going to pull the shade of flesh over itself again, I was completely ready to run screaming from the shop.

Nothing happened. I blew out a long sigh. Too much craziness in one day. It wasn't good for the nerves.

The bell chimed over the shop door and I spun to see a familiar face standing just this side of the threshold. Sherry looked happy and healthy and my consternation over the mask and the tingling in my arms disappeared as I rushed to greet her.

"I'm so glad to see you." I waved her over, signaling that she should sit in the wing back chair I'd just vacated. "How are you? You look great."

She smiled broadly and hooked a gorgeous yellow purse over her shoulder. "I am great," she said. "Whatever you did, it worked. I haven't seen him for weeks."

Him was the ghost of her father, whom she'd paid me to contact during a séance and then immediately freaked out when the mushrooms took effect and she'd caught sight of him in the dark corners of my shop. To be honest, I'd cast no magic except to toss a light dose of psilocybin mushroom dust in her tea.

I peered over the top of the wingback chair as she settled into the seat and tucked her purse alongside her thighs as she looked up at me. The man hovering behind her watched her as though he thought she would break if she moved the wrong way. With salt and pepper hair and a stomach that rose like a bowl of bread dough over his belt, I presumed he would need a chair long before he'd ask for one.

I kicked the ottoman toward him but he didn't so much as glance at it.

Sherry crossed her hands in her lap. "I was hoping maybe I could book another session."

I blinked at her stupidly.

"Is it for you or for your friend" I nodded in the direction of the man lurking behind her chair.

She angled her head at me in confusion. "My best friend," she said. "My sister."

Her sister. Not the man standing behind her. A man she wasn't even acknowledging, now that I paid closer attention. A man who rocked side to side as though he were struggling to stand straight without collapsing, a big bulk of man who seemed to feel as though he was balancing on a pinpoint.

I shivered as the man lifted his gaze to mine. The tattoos across my breast bone tingled.

Dead, they seemed to say. The man was dead. Her father. She wasn't seeing him, but I was.

I swallowed down the nausea at the realization and determined to show her a normal face, the way one would look if it wasn't being stared down by a dead man.

"What can I do for your sister?" I said, scratching through the notes in my brain for something I might be able to do that wouldn't need another shot of drugged tea. I hoped it wasn't another exorcism. I'd not learned yet how to do make them seem real without the psilocybin. The fraudulent supports I'd used in the past to make myself look more authentic had been a crutch I'd leaned on with relish. Now that I was clean of that addiction, I was on my own.

I'd used the mushroom tea to make her think she was really free of her father's ghost. And here I'd thought she'd been tripping when she'd addressed him in my back room. Maybe he'd been there all along and I had been the one who couldn't see him.

"Does she want to cast off your dad too?" I looked directly into the ghost's eyes at that and he glared back.

Sherry grinned. "No. Nothing like that."

She fidgeted in the chair, pulling out the cushion from behind her and tossing it onto the floor next to the chair. "My sister lost a child two years ago. She was nine. Her daughter, I mean. They've never found her. Not a trace. No clothing. No body. No leads."

The man standing behind her screamed soundlessly. I had to drag my gaze away from him just to keep from freaking out. My voice was far more level than I expected it to be when I asked her, "And you think I can locate her where the police have failed."

It was tricky business getting involved in cold cases. I didn't mind pretending to cast off shades of haunting family members or reading futures from obvious details, but to get a woman's hopes up that I might be able to find a missing child? That would be cruel.

Sherry opened up the mouth of her purse and started digging inside as I struggled to find a response that would keep me out of the inevitable train wreck I'd find myself in if I agreed. Watching her, I realized that she might be able to help me.

"I'm not sure if I could manage to find a missing kid," I said with as much kindness as I could find to warm the 'no' that was coming. "I wouldn't want to fail her." I reached over and closed her purse.

She looked up at me and I smiled as I eased the purse away from her grip, her hand slipping out to rest on her lap. "But I wonder if you might be able to do something for me. It's not a big deal. Just a quick look at a picture."

Seeing her again had sparked the memories of the vandal who had graffitied my shop. At the time, I'd thought the vandal had been Sherry's partner, an angry husband irate that I'd duped her, and out for revenge.

Later, I'd found the man in a photo in one of my mother's trunks. In it, he stood with several women in front of a building with a Hecate wheel painted over the door. I'd assumed they couldn't be the same man because the picture was over thirty years old and the man hadn't changed one bit.

So he had to be a relative. A doppelganger from his own gene pool. But his actions had always bothered me. He had no connection to me or my shop or any of my clients that I knew of. I kept thinking there must be some connection I'd overlooked. Maybe that connection was Sherry.

"Wait here," I said and raced for the back room where I'd stored much of the ephemera in totes to keep them from deteriorating or getting damp. I'd not had any time to look the stuff over past the first initial unpacking and after the scythe man tried to kill me in my store, I didn't have the energy to even look at the stuff. But now, the time might be just right.

"It's just one photo and I'd like to see if you know the man in it."

I found the photo easily enough since I had found it peculiar and kept it at the top of the stack along with others that seemed to be from the same era. A time when my mother was young and what looked like a group of very chummy but peculiar looking people.

The thread that connected Sherry to the man who had vandalized my shop was a thin one and I knew it. He'd been enraged at the thought I was a charlatan and the only person I'd done business with around that time was Sherry.

It didn't explain why the man looked exactly the same in the photo as he did when he'd been in my shop, but hey, a whole hell of a lot of strange things had been happening lately, and I badly wanted to figure out why he'd come to my shop in the first place. Why he'd wanted my amulet so badly he tried to yank it off my neck and later stole it.

I plucked the photo from the pile and carried it back to Sherry who had stood up by the time I'd returned. She was running her finger down along the gouge in my counter.

She looked up sharply when I breezed over to her.

"Here," I said, pointing at the tall wiry looking man I'd presumed at first was her partner. I laid the photo onto the dig in the wood, covering it up so I wouldn't have to look at it.

"Do you know this guy at all? Ever seen him before?"

I knew it was a long shot, and when she shook her head, I felt a strange sense of relief.

"You're sure you don't know him?" I said. "He's not a relative of your husband's or anything? A friend of a friend? An uncle? A grandfather?"

She shook her head. "I've never seen him before or anyone who even remotely resembles him."

I smiled at her and tucked the photo into my pocket because the ghost was staring at it too intently. "Thanks," I said. "You've been very helpful."

"It's an awfully old picture," she said. "Maybe someone at the library archives has some information. They should at least have a record of the hotel in the picture. Maybe some of the other people."

I fingered the photo, running the pad of a finger over the tacky backing.

She hooked her purse over her arm. "Anyone in the photo your people?"

"No," I said. "I don't know any of them. Except for the man I showed you. He came to my shop a few weeks ago." I didn't say why he'd come and I wasn't sure why I'd even admitted that much.

The man had injected himself into my life for some unknown reason and he'd died a horrible death as a result of it.

"Wow," she said. "If he came here, he'd have to be ancient."

My eyebrows squirreled together at the thought, because yes, indeed. He would have to be ancient. And yet he hadn't been old at all. He'd looked exactly the same age as he had in the photo. I would put him in his early thirties.

"So you can't do anything for my sister?" she said.

I shook my head. "I'm sorry." I felt the urge to touch her shoulder to ease the refusal. "I wish I could." It was true, at least. I tried not to imagine the cash that I'd just turned down. At least the ghost looked relieved. He even started to fade a little, which helped my nerves a hell of a lot.

Sherry nodded politely and if she looked disappointed, she didn't let it weigh her shoulders down. She really did look better, and as she left the shop, her father trailed along behind her. I waited until they were gone before I sank into the chair for a long while, pondering things.

And as I stared off into space, I gradually became aware that someone was standing in the middle of my shop watching me. It took me several more moments to realize that it wasn't just a man from off the street, but a man who was dead. A man whose body I had seen beneath Layne's jacket as he lay dead at the hands of the psychotic killer who had attacked me in my shop.

The exact same man as in the photo I'd just shown Sherry.

Chapter Fifteen

I woke with the strange sensation that I'd lost time. Confusion swam around me, and it took several long blinks to realize I'd blacked out the moment I caught sight of the dead man. Several blinks more and I discovered I wasn't in my shop any longer.

I was standing in front of the wall of runes at the crime scene I'd visited with Parrish the night before. The floodlights were not lit in the flophouse, but the streetlights cast enough illumination for me to know exactly where I was. If I doubted it, the smell of garlic and herbs and old blood was enough to confirm it for me.

It was dark outside, which meant I'd been out for several hours and managed to sleep walk from my shop all the way across town to pass through security guards at the crime scene.

To say I was freaked out would be an understatement.

With a mincing backward step, I eased myself away from the wall far enough that I could see the expanse of it. The stink of death clawed its way down my throat. And another smell accompanied it. Without trying to pinpoint where it was coming from, I inhaled through my nose, telling myself I would not scream when I let the breath go. I would calmly and sedately, like any other day, just exhale.

I dragged in another breath when that one whistled into and out of my nose, and then I was able to identify that other aroma. Wet dog, maybe, or manky fur.

Right about the time I recognized the smell, I realized my fingers were clenched into fists at my side and one hand was holding onto something. There was no give to the clunky object, just hard surface.

I looked down, lifting the fist to my gaze and uncurled my fingers.

There, in the middle of my palm rested a small but ornately decorated knife handle. Even more frightening than finding a handle in my grip was wondering where the blade was gone if it wasn't stuck in its handle.

Something wet and cold ran down my arms beneath my sleeves. The pretty sleeveless shirt clung to me at the chest.

It didn't take long to figure out the liquid was blood. In a haze, I looked downward and caught sight of droplets all over the floor around me.

My own? Someone else's? The answer either way clamped cold fingers around my heart.

"Shit," I said, and then, prudently terrified I wasn't alone, I swung around to face the room.

The waning moonlight wasn't enough to light the room, but the street lamps outside filtered in enough through the window that I could make out the floods and the derelict condition of the interior. The sound of my own rasping breath echoed back at me.

I swallowed hard, trying to force the clump of fear back down into my throat. I was alone. I wasn't in immediate danger. I could gather my wits if I wanted to.

But it was hard. So hard. I forced myself to sneak over to the window to check for security. On my way to the window, I stopped at the door. Tried the knob. It turned easily. So not locked. At least I hadn't beamed into the living room of the flop house. I could rule out aliens at least.

I tittered out of nerves and started to hug myself to quell the trembling. Then I realized I still held the knife handle. I held out my hand to the breath of light and confirmed my suspicions. Dark smears of viscous looking fluid ran down to my palms and in between my fingers.

I checked the knife handle again, angling it in the light coming in from the window. Yes. It was a handle only. No blade. I didn't want to think where the blade itself might be, stuck in the back of some poor innocent. I told myself if I'd killed someone I would know. I'd remember that.

A cautious check of the window showed the security guards were still there, chatting with each other. Another laugh escaped me. Manic sounding.

I clamped it off with a bite down on my lip.

For a moment I considered slipping out the door, but then I realized they would see me leave if they hadn't seen me enter. I leaned my back against the door and decided the smart thing to do was call someone. If I'd been conscious enough to pick up a knife before I came here, maybe I'd been smart enough to leave my phone in my pocket.

I didn't dare drop the knife handle. I held onto it as, with trembling fingers, I dipped into my jeans pocket. The sigh of relief when it touched the familiar case came of its own accord, a long rasping 'fuck' of relief.

I replaced the phone with the knife handle and swiped the screen, angling it toward me so it would dampen the light and not draw attention from the guards. Then I sank down onto my haunches, out of sight. Calling Layne was out of the question. I didn't know how I'd explain this to him and I wasn't sure I wanted to right then. That left just one more person in my contacts.

Parrish.

She'd brought me here originally. If anyone could get me out again without too many questions or suspicions, it would be her. It seemed a rational enough decision until I heard the phone start to ring. Then I panicked. I couldn't talk to her. I couldn't talk to anyone right then.

I clicked off and shot off a text instead. Simple. To the point. "Come to the flop house. I need you."

The response was short and terse. K. And I waited only a moment before it flickered over the screen. She was up. So it couldn't be too late. A quick check of my phone indicated it was a few minutes after midnight. I tried to calculate how long it had taken us to get here the first time and my brain coughed a bit like a dusty engine, then simply gave up.

I decided to give up too. It seemed the best plan of attack to use my energy to keep from going batshit. I leaned my head against the wall and made a concerted effort to simply breathe. In and out and in and out and rinse and repeat.

The whole time I waited, I clenched that knife blade and my phone, terrified if I moved at all, everything would evaporate and I'd find myself back in my shop. Or somewhere worse.

It took forever to hear Parrish's laugh coming from outside, but when I caught the sure, tonal sound of it, and realized it was just a little off kilter to be her usual casual laugh, I scrambled to my feet and moved away from the door.

I waited until it opened and she stood bathed in the streetlight glow before I broke down. A cold breeze wafted in, colder than the air in the room. Gooseflesh tracked my skin and made my teeth chatter. My legs went to water as she closed the door with an audible click.

She caught me by the elbow as I went down, sobbing.

"What in the holy fuck is going on?" In one glance, she took in the blood on my arms, the tears on my face, and no doubt the stink of dog that still permeated air by the way her nostrils flared, and she pulled me sideways, out of reach of the streetlights. "And what pray tell is that God-awful stink?"

Count on her to distill the issue down to the most critical. Not, why are you here, what do you want, or why are you covered in blood. Bless her heart, she didn't even consider I might be a killer. Or maybe she wasn't worried I could hurt her if I was.

"Dog," I said and gestured over my shoulder. I'd caught sight of it crouching in the corner shadows moments before she arrived. I'd tried talking to it once as it hunkered into the shadows, watching me. But it merely grumbled low in its throat and disappeared into the darkness. A chill swept through the air and I realized whatever magic had brought it to me had taken it back. I tried not to panic.

"No dog I know smells like that." She released me to my own power and waved her hand in front of her face. "You feeding it rotten eggs or something."

"It's gone," I said because I knew if she looked for the beast, she wouldn't find it.

She sent me a peculiar glance before reaching for the plug to the floodlight nearest her, but I stopped her.

"Don't," I said.

She canted her head at me, but jammed the plug into the outlet anyway. "I don't take don'ts," she said as the space flooded with blue light. "Now. Mind telling me why in the bright blue hell you are here?"

Her eye roamed my arms down to my clenched fist still holding the knife blade. I shuffled on my feet, noting that she was dressed for bed. I blinked stupidly at the wool socks shoved into sandals she wore, trying to formulate my answer. Any answer.

"I don't know."

"You don't know if you mind telling me or you don't know why you are here?"

"Both, I guess."

She pressed her lips together and scanned the room. "Does Layne know you're here?"

I shook my head and she nodded hers as though she thought it was a good thing he didn't. With a heavy sigh she dug beneath the flannel shirt that she'd thrown on over the white tank top to scratch thoughtfully at her chest.

Her nipples showed through the material and I averted my gaze. She caught the movement and brushed at her tank top.

"Good thing I was just chilling with a Harlequin and not a pillow queen or I'd be dressed a bit more scantily."

I had no idea what a pillow queen was, but I gathered she'd been reading. I wouldn't have taken her for the romance type.

"So?" she said.

I flung my arms up in frustration. "I don't know, I told you. One minute I was sitting in my shop, staring off into space and the next, I'm standing here staring at that damned symbol." I gestured wildly at the wall. "And to top it off I'm covered in..." my voice failed there as I choked on the words and looked down at myself. I swallowed and swallowed, working at the clump of terror and adrenaline that fisted itself into my throat.

She reached out and touched the top of my head so gently, that the tears finally spilled over.

"It's alright," she said in a shushing tone. "I see it. I smell it. But whose is it?"

I shook my head and she let go a soft groan.

"Well, that's not helpful at all."

She hovered near me as though she wanted to pull me in for a hug but held back because of the blood. Maybe she was worried it was evidence of a sort and didn't want to contaminate it or her. Whatever her reasons, she did not embrace me and I sensed not doing so bothered her. That alone helped me gather my wits.

I stood rigidly still as she lifted the nearby floodlight and panned it over my arms.

"Yours, I think," she said. "The direction is down, so it's come from you not someone else." She lifted the collar away from my neck and peered down my shirt as I sucked in a breath. When she looked at me next, she was so close I could make out the white hair in her eyebrow.

"Your chest is bleeding too."

I peered down as she lifted the flood. The light clawed its way into my shirt and for the first time, I realized my runes were bleeding. That was the source of the blood. I hadn't killed someone. I had hurt myself.

I knocked the light and her hand away, not wanting to see more. "The marks are bleeding."

"Marks?" she said as she leaned closer. When she peered up at me, it was with an expression of bewilderment. "There are no marks. Just a lot of blood." She waved her hand between us. "And that awful stink. It's not wet dog. I know the smell of wet dog." She grinned as though she'd made a stupid joke but then pressed on. "It's rotten eggs. I know that smell too."

"Sulfur," I said. "Someone has been casting." I put my fingers to my temples. The mother of a headache had begun to pound between my ears. "Plus, I think I saw a ghost. A man. He showed up just before I blacked out."

"A ghost?"

I explained what I could about the shade man, as I'd begun to think of him. She waited, listening patiently even as her expression clouded with concern. The trouble was, I couldn't be sure her concern was over the shade man or my mental health or the whole damn situation.

She pulled off her flannel shirt and draped it over me the way Layne had his jacket all those weeks ago. I sent her a sharp look and she smiled broad enough that I saw all her front teeth.

"Not to worry," she said. "I've no lesbian designs on you. It just seemed the right thing to do what with you shaking enough to jiggle your way right out of your pants."

"I know," I said. "I'm just...I'm just a mess is all. Not thinking straight. All this blood and God only knows how--"

My words cut off as she whipped the shirt back off my shoulders and started rubbing at my arms, scraping hard enough to remove the dried on blood. I had the feeling my skin would end up red and raw by the time she was done but I didn't care. I just watched her, aloof and dead-minded, until she seemed satisfied she'd got it all.

She stood back and balled her shirt up in her fist. "It's not like it's evidence," she mumbled. "No sense letting it dry there."

"Thank you," I said and she shrugged.

"I should have done it first thing." As though she was uncomfortable with her own forgetfulness, she started making rounds of the room, talking as she went.

"Those bastards out there will ask about you," she said, jerking her thumb toward the door. "I had a hard time convincing them I forgot something in here." She looked down at her white tank top. "Me being in my jammies and all. What did you say to them that they let you in? I might be able to use that."

I barked out a laugh and tapped my chest. "Fugue state, remember?"

She gawked at me. "You really don't remember? Well, they didn't mention you to me, so maybe they just didn't see you go past. Gonna make it a hell of a lot harder explaining you when we leave." She leaned sideways to peer out the window. "Maybe I can distract them long enough for you to bolt." She tossed a look at me over her shoulder, squinting. "Can you run? I mean really run? Like can you make it to the sidewalk without breaking a sweat?" She waved her hand in a dismissing gesture. "Never mind. I know your type. All bedroom athletics and zero stamina for much else."

I was about to protest when she held up her hand to stop me talking.

"Layne," she said. "We've got no choice. We have to call him. He's the lead on this. He can send the men home or out for a snack or something."

I really didn't want to bring Layne into this. I didn't want him to see me the way I probably looked. My eyes all bugged out and terrified, my skin swollen and red from the scrubbing, the soaking of adrenaline that was making me so edgy I was barely coherent.

I was about to say so when I leaned against the wall for a moment to catch my breath, my palm flattening against the old plaster. That's when a searing pain swept up my arm.

In seconds, it felt like they were on fire.

Chapter Sixteen

IF HAVING ELECTRIC JOLTS ratcheting up my arm was terrifying, the things I saw between the waves of pain was much, much worse. Visions flashed through my mind like a kaleidoscope on crack. The swiftness of the transitions and the blurring of colors made me nauseous. I must have staggered under the suddenness of it all because Parrish caught me by the waist as I sagged against her like a sack of potatoes. Her warmth and solid muscle put some stiffness back into my knees.

"What in the name of sweet fuck is going on with you?" she said as she peered askance at me. "You on dope or something?"

I laid a palm against her ribs to steady myself. I couldn't be indignant at the question, not when I'd used dope to help my customers get what they paid for.

"I have no idea." The words came out a bit breathy, as though all the wind had been slammed out of me. "I just. I think I just saw the killer." My hand went to my head. It wasn't dizzy anymore but it hurt like a mother. "Killings." I corrected myself. "I think I just saw the murders. None of them fought their deaths at all. They just let all that happen to them."

"That's it," she said and dropped her hand from my waist to pull out her phone. "I'm calling Layne."

I reeled away, holding my head in my hands because now it really hurt. I wouldn't be surprised if some evil demon was chiseling away at my skull from inside. The pain was so great, I was vaguely aware of her voice as she addressed the person on the other end of the line, Layne presumably. Whatever he was saying on his end had her cursing more than she was talking.

At one point, I heard her say, "OK. Hold on." And then a bright light shone in my face. I squinted back at it, realizing she was holding her phone with the torch turned on.

With my hand shielding my eyes, I growled at her. "What's up with that?"

"There," she said. "You see?" This directed into her phone.

When Layne responded, I heard him through the phone. Angry or worried or afraid, I couldn't be sure. He swore. "Keep her there for Pete's sake and don't touch a single thing."

"Do you think making dust angels on the floor counts for touching things?" she said as she eyed me.

I'd already sunk to the floor and stretched my legs out and was just leaning back because my torso, my head, and my shoulders had just got way too heavy to hold up anymore.

"Fuck," Layne said through the phone and Parrish echoed the sentiment before powering down the screen and tucking it back into the waistband of her pajama pants.

She crossed her arms as she studied me.

"He says not to move."

"No worries there," I said.

"He says we need to stay put till he gets here."

I tucked my chin into my chest so I could see over it to her face. It had clouded over with concern and maybe a bit of annoyance.

"He's coming?" I said, feeling both anxious and relieved at the news.

"Oh, he's coming. He said he'll be here in less than ten minutes."

Somehow that sounded like a threat.

"I didn't do anything," I said. "I told you. I just woke up here."

She edged close enough to crouch beside me. Her fingers tapped my knee.

"You see," she said. "One does not simply walk around a crime scene in the middle of the night without proper credentials and not get pinned as a suspect. You've heard of killers returning to the scene of the crime? Well, what we have here, is a woman whose jewelry was found at the scene, who seems to understand the inner workings of a satanic cult, who just told me details about the murders that only the killer would know."

I closed my eyes. This couldn't be happening. "But I didn't do it."

"I know, Hun," she said. "But we're going to have a hell of a time convincing anyone else unless we can think of a way to explain it all, and Layne isn't one to trust easily."

I lifted my arm. "Help me up?"

She put her weight into heaving me back to my feet and though I was weak, at least the headache had started to abate. I stood on my own steam next to her and felt pretty solid considering the awful things I'd just seen.

"I'm not a member of a satanic cult."

She gestured to the wall with its Hecate symbol drawn in blood, the altar inside the fireplace, then the floor where blood stains from the murders were still evident even in the gloomy light filtering in from the street lamps.

"What do you think the media will call it?"

I stuck my chin out. "Someone with a psychotic break?"

She barked out a laugh. "You lived in Canada too long. Satan worship gives one the whiff of money. If they can't pin it on Satan, they'll find some black magic coven to blame it on. Witches are just sexy." She shrugged in her white tank top. "Sorry. Present witch company excluded."

"I'm not a witch," I said and hugged myself. "I'm a—"

"Woman of power," Parrish said, interrupting me. "I know. You think that will play? Hell, they already played out the psycho angle the last time but that's not as exciting as dogs getting shamed on social media. So my guess is once the media gets hold of all this, your shop will either get a hell of a lot of patronage or none at all."

I thought about all the customers I'd wanted, the reason I'd agreed to help Layne in the first place and decided maybe I shouldn't have wished too hard to get what I wanted. I might well end up a pariah instead of a psychic with street cred.

I sighed heavily and started to reach out for the wall to lean against when Parrish caught my hand.

"Don't touch anything else," she said. "I'm going to have a hell of a time explaining your juju all over the place as it is. Are you sure you don't remember any-thing?"

My hand crept up to my throat. "I'm not sure I want to remember after what I just saw."

She canted her head at me. "Which was what exactly?"

I clamped my mouth closed. The truth was it was just shades and shadows, blurred images and emotions. But they were strong enough to affect me right to the core. One thing had stuck with me, though, and it was the dreadful sense that my mother had been involved somehow. I felt her so intimately she might have been standing behind me.

I decided that small tidbit I could keep to myself because it didn't exactly help my case.

When the doorknob rattled, both of us started even though we'd been expecting Layne to arrive. He stood haloed in the light of the door frame for one moment, surveying the room, before he stepped inside and closed the door tightly behind him.

It took him three long minutes—I counted—before he spoke. In all the time, his eyes glowed through the gloom like neon signs and his jaw worked back and forth as he chewed his gum so furiously I thought he'd break a tooth. But his voice when he spoke carried an edge that made me cringe.

"Why did you come here?"

I clenched my fists at my sides. Parrish had shown me compassion. Layne nearly vibrated with suspicion. "I heard Parrish tell you I woke up here. Very different than coming here."

He pinched the bridge of his nose and whistled out a note of barely suppressed irritation.

"This does not look good, Brie."

"It's worse than it looks," Parrish said and I swung to face her. Traitor, I thought, until she visibly softened and explained. "She's not well, Layne. Did you even glance at the photo I sent? Look at her."

So that was why she'd shone the light in my face. She'd been snapping a photo. That I didn't look well when I was feeling much better was news to me, but I stood rigid beneath his scrutiny as he grabbed the floodlight and played it over my face.

He made thoughtful sounds deep in his throat but other than that, his voice revealed nothing. I wished I could see him through the shadows behind the light, but all I got was that voice and enough lumens to make my eyes hurt.

"She's right," he finally said to me. "You look like shit."

That did it. I opened my mouth to deliver a sassy retort but what came out, I was horrified to hear, was a long, wailing sob. They let me stand there, crying, for several seconds before one of them—Parrish—enfolded me in an embrace.

I'd have fought Layne, so I was grateful it was her. She rubbed my back and shushed me. Then, as if she had just caught herself doing something uncharacteristic and awkward, she peeled herself away and brushed the front of her shirt.

"You got blood all over my boobs," she said.

"If you'd worn a bra, the blood wouldn't have soaked through," Layne said and Parrish flicked an F-you finger at him.

"This is my lucky shirt," she said. "Shows my nipples at their very best. You expect me to pad down my best feature?"

He ran both hands over the top of his hair and swore. "Look," he said. "I managed to get the guards to take ten." He cranked his wrist over to look at his watch as he set the floodlight back down. "We have probably five minutes to get out of here without her being seen." He flicked his chin in my direction but wouldn't look me in the eye. "Is there anything here she can use to help before we flee the scene? Anything she thinks is important enough for me to snap with my phone camera? Speak now or forever hold your fuckin' peace."

That he was talking about me as if I wasn't there was a good indicator of how he felt right then, and if I wasn't sure, then the gratuitous swearing that accompanied his words nailed it for me.

I raised my hand to gain his attention, then realizing that what I was doing was asking his permission to speak instead of acting like an adult, lowered it and faced him with all the calm I could muster.

"I think *she* bled all over the floor." I scraped around with my toe, trying to find droplets without covering them over with dust. "Does *she* need to worry about that?"

He caught my eye and held it. "Not unless *she* killed those people."

I blinked to hold back the sting of tears that burned my eyes at the subtle insinuation. "I most certainly did not."

He shrugged at the shift in pronoun, but I wasn't sure it was as casual a motion as he wanted me to think it was. "Then you have nothing to worry about. We'll say you cut yourself on something in here when you were here with Parrish."

He glared at Parrish then who crossed her arms defensively.

"We had reason to believe we could find something useful here in the absence of the detective who should have been investigating but was MI fuckin' A," she said.

He averted his gaze from hers, but I didn't miss the communication that sailed through the space between them. I had the feeling they'd had words over his lengthy absence and neither one of them had recovered from it.

I ran a hand over the back of my neck. I was past exhausted. Whatever was going on between her and Layne was their business. I had no energy to dissect it.

"Can we just go now?" I said.

"Best thing you've said all night," he said and guided me toward the door. "Get the light, Parrish." It wasn't exactly a reprimand, but the words had the sound of punishment just the same.

The floodlights went black before we were through the door. I had every intention of hopping in with Parrish in her little wreck of a car, but Layne kept guiding me to his. He left me to open the door for myself, but waited until I got in before he rounded the car to his side and shoved in behind the wheel.

He said nothing as he started the engine. The ride home was tense and electric. If I wanted to speak to him, which I didn't, I doubted he'd respond. So, I sat in mindful silence on my side while he kept a sullen silence on his.

When he pulled up to the curb outside my apartment, I had already decided to flee the car without saying goodnight. But when I started to open the door, his hand gripped my elbow.

"Sit still," he hissed and I wrenched my arm away as I glared over my shoulder at him.

"You can't order me," I said. "I didn't do anything wrong and I'm not a pack member and I'm not even an official suspect."

If he heard me, I couldn't know because he had already leaped from his side of the car and was rounding the vehicle toward my front porch.

And then I realized exactly why he'd ordered me to stay put.

The front door of my apartment was completely ajar.

CHAPTER SEVENTEEN

I SANK INTO THE car seat as I watched Layne pull his gun and head toward my apartment. All I could think as a light flooded the cabin from behind was that someone had broken in to my home. If I hadn't sleep-walked or sleep cab rode all the way to the flophouse, I'd have gone home like normal and been inside my apartment when he broke in.

I wasn't sure which was the best alternative.

Not sure where the light was coming from, I dropped down in the seat, and I stayed there until Parrish yanked open the door on my side of the vehicle.

"What's up?" she said as she shoved me over and climbed into the bucket seat with me.

It was a tight fit, enough that I ended up hanging one leg over the gear shift and hoisted one butt cheek onto her thigh.

"What did he see?" she said. "Should I let my wolf out? Did he?"

"Too many questions," I hissed at her. "All I know is he took off running." My voice sounded small and weak and I coughed to cover it up. "He didn't shift. That has to be a good sign, right?"

She had already yanked the door closed with a thunk and the interior light had blinked off, so I couldn't see her face when she answered. Her tone, however, spoke volumes.

"A wolf can't carry a gun," she said. "So all that tells us is that his wolf might be planning to eat whoever he finds in there."

The comment made me grip my stomach. "You eat people?" I said, aghast and then, afraid I'd hurt her feelings, changed topic to the real issue. "Maybe my door just got caught by the wind this morning. Maybe I left it open."

"Maybe," she said in an unconvinced voice.

The gear shift dug into the tender parts of my thigh. I decided it would be far more comfortable to wait in the driver's seat and started clambering awkwardly sideways so I could see and sit without wincing every time I breathed.

"You'd think you would have got into the back," I complained as I whacked my knee on the dash during the awkward maneuvering.

"No chance of that," she said thoughtfully. "I saw how fast he was running."

"What's that got to do with anything?"

"You think I'd leave you sitting here like a fucking rubber duck at a carnival fair? Someone's coming for you, they're going through me to get you."

The warmth that swam over me at that comment made up for the uncomfortable positioning.

"Here he comes," she said and pushed out of the car before I even caught sight of him.

She sped up the walk and met him halfway. I watched their animated conversation, both of them in turns taking a look toward the car where I sat wringing my hands if I cared to look down at my lap. Some woman of power I was, cringing in the darkness of a car's interior.

That thought was what drove me out of the vehicle and heading up the walk toward them. Layne caught sight of me and waved me over.

"So?" I asked, trying my best for a casual tone and failing miserably. "Do I need to move?"

"You tell me," he said and stepped back so I could walk between him and Parrish as we approached the doorstep.

I looked at the doorknob, curious if I'd see evidence of a break in. Not that I'd know what to look for.

"No one jimmied the lock that I can see," he said, answering the question for me. "But it's important to know if anything is missing."

"No one is inside?" I said.

"Do you mean 'Is someone currently lying in a pool of his own blood in your living room after being shot by a silent bullet from my gun?'"

In the light coming from the foyer, I could see a tug of smile playing at the corner of his mouth.

"Come on, Brie," he said when I didn't smile back. "You think I'd herd you back into your apartment if a threat waited inside?"

"You might if you thought I was a killer and wanted to trap me."

Parrish had the grace to chortle into her hand but Layne did not find it the least bit funny. I hadn't meant it to be. I was earnestly serious.

He pushed me inside and closed the door on Parrish before she could step over the threshold.

"Go," he said in a commanding tone that I figured he'd use if he were the alpha of his pack ordering his minions about. Funny thing was, I felt very much like obeying. "Check things out. I'll follow you."

I studied his face for a moment before turning to do exactly as he bid. I heard Parrish enter behind me but she didn't say anything, just followed along with Layne as I crept through my own apartment as though it were the insides of a bomb.

"Tell me everything that happened from the time you last remember to the time you woke up at the murder scene."

I froze at the words murder scene, my hand on the back of my sofa as I scanned the living room. I knew people and I knew behavior. He might not think I was a killer, but he was still pissed I'd gone there. Didn't matter if I hadn't done it intentionally. His use of the official term was a means to create distance for himself, so he could scold me without feeling the empathy that might encourage his forgiveness.

"Well," he said.

I sighed and turned on him. Parrish lurked a few feet away, her posture rigid.

"Nothing seems amiss," I said.

He nodded as though he expected as much. "There's no one in the house. No sign of break in. You must have left the door open."

I bit my lip and nodded.

"That's a good thing," he said, his voice softening. I guessed it had something to do with the way my face was crumbling, so I nodded again. I didn't trust my voice.

"Tell him about the man," Parrish said. "And the things you saw."

It was Layne's turn to go rigid. "What man? What things?"

I sank onto the sofa and sagged over my knees. "Can't this wait till tomorrow?"

I felt his weight sink down into the cushions beside me. Parrish mosied off toward the kitchen. Water started running from the tap. Cupboard doors opened and closed. The telltale sound of ice clinked into glasses.

I didn't look up from my feet until she pushed a glass of water into my hand. I eased my eyes closed at the thought of running through everything, things I wanted to just forget. I was aware I was stalling when I took a large gulp of water without swallowing it. My cheeks billowed out as my throat refused to let the water slide down.

"Brie," Layne said in a soothing voice. "It's alright. I know you're not a killer. I know you're just a victim of all this. I won't let anything hurt you."

"Damn straight," Parrish echoed and I swallowed finally.

"Go ahead." Layne was careful not to move too quickly when he reached out to run his palm down my arm. I felt like a rabbit in a snare beneath his gaze. "You're safe. Just tell me everything."

Something in his voice, probably the alpha power, pulsed with command, enough that although I wasn't keen on revisiting the episode, I felt compelled to divulge it.

With a deep inhale I prepared the first sentence and then before I could think of any way to sugar coat it, I spilled the entire afternoon from the time I sank into the chair at my shop to the moment I opened my eyes in the flophouse.

I watched his face shift several times from concern to anger to worry and back again as I explained about the man we both knew was dead visiting me. I confessed the fear I felt as I discovered myself in the flophouse, a place I'd not remembered going to. I stopped short at the images that ran through my mind and Parrish had to prod me.

She had been pacing the living room, picking up things and setting them down again but stopped when I finished speaking. "Tell him about the murders."

My gaze flicked to Layne's when she said it because although he said nothing, his entire body tightened. I knew he wanted to ask me what she meant but was being careful not to press me too hard.

"I think I saw it happen," I said and rubbed at my arms in memory. "My arms started to burn and then everything went all shadowy in my vision. I don't know for sure, but I think I saw three figures. They were...they had brought knives and...well, all I could smell was sulfur and death."

"And then you just collapsed like a God damned Carol Burnett character and started making dirt angels on the floor," Parrish interjected when she saw I was struggling. "Fuck." She swung her gaze to Layne. "I told you it was a mess."

Layne heaved himself to his feet and stared down at me with his hands on his hips. "She does look pretty awful."

"*She* is crazy tired," I said, using the pronoun again to indicate I did not like being spoke of as if I weren't in the room. I laid my forehead into my palms as I leaned my elbows against my knees. "I just want this night to be over. Can't you guys just go home and pick at my brain tomorrow?"

"Oh, we're not going home," he said.

My head snapped up at that. "The hell you aren't. I'm so exhausted I can barely blink. I have to work tomorrow. You aren't questioning me anymore till I get some sleep."

He crouched in front of me, his knees popping. "It's best to get the details as quickly after an event as possible," he said. "It protects the truest recollection. Our memories are pretty fluid. Changeable. You might have even altered your own memory just by retelling the story."

"I did not exaggerate."

"I'm sure you think you've given us accurate information."

"It happened just as I said." I hugged my chest and he nodded sympathetically.

"You've given us what you can, and that's good. We'll revisit it all later. You do need your sleep, and we need some time to process what you've told us."

"Good. So you are leaving," I said, not sure he really believed it all but too exhausted to argue any longer. "I need to hit the hay. I might even fall asleep right here in the chair. Lock the door on the way out, will you."

He gave me a look like he expected fireworks in the next second. "I'm staying here tonight," he said in a tone that broached no refusal. That alpha tone again, I supposed, but I'd be damned if I'd let him bully me with it.

I shook my head, the residual dizziness swashing against my skull.

"No way. I don't need a nursemaid. And with you laying there next to me, I'll never get a second of sleep."

Parrish's low chuckle warbled toward me and I looked askance at her.

"You have a sofa, Brie," she said with a hint of a smile playing on her lips. "But if you want him to sleep with you, maybe you best forgo the sexy lingerie just for tonight."

My face heated to an uncomfortable temperature as I realized what I said. The suggestion that I expected him to sleep with me wasn't one I could come back from easily. A quick glance at Layne revealed his smug expression. He'd heard the Freudian slip just as Parrish had. The mention of lingerie brought back Layne's dad's visit to my shop and his request that I accompany him to dinner wearing lingerie beneath my clothes that he'd paid for, and it was all too much.

"I'm fucking tired," I growled and shot to my feet with more energy than I could expend in the moment. I swayed for a second and Layne's hand gripped my calf.

"I'm humbled you think I belong in your bed, Brie," he purred and then that hand slid up my leg as he stood. "But I think it's best for both of us if I take the sofa as Parrish suggested."

I glared at both of them for a moment before I stormed to the hallway closet, leaving them both talking in low tones behind me. I didn't think they were mocking me because the humor had left their voices, but I didn't care. I'd had enough.

I rummaged through and yanked out a scratchy crocheted blanket and slung it over my arm. Then I dug out a ratty feather pillow that had seen a generation of oily heads and carried both back to the living room. I tossed the pile on the arm of the sofa and spun on my heel.

"If you snore, please stuff your socks in your mouth," I said and in a flash of inspiration, dug into my pocket to extract the knife handle. This, I slapped into his fist and spun on my heel to leave him gaping at it. Teach him to doubt my memory.

Parrish shot Layne a conspiratorial look before heading for the door, and I caught it as I spun around.

I was already striding to my bedroom when she said she'd let herself out.

"Don't worry, Brie," she said. "He doesn't snore. Just sort of yips and kicks his little legs like he's chasing rabbits."

"Go the hell home, Parrish," Layne growled, and though she retorted with something that made him swear, I didn't hear it because I was already in my bedroom and closing the door.

I didn't bother with my slippers or my clothes. I fell onto the bed face first and curled into a ball. I probably fell asleep immediately.

I only woke up when I felt myself being watched.

Chapter Eighteen

THE BIG BLACK BEAST on the bed beside me smelled of sulfur. Its red eyes peered at me without blinking and even though the room was flooded with morning light, it still looked swathed in shadow. It took me all of three seconds to shriek and jump out of bed.

Layne burst through the door and into the room a heartbeat later. His gun was drawn. With his torso naked from the waist up, every muscle stood out on his chest like ropes of hard knots. In one second, he had assessed where I stood cringing in the corner and found the threat of the huge black dog still sitting on the middle of my mattress, looking out at the room as though it found the whole situation funny.

"Are you alright?" Layne said but he didn't lower his pistol. In fact, it was aimed directly at the dog, which started panting. The tilt of its mouth might make a gal think it was laughing.

I patted down my body in case the dog had taken a bite of me while I slept. "I think so." I didn't dare look down at myself. Instead, my eyes pinned to the dog who shuffled on the bed restlessly.

"I didn't know you had a dog," Layne said.

"I don't."

The dog licked its jowls and whined.

"Well," I corrected myself. "I don't have a real dog."

"What the hell is that supposed to mean?" Layne demanded without lowering his gun one inch. The dog didn't seem overly concerned that it might get shot.

I crept out from the corner, approaching Layne slowly so he didn't pull the trigger by accident. "Remember the dog I wanted you to help me with?" I asked. "The one I thought was dead?"

"The dog that wasn't there," he said thoughtfully. "I remember. This is that dog?"

Weeks earlier, it seemed I'd been the only one who could see the beast. At one point, it had appeared to me on the street, looking as dead as any of the dogs my mother had killed in her rituals she practiced in the basement of our home.

Now, the beast had become visible to more than just me. Parrish had seen it lurking outside my shop after the ordeal when magic burst from my mother's grimoire and killed the man we thought was the murderer. If Layne could see it now, I had no doubt it had found a way to remain corporeal when it wanted.

I laid a hand on Layne's wrist, urging him to lower the gun. "It's the same dog. I don't think it's here to harm me," I said. "It would have done something by now."

Layne lowered the gun but he didn't take his eyes off the dog. "Maybe it just couldn't before," he said. "Maybe it just needed something to give it enough form to attack."

"It defended me against the killer," I said. "Those weeks ago when you followed me home and ended up fighting him."

"It stinks," he said, still not averting his gaze. The dog pawed the covers but it too refused to take its eyes off Layne. I had the feeling they were sizing each other up.

"Dominance contests later," I said, feeling the let down of adrenaline in the grumbling of my stomach. "I need to get to work."

As I released his hand, my fingers whispered against his waist. I'd forgotten for a moment he was sporting skin from the waist up.

He looked sideways at me, catching my eye with a hint of a smirk that made me back away a step.

"What's the stink eye for?" he said, looking me up and down. "Most normal people don't go to bed in their clothes, especially clothes full of their own blood."

I peered down at myself, noting I was indeed still dressed in my clothes from the night before.

"I told you I was exhausted. You couldn't sleep one night in a shirt?"

"I was naked, actually," he said. "I pulled my pants on so I wouldn't scare you."

I blew through my lips. "You're pretty cocky about your equipment's ability to scare a gal."

"I'm glad you agree it's cocky," he said and I might have spit out a comeback but he had already turned from me and was approaching my bed. He held the pistol by his side, his fingers twitching along the side of the barrel.

The dog backed up and bared its teeth. Layne raised the pistol again and the dog growled low in its throat.

"Don't," I said, but it didn't matter. The beast dissolved into shadow and then was gone in a breath.

Layne dropped his pistol and flicked the safety back on.

"I swear things are getting curiouser and curiouser."

"You're telling me," I said and sighed. "I'm not sure I can take one more strange thing."

I stooped to gather up a pile of clothes from the laundry basket that I'd managed to wash and carry all twenty steps to the dresser before dropping it onto the floor. I dug for underwear and a bra.

"I need a shower. Thanks for staying the night and keeping me safe from all harm, but I'm good now." A glance at the clock indicated I'd already slept through the first hour of Friday shop time. "I'm late."

He stopped me before I got to the door.

"I'm coming with you today," he said.

I looked at him over my shoulder. His jaw had a smudge of charcoal shadow and his shoulder muscles twitched as my eye started to roam of its own accord to his chest. I swallowed down the primal lust that seemed to have risen in the face of seeming danger, one made worse by the early hour and deep sleep hangover.

"Shouldn't you be getting to your own job?" I said with a bit more temper than I needed.

"What do you think this is?" He closed the distance between us and gave me a gentle shove through the gaping bedroom door. "Go shower. I'll pull on a shirt so you're not distracted any more than you need to be. Then we'll leave together."

I heaved a sigh. "Suit yourself," I said. "But don't be surprised when all that happens in my little shop is a bit of dusting."

"Spoken like a true woman of power," he said with a wink and I fled to the bathroom because I'd pretty much just admitted I was as powerful as a maid.

I stripped off the clothes from the night before and ran the material of my shirt through my fingers. Blood stains peppered the fabric. I considered soaking the shirt in the sink then thought better of it. I had no desire to remember the night in any way.

The shirt went into the trash, and I tossed a handful of tissues over top to hide the offending material from a casual glance.

Naked, I felt cold even when the steam from the shower billowed around me. I knew from experience the shower would take a few moments to come to full temperature so I swiped at the fog on the mirror out of habit. The face that stared back at me looked haunted. No wonder Parrish had said I looked awful.

My eyes were red-rimmed and the circles that carved out hollows of shadow beneath my eyes had a bluish cast. The pallor of my skin was decidedly pasty. I couldn't fool myself into thinking it was the lighting because even my eyes had lost their luster.

In a nutshell I looked like death warmed over.

Even the tattoos that no one saw but me held a grayish tint. Except for the edges. The edges looked strangely brownish. I leaned closer to the mirror so I could see better and was surprised to discover they looked scabbed over.

Curious, I lifted an arm up to my face and scanned the markings that ran the length from collar bone to wrist. Yes. Definitely edged in fine-lined scabs. I ran a finger over the line to feel the raised edges. If I didn't know better, I'd guess someone had drawn an outline of each mark with a razor and that overnight the skin had knit back together, leaving a hairline scab as its only evidence.

Anxiety climbed my spine. I was sure I'd feel someone slicing into my skin even if I'd been in some sort of fugue state. I stooped to dig back into the trash for my shirt and snatched it out of the bin. In my exhaustion the night before along with all the other strangeness, I hadn't had much time to consider why I'd been covered in my own blood, and when Parrish had wiped it off me with her own shirt, I presumed she was similarly preoccupied.

Now in the light of a new day, I wanted to know exactly how I'd managed to bleed without cutting myself. I was sure if my shirt had fine cuts in the material I'd have noticed. But maybe I'd just been too out of it. Because how else would I cut myself with a shirt on and have no evidence in the clothing itself?

But when I fished the shirt out of the garbage, there were no signs of any holes of any sort in the material. I chewed my lip in thought as the steam wrapped about me. There was no way I'd have taken off my shirt and traced the outlines of those tattoos so perfectly and not remembered. I didn't care what kind of fugue I was in. It would have hurt.

That left one possibility. Someone must have drugged me, taken off my shirt, cut me, and brought me to the murder scene. I wasn't sure how they'd done it, but it was the only rational possibility. Except that left one more disturbing question.

Why hadn't either Parrish or Layne considered those possibilities?

Unless they had considered them and were afraid to tell me, because if that was true, then the open door to my apartment the night before was most definitely not the result of me leaving it ajar.

A trail of goosebumps lifted on my spine and traveled to the base of my hairline. They knew. That was the conspiratorial exchanges of glances between the two of them. That was why Layne stayed with me through the night. Why he'd barreled into my bedroom with his gun drawn, why he planned to stay with me at work.

He believed someone had attacked me.

Despite the steam all around me, the heat that even then was wetting my hair, I shivered. My mouth went dry.

I took another look at the trash can. Something about the way it looked made the fear start clomping around in my brain with army boots.

But for the tissues I'd wadded on top of my shirt, my trash was empty.

It had been half full the day before.

Only when I rammed my heel into the skirting of the sink vanity did I realize I'd back-stepped across the floor. The shirt had slipped from my grasp and fallen into a puddle of fabric at my feet. One single thought kept bouncing around my brain like a pickle ball.

I'd clipped my nails, waxed my legs and underarms just two days ago. I knew I'd tossed the refuse into that bin because trash day was not for another three days and I didn't like having all that stuff littering the sidewalk beside my house.

My chest started to hitch along with my breath. When my knees buckled, I was already reaching for the toilet tank and I sank down on the seat with a loud thud. I gripped the side of the vanity to keep myself from sagging right off the damn toilet bowl.

Layne pounded on the door a moment later and in a stupor, I lifted my gaze to the steam around me, that all but obliterated the knob. It was turning. I blinked as I tried to remember if I'd locked it or not and then it didn't matter because he was barging in.

"What's wrong?" he shouted. His eyes glowed that unholy yellow again, piercing me through the vapors. The wolf was high on alert.

It took a single second for him to see me splayed over the toilet lid with my knees buckled in and my arm slung across the vanity top before he barreled across the space. It wasn't a big bathroom, just room enough for a tub and shower, a vanity, and a toilet, so everything seemed to happen at once.

Definitely not a pleasant thing for a woman on melt-down.

At his entrance, I tightened into a ball instinctively, laying one arm across my breasts and curling into a tighter ball to hide all the other bits of vulnerability a man shouldn't see unless you were feeling pretty damned confident it was a good naked.

"What the hell?" I demanded. "Naked here." Fear of humiliation momentarily superseded the fear of some unknown intruder doing nasty things to me. Priorities shifted, I guess, in the face of naked skin.

"It's not like I haven't seen a nipple before," he drawled but he averted his gaze to the tub as he asked. "Are you alright?"

I grabbed for a towel. "I don't care how many hussies' nipples you've subjected to your rudeness. In polite society, we knock before we enter a bathroom."

Without bothering to get up because the towel was a small one, I laid it over my chest, letting it drape to my thighs. I didn't want to admit that I was glad he was there. He loomed over me with his fists clenching and unclenching while I did my best to reach for my robe without letting the towel slip.

"Little help?" I said, finally, when I couldn't grasp the edge of the housecoat as it hung on its hook behind the door.

He blinked and his nostrils widened and I could almost imagine him shaking his head like a wet dog before he spun around and yanked the robe from its hook. When I thought he'd just toss it at me, he laid it gently over my shoulder and tugged down the shoulder to drape over me enough that I could slip an arm into the sleeve without baring my goods.

"I thought someone had knocked you out or something," he said.

I lifted one eyebrow, indicating I thought he'd just revealed information he was keeping from me. "As opposed to me just falling down in here? I wonder why you'd think that."

I pushed off from the lid and ducked by him so I could turn off the shower. It was too steamy and if we were going to have this talk, I didn't want to end up paying for it in my water bill.

The taps squeaked off, making a shriek as loud as a cat in heat.

"You figured that out, huh?" He angled his head so I couldn't see his eyes anymore. I had to go round his back and open the door then turn to face him to see him full on.

"I'm not the complete idiot you think I am," I said and hugged myself over the robe self-consciously. It was my favorite bit of my wardrobe because it had a thick pile and appliquéd kittens and puppies on it. The pockets had started to come unstitched at the sides and hung down with the threat of tearing straight off with the breeze from a fast walk.

I hated that he had to see me in it.

"I don't think you're an idiot, Brie," he said.

"Just a fool."

He grinned playfully. "Maybe you're cunning enough to know a werewolf like me would rush to your naked aid if he heard what sounded like dead weight falling off a big perch."

"I didn't—" I waved at him in dismissal. "Never mind," I said. "What's important is that both of you, you and Parrish, knew someone had broken in here and yet you pretended it was me all along."

I tried to shove my way through the door into my kitchen but he snagged my elbow and tugged with enough force to spin me back around. I caught at the edge of the towel as it tried to slip down. The smile that had played over his features a second earlier was gone. His gaze had grown hard and suspicious.

"What makes you think someone broke in here?"

I wrenched my elbow from his grasp and pointed at the bathroom. "My stuff," I said, not wanting to admit the things that I'd noticed were missing from the trash because I didn't want him to imagine me with hair all over my legs and sundries. "All of it missing. I haven't taken out the trash this week. But the bin is empty."

He looked in the direction of the bathroom, his expression clouding with thought.

"What sort of stuff?"

"Someone drugged me," I said, avoiding the question as neatly as I could and headed to my bedroom to get dressed. "They date rape drugged me and brought me to that flophouse and probably made a pit stop here to pick through my trash. Who knows what else they took."

His eyebrows both climbed an inch.

"You think someone drugged you so they could collect your trash? What was in there that was worth stealing?"

I planted my bare feet on the kitchen floor, rooted there as I hugged myself all the tighter. It did sound far-fetched.

"Who knows what psychos find valuable." My shoulder blades knit together beneath the towel with each second. Soon, I wouldn't be able to unravel the knots. "You've got an unknown number of killers who shove statues of goddesses in women's stomachs, who burn the bodies of dead dogs on altars they make out of earth and stone, killers who paint symbols in blood on walls and you wonder why they might go through a psychic's trash?"

"Yeah," he said. "Let's put aside the accusation that we think someone broke in here when all I smell in this entire apartment is you, your soap, a stinking invisible dog, werewolf pheromones which no doubt are me and Parrish, and a bit of overripe cheese you have in your fridge. Yeah, I do wonder what a psycho who killed four psychics would find valuable. Don't you?"

I stared at him as my mind reeled through his words.

It came to me in a flash so sudden, a gasp escaped me.

"Oh my God," I said. "I know. I do know."

And I did. The things that had gone missing. They weren't just personal effects. They were intimate effects. My hair. Nail clippings.

For a moment, my mind flashed me a memory of me sitting on the floor of the attic as I sorted through my mother's ephemera. I'd found the picture of the shade man there along with all those newspaper stories my mother had kept about the Cult of Blackburn who had killed their own members and tried to raise them from the dead. The media thought that with the imprisonment of the cult's leader, the members had scattered and disbanded.

My memory pulled out those clippings for me as I stood there, the horror of knowing my personal effects had been stolen. It scanned the headlines, and I knew beyond a shadow of doubt that they weren't disbanded at all.

"They're back," I murmured. "They're back and they've bewitched me."

Chapter Nineteen

THERE WAS ONE THING more powerful to a witch than hair. Blood.

While a witch's hair held a strong connection to her power, in truth, it wasn't just a witch who was vulnerable to spells cast with pieces of her hair. Any victim could be controlled in various ways using their hair or nails. There was power in the intimate. A pubic hair could create the foundation of a love spell. A bit of nail clipping could be buried and secure the wasting of the host they were taken from.

But blood held the strongest connection. Spells woven with blood had untold power. Blood opened portals, it called dark forces. If hair and nails were the tinder to a magic fire, blood was gasoline.

"They have my blood," I said in a voice that had risen to a pitch I didn't recognize. Once I got through the horror of knowing someone had stolen my hair and nail clippings, my mind meandered all the way back to the flop house and the blood that ran down my arms and wrists to the floor.

"There's no telling how long they had me," I said with a sick feeling in my throat. "They could have bled me for as long as they wanted and collected what they needed." It was bad enough I woke in that house, but to think of unknown numbers of people bleeding me like a lamb for slaughter made my teeth ache.

Layne held his hand up. "Wait," he said. "What makes you think they—whoever they are—have your blood? And what would they do with it?"

"The Cult of Blackburn," I said as I held my arms out to show him. "You saw the blood." I tried to remember if he had seen it at all. I struggled with the time frame, trying to recall when Parrish had wiped my arms clean. "Any witch can do any number of things with blood or nail clippings." I felt like I was choking on the words. "A black witch gathering energy from blood and death? There's no end to what they might do."

"You're saying this cult is really a coven of witches."

I nodded. "Black witches."

"Fuck," he said, and gripped the back of his neck as he stared at me. "I just wanted to be here in case you sleep walked."

I wrung my hands together at the very distinct possibility that I'd been hexed or marked for sacrifice or God only knew what else. "I'm not equipped for this. I have no idea how to counter, to protect myself." I was rambling now, and realizing I was admitting to being pretty ignorant, which I knew I might care about later. But right then, I was panicking. "And my amulet. It cloaks me. You remember. It made me invisible back at the docks. I don't have it." My voice had a screeching sound to it that made me feel like I was clawing at an old schoolhouse blackboard. "I need it."

"OK," he said a tone he no doubt used to great effect in his detective work. "Let's just stay calm. There isn't anything happening right now."

"How do you know?" I said, spinning in place, scanning the kitchen for sharp objects in case I went into a fugue again, one instigated by a person or persons who wanted God only knew what from me. "They could be casting right now. I could be in danger. You could be in danger if they try to control me." I thought of the knife handle I'd found in my grip.

He snorted. "No offense, Brie, but I'm pretty sure I can take you." He closed the distance between us and laid his hands on my shoulders. When he caught my eye and held it, I felt the panic subside.

I inhaled slowly, feeling my rib cage expand. He nodded silently as though he knew what effect he was having on me.

"Good," he said. "Good. Now, you go get that shower. I'll case your apartment for anything that might indicate someone has broken in and then we'll go to your shop. You have the grimoire there, right?"

I nodded mutely. Yes. The grimoire. Maybe it could provide some answers, or maybe a spell to protect me from unwanted and threatening magic while the amulet was in police evidence. It was a hope, at least. I headed to the shower with the hope quelling the tide of panic.

The shower smoothed out more of the jagged edges of anxiety. A normal, everyday, non-magic activity. I dressed in a tunic top with long bell sleeves and joggings. Normal, everyday wear. Just like the very normal act of opening up and doing regular things helped even more.

What did not help was having Layne lurking around the store while I worked. Twice, I had to drop my finger down onto a page in the grimoire and ask him to stop touching things. He did not take orders well, no matter how small, and whether he did it to get on my nerves or because he was antsy, I didn't know. I just knew it was terribly distracting.

"There's something odd about the book," I said as I drew my finger down along a page that didn't look like a spell at all. There was no listing of ingredients or Latin phrases like I'd seen before. As I flipped through the pages, I noted some had spells and incantations, but most were empty.

I looked up because Layne had been skulking a bit too close for me a moment earlier and I expected his response to come from somewhere near, but got I nothing. I spied him at the counter, staring at the death mask.

"Don't touch it," I said.

He didn't touch it, but neither did he pull his gaze away when he replied. "It's creepy."

"Yeah, well, if you touch it and break it, you'll end up ruining my chances of paying the mortgage next month."

He looked at me then, tilting his head just enough to catch me collapsing into one of the wingback chairs with the grimoire spread on my lap.

"Is that a subtle way for you to ask me to buy more junk?"

"You're a funny man," I said. "I have no idea why you don't take that act on the road."

He grinned then sobered as he glanced at the mask again. "Who keeps a creepy thing like that? It's even got hair stuck in it. You think it was the hair from the dead person?"

I rolled my eyes. "It's a death mask," I said. "Of course it's from the dead person."

"Well, it's creepy."

"I think we've determined you think it's creepy by the constant use of the word 'creepy'." I flipped a page and ran my hand down the vellum. "I'm beginning to see why you became a police officer. You are incredibly astute."

"It's staring at me," he said in an offhand tone. "I don't like it."

My head snapped up at that comment and my hand froze on the page as I looked at him. Shades of the night before crept along the dark halls of my mind.

"What do you mean, staring at you?"

He jerked a thumb at it as he edged away from the counter. "Take a look."

I put the grimoire down on the chair and went over to where he stood, giving the death mask a nasty glare. As I squinted and leaned in, something behind the mask blinked, like a shutter closing or an eyelid. I waited several seconds without moving, holding my hand up so Layne wouldn't move either.

A moment later, the shutter behind the mask's eyes moved again, and this time I saw very clearly two hazel eyes looking back at me.

"What do you see when you look at the mask?" I asked Layne in a hoarse whisper. I had the disquieting thought that like Maureen, he merely thought it was watching him, that he hadn't seen the eyes or the fleshy lids that blinked at me every few seconds.

Even as I asked Layne the question, the mask seemed to become more and more human. The plaster had the distinct tinge of skin tones, the hardness softened enough that I was sure if I reached out to touch it, the mask would feel pliant. And I wanted to touch it. More than anything in that moment, something compelled me to reach for it. I had the urge to stroke its cheek or wipe away an invisible tear.

But it was Layne who reached for it, not me. In a flash, before his hand came down on the mask, I brushed it aside, and pinned it beneath mine to the counter next to the mask.

Maureen had told me she wasn't always afraid of the mask. But I was pretty sure that while she felt it watching her she probably hadn't seen the mask turn into a young girl's face.

"Maybe we shouldn't mess with the thing," I said, not sure I should tell him what I was seeing because it was obvious I was seeing more than he was, that whatever was happening with the mask, he had a sense of it, like when the hair raises on the back of a neck when someone is watching, but that was all he was getting.

I expected him to pull his hand out from beneath mine, but instead he turned it over and laced his fingers through mine. "Your hand is hot," he said in a tight voice.

The air around us was electric enough in that second that a spark might have sizzled my hair. His gaze was locked on mine for a moment but it trailed down to my lips, then dipped to my throat. The hammering of my pulse held his attention for a long moment and I almost stepped closer, just enough to touch his shoes with my own, just to test his intentions.

His thumb stroked the belly of my palm and I struggled not to ease my eyes closed and imagine the way that thumb might feel on other parts of my body.

Then he yanked his hand away as though I burned him. I shoved my hand in my pocket, feeling slighted until I felt the heat through my pants. He was right. My hand was burning, my entire body was burning. I couldn't just tell myself it was the heat he drew from me. The sensation was too strong to be lust.

"What the heck?" he said. "That's really hot."

I cleared my throat as I willed self-assurance into my voice. "I think," I said, taking a step backward. "I think it's from the mask."

I rocked back on my heels, happy to distract us both from the awkward silence a moment earlier. "I have no idea what will happen if you touch it, but it makes me feel strange."

"Then you shouldn't touch it either," he said.

"This is what I do, Layne," I said. "It's what people pay me for."

"People pay you to cast demons from possessed things?" He shoved his own hand into his pocket too, and I noticed it was balled up in there, a perfect echo of my own.

"You think it's possessed?" I said. I was beginning to believe that was exactly the case, and yet, it didn't feel demonic.

He shrugged. "What else?"

I laughed because it seemed the best alternative considering all the other horrible things that I had on my plate at the moment. The last thing I needed was a demon waiting to clutch at my soul.

"I think if it was a demon, it would have done something by now. Like maybe possessing human flesh." I put on a thoughtful expression, not just for his benefit. "Maybe it's just waiting for someone to touch it to make the connection." That last was for his sake, though. Deflect and distract. Good tools of the trade. Sometimes they even worked on the practitioner.

He shuddered visibly, and although I was joking, I lifted a scarf from a nearby shelf and tossed it over the hunk of plaster. I had no idea what to do with the thing, and even if his assessment of it was that it was creepy, I didn't get the same vibe. I felt sad and mournful, but nothing else.

Layne's shoulders sagged when it was out of sight.

"Big bad wolf worried about a little granny mask?"

"Very funny," he said but he paced away from the counter and started circling the shop again. I went back to my chair and lifted the grimoire onto my lap. He muttered to himself loudly enough that I groaned and slapped the pages of the book to get his attention.

"You know, I could use my amulet back," I said. "Maybe it would be more helpful if you contacted your partner and asked him to return it."

A woman came into the shop before he could answer, and he backed away to give her space to meander. Either his cop vibe was strong, or his werewolf mojo was because she took one short spin around the store and then left with the bell jangling behind her like a reproach.

"OK," I said. "Now you're queering my business."

He sent me a withering look that informed me he wasn't leaving or disappearing no matter what I said. I aimed to change that. I was tired of his hovering over me. It was hard enough trying to find some sense of what was going on, trying to find some sort of information in a grimoire I didn't understand, let alone having him hanging around like a bat with no perch.

"I don't think anything is going to happen to me," I said, leaning back. "I mean, it's mid-day. What kind of witch coven would do their dirty deeds in the middle of a sunny afternoon?" I flipped a page and ran my hand down along the vellum as I spoke. "Any witch worth her salt will do her casting on a waning moon."

"Spoken like a true witch?" he said, and I looked up to see him standing in front of me. I hadn't heard him approach and considered putting a bell on him. "You do your work during the day. Maybe you're not worth your salt."

"If you're trying to hurt my feelings, it's going to take more than an accusation of charlatanry," I said blandly. "I was raised by a witch who killed puppies and burned their bodies in our basement. I have a pretty hard wall built inside."

I thumped my chest to indicate just how hard the wall was and at the moment I touched my own skin to skin, the page I was studying started to smoke. A gasp escaped me as a searing pain burned its way into my core. A spark started jumping down my arms as though it was grease on a hot griddle.

Next thing I knew, the blank page started to fill with symbols just like the ones on my skin, the ones I saw in the mirror each morning since I'd left that flophouse the first time and touched the wall, those symbols burned themselves onto the page.

In one movement, more from the pain of the burning than fear, I shoved the grimoire off my lap and onto the floor as I leapt to my feet. The book landed with a large thud that had Layne beating a hasty trail across the floor, his brows furrowed in alarm.

I gawked at him, knowing my mouth hung open and my eyes were probably hanging on my cheeks. My mouth was too dry to speak, but I pointed at the book as it lay open between us on the floorboards.

Now that I was on my feet, it all seemed so ridiculous that I sank back onto the chair cushion.

"Burned me," I managed in a throat so raspy, it might have been exposed to a smoke filled room. I coughed out of sympathetic response.

"Did more than that," he said and dropped to his knees beside me. He grabbed for my arm and pushed my sleeve above my elbow. Bunched above the joint, the material looked singed and brown.

And bloody.

"Sweet Jesus," I said as my gaze pinned to the skin below my elbow. It was bleeding, and the tattoos looked more like brandings than ink.

"What the hell is happening?" I tore my eyes from the sight of the markings to lift my gaze to his. He looked as freaked out as I felt.

The trouble was, he wasn't looking at me. He was looking over my shoulder.

And though dread climbed my spine like a spider up a leaking faucet, I forced myself to twist to see what he was looking at.

"Is that the man who vandalized your shop?" he said in a tight voice filled with something that I would have to label as the sort of primal fear a man gets when he knows he's facing something that has no conceivable reason to exist.

"Yes," I said because it was the same man. While I'd thought he was a ghost before, it was clear Layne was seeing him now.

And we both knew he was dead.

CHAPTER TWENTY

THE MAN DISAPPEARED ALMOST instantly, but the room had grown so hot I started to perspire. I tugged at the collar of my tunic. Dizziness swept over me and I could just make out the edges of black creeping into my vision.

"Stay with me," Layne said, but his voice was so distant, it might have been coming through water. I swung my gaze to him, stupefied as I tried to remember what I'd been doing just moments before.

"It's alright, Brie," he said. Warm hands ran down my throat, soft strokes like he was trying to get me to swallow a pill. I pushed his hands away irritably.

"Stop," I said and tried to get up. I realized I was on the floor and not in the chair like I'd been a moment earlier.

Those hands moved beneath my head to cup the nape of my neck as he cradled me into a sitting position. I leaned against the warmth of his arm until the room stopped swirling around me.

"What in the hell happened?" he demanded. His eyes were peering into mine a little too close. The yellow swirled within, a threat that the wolf was uncomfortable or afraid or both. That couldn't be good.

I rolled to the side, fully intending to extricate myself from his arms because he was hot, so hot. The heat came off him in waves and I was getting sticky with it. He resisted my movement and I growled at him.

"Let me the fuck go," I said.

He dropped his arms so fast I fell backwards and hit my head. I yelped.

"Serves you right," he grumbled but he didn't move to help me up. Didn't matter. I just laid there with my arm slung over my forehead. I didn't have the energy to move.

"I'm sorry," I said. "Everything was just so..."

"I know," he said. "I'm sorry too. But what in the sweet hell was that? Did we just see the same thing?"

"I think so."

I peered out at him from beneath my forearm. He looked calmer, but not much more relaxed. The tension riding his shoulders made them rigid enough that a skateboarder could have done tricks off them.

"Are you going to attack me?" I said.

He swept me with a glance that made me feel even warmer. "If my wolf was going to attack you, it wouldn't be for the reasons you think."

With a pinch at the bridge of my nose, I squeezed my eyes closed. "This is not happening," I mumbled. "This just is not happening."

"You mean the dead guy at the door of your shop or the fact that your tattoos are bleeding."

So he'd seen the shade man too, as I'd come to think of him. Much like the shade of my mother that had appeared to me when I'd been cleaning out her trunks.

He'd also seen the tattoos. I lifted my arm an inch from my face so I could inspect the marks that trailed from the middle of my chest all the way down to my wrist. My skin was smeared with blood. That had to mean my face was now too.

I must have winced at the sight because he said, "I'll get a wash cloth," and then got up with a creaking of his knees. I laid there while I listened to him running water in the restroom, perfectly happy to wait on the floor for him to come back.

Then I realized that if someone came in, they'd see me lying there all bloody and weak. That was the last thing I needed a customer to see from me. Whether or not I had the wherewithal, I had to get up.

I was rolled over to my knees when Layne returned but I couldn't manage much more. His steady hand rested on my shoulder as my head hung between my shoulders. Without me asking, he dropped the wet cloth onto the back of my neck, cooling me down.

I sighed in blissful relief as he ran the wet cloth over my skin, washing the blood away and cooling me down.

"Holy hell," he said. "I think there's steam coming off it."

"That helps," I said and lifted my face to see him crouching in front of me.

The yellow had gone from his eyes, but there was a nervous tick at the corner.

"I think I can get up now," I said.

He nodded and cupped the triceps of my arm so I'd have some leverage when I tried to stand. Not that I needed leverage because he did more to lift me than I did to stand.

"I'm not always like this, you know," I said as I weaved on my feet.

"Like what? All hopped up on magic?" he tried to smile but it didn't take.

I rubbed the back of my neck. "Seems like I'm always fainting or puking or bleeding when you're around." I remembered his first comment about not being into damsels in distress and felt decidedly damsel-like.

He shrugged. "It's a nice change from dead bodies."

I wobbled over to the door of the shop and turned the sign over to closed. There was no way I was going to be in the right state of mind to sell a candle. Plus, my shirt was all stained. I'd have to find something to wear over it. Perhaps I had a spare shirt here left over from the days I'd worked and slept here as I got the building in shipshape.

I was considering it as I watched him shove his hands into his pockets. His jaw seesawed back and forth.

"What?" I said, knowing he wanted to say something but was afraid to come right out with it.

He started to speak, shook his head, then yanked his hands from his pockets before standing there with them clenching and unclenching at his sides.

"Out with it."

"Can you do it again?" he asked. "Duplicate the conditions. Try to make it happen again."

"Are you insane?" I demanded as I found energy from annoyance to cross the room again. "I don't even know what I did, let alone want to repeat it."

He followed me to the apothecary gallery, where I kept the tin of coffee grounds—real coffee, not the psilocybin mix I'd used in the weeks before I'd met him. I felt him lurking behind me as I dug out a mug from the bottom cupboard and plopped it next to the tin of Java. I knew he wanted to continue the conversation but I'd be damned if I'd do it without at least a hit of caffeine.

He waited while I carried the whole kit to the sink in the back room. He didn't leave his spot, but I could see him lean sideways to keep me in his line of sight as I prepped the pot. It was steaming and burping before he finally followed me into the back room.

"I've never been in here," he said, stalling, I thought.

"You have been in here," I said in a bald tone. "You chased me through the room out the back alley if you remember correctly."

He smirked as though he'd trapped me into talking when I didn't want to.

"I didn't exactly see it all, though," he said. "That little dress of yours blew up when you lit out of here." He pointed at the door. "Windy day," he added with another smile. "Couldn't see anything else with that pretty little ass bared to the world."

I sighed because I knew it had not been windy at all but I wasn't about to contradict him. For whatever reason, he was trying to get a rise out of me. Instead, I poured a mug of coffee and lifted it to my lips.

He grimaced. "No cream or sugar?"

I shook my head. "Black. Like my witch's heart."

"I thought you weren't a witch."

I eyed him over the rim of the mug as I slurped at the edge. I figured I'd let him think he'd won me over. Make him find a way to traverse the territory he so badly wanted, because I had no intention of bringing up the subject. I might give it some thought later, I might even try to figure out what had happened so I could avoid it happening again, but I was most definitely not going to try to repeat it.

"Brie," he said but got no farther because I held up a finger to stop him from saying more.

"Coffee first, kicking black magic second," I said.

He crossed his arms over his chest and I tried not to look at the way his biceps bulged and let go as he did so. Damn him and his hot body trying to distract me.

I carried the coffee past him to the main shop so I could get out of the silent examination he was giving me. As I brushed past him, his fingers hooked into my elbow. Not unkindly, he held me fast in his arms, and made me turn to face him. His expression softened when I caught his eye.

The tension in the air was electric. His warm body against mine, the feel of his arms corralling me like a shepherd penning in. I wanted to sag against him and knowing it made me irritable because I knew he was toying with me to get his way.

"I won't let anything hurt you, Brie," he said in a throaty voice. "I'll be right here with you."

"You mean like you were when it happened just a few minutes ago? That's very comforting."

I didn't mean for it to sound so mean, but there it was. I only realized I was ticked off about it when I the words came out of my mouth.

There was a long moment when he held me maybe a little too tightly, when I leaned into him out of reflex or instinct, and when I thought he might find a way to soothe the ache that had started up in my throat, the one that told me if we didn't do something in a short moment, I was going to kiss him.

But then he let me go and the coffee ebbed up over the rim of the mug and spilled onto the floor. Seeing it, my eyes welled up for some reason and I turned away from him and the puddle. I was all the way to the counter, intending to grab the cloth we'd left beside the cash register, when he groaned and did what he always did.

Became a prick.

"If you don't try to figure out what's happening, you might just end up behind bars."

I whipped around, ignoring the mug in my hand and was lucky it didn't spill all over my feet. "If I end up behind bars it's because you aren't doing your God damned job."

"Just try for Pete's sake. Don't you want to know what's happening to you?" He gestured to my arms, still bloody but drying into an itchy bit of crust. "Don't you want to know who's doing that to you, or are you content to let them bleed you bit by bit until you're comatose?"

"I thought you said you thought I did this," I angled my arms toward him, making the crusted over tattoos much more visible. "I thought you wanted me to repeat it."

He came closer then, his brow furrowing in worry. "Don't you see, Brie? If you can't repeat it, then it means someone else is doing this to you." He waved his hand in the direction of the grimoire then the door. "Maybe it's the damn dead guy doing it and not you. Maybe he's the one who broke into your apartment."

"Ghosts don't break in," I said.

He dropped his head back onto his shoulders. "Not the point and you know it. Repeat it. Test it. If you can't do it again, then it's something else. Some other force messing with you."

He didn't need to say more than that. The thought that some 'other' force was messing with me was what had got me upset in the first place and drove me to dig through my mother's grimoire. It was becoming horribly clear that all that witchcraft and spell work I'd grown up with actually had power. And now that power had landed at my doorstep.

He was right. I did need to try again.

"I have no idea where to start," I said.

"Start with the grimoire." He brushed past me to retrieve it from the floor and placed it reverently, carefully, on the counter. I noticed he placed it directly over the gouge in the surface.

It was open, but not to the page I'd seen when things had gone all shady. With a sigh, I started to flip through the pages.

"I was looking at this," I said as I found the page. "It was blank."

I peered up at him and he gave me an expectant look. "So? You were just looking at it and it changed?"

My brow furrowed along with his as I tried to remember. "I think so. It started to smoke and then that man showed up."

"No," he said. "You touched your chest."

I pursed my lips in thought. "Yes," I said hesitantly, "but the page was blank when I did that. It started to smoke before the letters came."

I looked down at them as I braced myself. "Hold on," I said in warning and whacked my chest again.

Nothing. My knees were grateful.

He blinked, obviously not ready despite my warning for him to hold on.

"Try again?" he said.

I eyed the book as I considered repeating the action. "I'm not sure that's all," I said. "I mean, the guy showed up after I touched my chest."

"You had your hand on the book, too," he said.

I had. Was that it? Was there some sort of physical connection that had to be made?

I swallowed down the anxiety as I spoke. "You think you could watch for the guy?" I said. "Make sure he doesn't hurt me?" I hated that my voice sounded so small, but he smiled gently.

"I will kill the person who tries to hurt you."

"Ghosts are already dead."

"Semantics," he said. "You get my point."

I nodded and drew in a long bracing breath as I placed my palm down on the lettering on the pages of the grimoire.

Then with a sharp exhale, I touched my chest with the other.

The next thing I knew, I was staring up at a pair of black eyes.

CHAPTER TWENTY-ONE

Parrish's red hair hung in my face. I brushed it away irritably and in doing so, noticed the blood pooling at my wrist.

"I was just about to kiss you awake," she said with a smile that showed a dimple in one corner of her mouth. "Save you from the poisoned apple our irritable wolf seems to have fed you."

"You're mixing up your fairytales," I murmured past a tongue that felt too big for my mouth. Where my throat managed to move, it felt like it was stuffed with Brillo pads.

Layne's face appeared next to Parrish's but his was not in the least bit relieved. He was irritable. Just like Parrish said.

"You're cranky I passed out when you're the one that convinced me to do it?" I said. At least it's what I tried to say. It came out more like a bunch of consonants without any vowels or breaks in between to make the individual words discernible.

"I take it our shopping trip is out," Parrish said as she leaned down far enough to worm her hands beneath my back and hoist me up without a single shred of gentleness. I flopped forward like a puppet before I could put enough steel in my spine to keep from falling straight over.

"What in the hell did you put in her coffee?" Parrish said to Layne.

"Long story," he said as he shoved her aside—with as much gentleness as she'd moved me—then scooped me beneath my knees and behind my back.

He stood, hoisting me with him as he straightened up. I felt very much the damsel and he the dashing hero.

The thought buzzed in my mind like a hornet in a jar. I needed to do something about that impression of my frailty.

I made a grab for Parrish's shirt, a plaid bit of flannel straight out of the 90s, and caught the edge of her sleeve.

"Ghost," I said, when I was pretty sure I planned to ask her to tell him to put me down.

Parrish screwed her eyebrows together and looked at Layne. "Coat? What's she going on about?"

Layne gently peeled my fingers off the flannel and tucked my hand between my ribs and his chest. "She accessed her magic," he said. "Pretty potent stuff, I'm guessing based on how flat it knocked her onto her ass."

I made a swipe for his face, thinking to hush his foolish mouth. "No magic," I said, realizing that too had come out wrong. I tried again and got the same result. "Ghost."

He carried me across the room and arranged me in the wingback chair but kept talking to Parrish as though I wasn't there. "It's my fault," he said in a choked voice. "I asked her to do it again and she screamed like a banshee then fell into a fit on the floor. It took me five minutes to rouse her."

Parrish gave me a long look. "Exactly what is 'it' that you keep yabbering about?"

He stood back and crossed his arms as he watched me trying to rearrange myself in the chair. When my hand slipped and I fell against the arm, whacking my chin on the hardest part, he scurried forward to help.

I managed to glare at him before he dropped to his knees next to me.

"I'm fine."

"She's fine," Parrish echoed as she laid her hand on his shoulder, holding him back. "Give her some space. You're being too clingy. Sheesh. Be a werewolf will ya?"

"I'm not clingy," he growled and whirled on her with enough force that she backed away a step. Even I cringed in the chair at the sound of fury in his voice.

Parrish held up her hands in surrender. "Hold on, now, Garder. Everything is fine. She's fine. You're fine. I'm fine. The Goddamn bell over top the Goddamn door is fine. No need to pull the alpha bitch out to play because your little girlfriend had a tizzy."

"I'm telling you she is not fine," he said, this time in a softer voice, but with all the heat of the earlier comment. "You didn't see what I saw. Her eyes rolled back in her head for Pete's sake. That only happens in the movies." There was a lengthy silence before he said, "And I'm not an alpha bitch."

She nodded as though she completely agreed. "So you made her do something she shouldn't have?"

"Yes." There was agony in his voice. "We were trying to repeat what happened earlier. It was too much. Too soon. I shouldn't have asked it of her." He went on to explain all that had transpired from the time I'd seen her last to the moment she'd come into the shop—I'd flipped the sign but neglected to lock the door, apparently—and he filled in things I'd not known had happened.

Like the shade man turning up again for several seconds after I collapsed. Like the sound of a large dog growling ferociously enough that the wolf in him nearly took over out of instinct. He'd kept it together though, and dutifully wiped away the blood that welled along the lines of the tattoos—which were as visible to him as they were to me for several long moments.

Apparently, I'd been out for longer than I thought. No wonder all my muscles ached. Losing blood probably drained my energy. I didn't think it was enough to be dangerous, but the bleeding itself was a worry.

I sat in the chair barely listening to their exchange, letting myself rest and my mind to wander. I had plenty of time to think as they argued about whether or not he should have pushed me. One thing was perfectly clear, even if my energy levels weren't up.

I'd made a connection to some magic when I'd touched the grimoire and my tattoos.

My mother's magic, I presumed. It was her grimoire, after all. Her amulet that was found at the scene at the flophouse. "Oh my God," I said aloud, surprising myself. "It makes perfect sense."

Layne peered down at me. "What's that?"

"Hecate. She's the goddess of death and magic and ghosts. My mother must have been a follower. Maybe they are sacrificing to their god."

"Satanic cult," Parrish declared. "I knew it. Didn't I say it was a satanic cult?"

"Hecate is not Satan," I said. "And what you said was the media would love it if it was."

"Tomayto Tomahto," she said, seesawing her hand back and forth.

I stared at her, working through her comment as it crystallized the issue for me. I'd never fully understood why connecting to the magic had such a strong effect on me, or why it seemed to be some sort of beacon for the shade man and the dog, but I did know some things about the goddess my mother professed to worship, and that helped me decipher the foundation of the power if nothing else. And it all had to do with the symbol on my amulet. The one on my shop windows and my logo.

The Hecate's wheel.

Hecate. The three-bodied goddess who could look at all directions of a crossroads at the same time. Where she was, a pack of dogs followed. Her legends referred to dogs being her familiars, and the animal she preferred for sacrifice.

Dogs. Crossroads. Three bodied female statuettes. All those numbers found at the crime scenes, numbers sacred to the goddess. We'd thought the killer was numbering his kills, but those numbers were associated with Hecate. Parrish's comment about the cult.

I should have seen it before. The connection was so clear.

The Hecate killers and the Cult of Blackburn were one and the same.

And while my mother had just stuck to small animals and stalking graveyards, this cult was after more. They were willing to sacrifice people to access death magic, the most powerful magic of all.

And if my mother, as part of that coven, had power to store all that magic in her grimoire and amulet, what then might an entire coven be able to accomplish with the kinds of sacrifices they were making.

I said as much to Layne and Parrish.

"You think they're killing people so the goddess will what? Bless them? Is that something I should be writing in my report?" She mimed holding a microphone to her mouth. "Subject appears to be thirty year old female with ties to an immortal goddess who requires her worshipers to mule little statues of her into the afterlife. Stomach linings optional and —"

Layne put his hand against her mouth to stop her from going on. "The DNA," he said. "Did you get the results back?"

She nodded beneath his palm.

"And if I take my hand away you are just going to give us facts and not an unfunny diatribe about satanic cults."

"Hecate cult," I said, correcting him but he ignored me as he waited for Parrish to nod again. "You sent a clipping of your shirt with Brie's blood on it along with a hair sample."

She nodded once more and her gaze flicked to mine. Dread tingled at the base of my spine. I would have expected if my blood was going to a lab somewhere, that I'd be informed or asked. But I had visions of my empty trash can at the mention of another sample.

Layne withdrew his hand and she worked her lips over her teeth to unstick them where his hand had mopped up any saliva.

"You taste like pizza," she said. "With anchovies."

I was aware my voice was very small when I spoke. "What DNA?"

Parrish turned slowly to face me head on. "The blood I wiped off you at the flophouse."

I noted she deftly avoided using the term murder scene.

"And the hair," I said. "Whose was that?"

She twisted the ankle of her combat boot as her mouth worked around the confession. "There were a couple of hairs on the shirt too," she finally said. "One was mine." She chuckled and shook out her hands before shoving them into the front pockets of her jeans. "Seems I'm going gray."

"And the other one?" I pressed. "I'm guessing it was mine."

"It's not because we think you're a suspect," she said hurriedly. "It's more to rule us out, you see. What with Farrel making a big stink and your amulet being at the scene and all. With you found at the crime scene, you know, with blood on you..."

My throat had a hard time swallowing around the clump that grew smack dab in the middle. "I didn't kill anyone," I said.

She nodded frantically, agreeing and wanting me to see how truly sincere that agreement was. "Yes, we know. I believe you, but the courts. Well, they can be a bit less naive when it comes to crime."

My back went rigid and she most have sensed it because she rushed to my side and gripped me by the shoulders so she could look me directly in the eyes. "I don't mean to imply you did it. Oh fuck. I'm ridiculous at this. Layne?"

She tossed him a helpless look and he lifted his brows in innocent query.

"You're doing fine," he said in a strangled voice. "Don't let me stop you."

"You're a prick," she said.

"I've been accused of that before," he said.

She glanced back at me as her hands loosed their death grip on my shoulders. "He's a prick."

I nodded. "I've said so."

She huffed out a bit of a sigh. "Listen, Brie. I'm sorry. I really should have told you but Layne—"

"Don't bring me into your mess," he said.

She ignored him. "We both wanted to clear you unequivocally, and then we were curious to know if maybe the blood might have been the victim's."

"Was it?" I said in a tight voice and she shook her head. I was sure my relief was palpable, except she didn't seem to react to it. That could only mean one thing.

"There's a problem, isn't there?" I said and the dread sang up my spine again.

Layne spit his gum into a tissue, coming to life again at the comment. "Is there a problem, Parrish?"

"A small one," she said without looking his way. "Well, maybe a bit larger than small. Big, actually."

I groaned because that did not sound encouraging at all. "What could possibly be wrong with my blood?"

She winced as she answered. "That's the thing," she said. "It's not your blood."

Chapter Twenty-Two

THE ONLY THING WORSE than not having my own blood on me at a murder scene, had to be having someone else's blood on me. I'd blacked out and came to in a house where multiple murders had been committed and the blood found on my arms was not my own. It didn't look good. In fact, it looked pretty damn incriminating.

My hands started to travel to my throat before I remembered the jolt I'd taken a few moments earlier. I didn't dare touch myself anywhere in the vicinity of the grimoire.

I pushed them down by my sides and stalked over to the door.

"You two need to leave," I said.

"Brie," Layne said in an infuriatingly gentle tone.

"Brie nothing," I said. "If the blood on me was not mine, then I'm pretty sure you shouldn't be hanging around carousing with a suspect. In fact, I don't want you hanging around." I nearly sobbed on the last and Parrish clomped over to me with a pace that might put a horse to shame.

"But that's just it," she said. "It's not yours. But it's not the victims either."

I waved my arm in a gesture that indicated it was all useless hope. "Doesn't matter," I said. "It's probably some other poor victim I murdered in my sleep somewhere and you just haven't found the body."

She pursed her lips as though she was trying not to laugh and it nearly broke me.

"Are you trying to drive me off the deep end?" I said, "because it sure seems like it."

Layne pushed past Parrish when she started for me. "She's not very good at this," he said and glared over his shoulder at her.

"You left me out on that limb, buster," she said. "Is it my fault I'm too much woman to be hanging by such a rotten branch?"

"I'm sorry, Brie." He made to touch me but I yanked my shoulder away and edged away from his reach. "We believe you," he said in a soothing voice. "Like she said, it was meant to clear you and her. But this new development makes things more interesting."

"Incriminating you mean."

"No. Interesting."

"I'll say," Parrish interjected. "I mean, the DNA from the hair indicates the blood is a mitochondrial match."

She grinned very wide as though she'd just handed us a big piece of Dutch chocolate.

Layne swore. "You couldn't say that like a week ago?"

"What week?" she countered his hyperbolic language with an equally infuriating bit of logic. "We were just discussing it."

"You're too literal to live," he said and she tossed an F-you finger up at him.

I put my fingers to my forehead and pressed against the headache blooming there. "Please," I said. "Stop the bickering and tell me what in the hell does all this mean. I'm sick, I ache, and I want to be done with this conversation."

Layne rocked back on his heels and dug into his pocket to extract a piece of gum. He unwrapped it as he spoke, doing it as thoughtfully as his words sounded.

"It means there's a maternal connection somewhere. Maternal DNA is very robust. It can't pinpoint individuals, but it can indicate that the person whose blood you had on you was related to you somehow." He shoved the gum into his mouth and chewed for a moment, watching me the whole time. When he'd gathered the rest of his thoughts, he planted the wad on the side of his mouth. "Do you have any brothers and sisters?"

I shook my head. "My dad died when I was a kid. My mother never remarried."

Saying it out loud, all the reasons why she'd never remarried tried to push their way out of the dark closet I'd shoved them into. I wrestled the familiar nasty images back in and took a deep breath so I could finish. If I missed a beat in the conversation, neither Layne nor Parrish indicated they'd noticed.

"She have any boyfriends? Lovers?"

I barked out a laugh at that. "Not sure who would take up with a mad woman who sacrificed puppies in her spare time. Ranting about power and burning her bones"

Parrish's ginger eyebrows climbed to her hairline. "Burning her bones?"

I nodded and felt my shoulders sag with the promise of release. All those sessions with my Canadian therapist, and I'd never once admitted the things I was about to tell these two.

"It's what I wanted to tell you before," I said and headed to the nearest wingback chair to sit down. I perched on the edge and waved at them to pull up a place to sit as well. Layne found a stool, and Parrish opted to hitch her butt onto the counter.

"Hecate is the goddess of death and reanimation. My mother spent months in our basement casting spells and making sacrifices. I thought she was trying to raise my father from the dead." I choked on the words and the memories but I kept on. "I was a kid. No more than six and it terrified me."

"As well it should," Parrish murmured.

I appreciated the sympathy. "I adored my dad. And my mother was never the same when he died. Freak accident, as far as I know. All these years, I've thought she was trying to raise him from the dead." I heaved a sigh of fear and exhaustion. "Now I find out she was just part of a cult of death worshipers.

"My mother always said that death magic has powers that blood or hair don't possess. Whatever they're trying to do, it's big."

Layne leaned back. "Doesn't explain why they're killing people, but at least we know what we're dealing with."

"Yeah," Parrish said. "A cult of black witches. Fun times."

The way she said it, sounded like she'd been through the same sorts of fun times before.

"We were guardians for a black coven," she said. "Long time ago."

I remembered that, but I'd thought it was dozens of years in the past. Maybe a century. She saw me watching her and grinned so expectantly, I thought maybe she was trying to deflect, but I squirreled the information away for study later.

"Our pack abandoned the coven when they began practicing black magic," Layne said. "It's why our alpha broke ties. It's in all our lore. That's what Parrish is trying to say." He looked past me to Parrish and she hurriedly agreed. Too acquiescent for her to be sincere. One more note to put in my mental file about Layne and his pack.

A sudden thought struck me. I remembered Layne saying Parrish was made back in the 60s. I don't know why it slipped my attention then, but I was sure it was a slip, that he'd not meant to mention any time line at all.

"You were turned in the 60s," I said, giving her an assessing look. When her gaze flicked to Layne's I knew they'd hoped I'd forgotten that. "You'd have to be over seventy years old but you don't look a day over thirty two."

She started to say something, but Layne put his hand down on her arm, stopping her. "We don't age like humans once we're turned," he said.

I narrowed my gaze at him. "Just how old are you?"

He picked at a piece of lint on his pants. "Older than Parrish."

"So you could be from the fifties?" I said, whistling quietly. "I knew you were older than me, but..."

"But you dig older men?" he said, his eyebrows waggling suggestively.

I knew he was trying to change the subject with his innuendo, but I wasn't about to let it go. Just file it away like the other things. A project for later when all this mess was cleared away.

"We were talking about your pack lore and it being the muscle for a black coven." The image of me trailing my mother's heel in a night graveyard rose to my mind and I shoved it determinedly back as I worked through the possibilities that had been brewing in my psyche.

"You think your mother was a member?" he asked.

"I'm guessing the people they are sacrificing have some affinity with the coven," I said, thinking of the pictures my mother kept, the one with the shade man who had attacked me and then died at the hands of the man who had murdered all the psychics weeks earlier. "They killed some of their own in the past. Who's to say they didn't do it again in the 60s and again during my childhood. My mom kept getting these strange calls when I was a kid. Maybe she was a defector or something." I hated the sound of hope in my voice. "Maybe she was targeted as well and made the amulet to protect herself. Maybe it's a cycle or something that they are repeating and that's what the murders are. I mean, those victims from the flophouse did not struggle."

"Maybe anything," Layne said. "We won't know until we catch them, but at least now we have a place to start."

"We do?"

He nodded. "We have your mother's clippings and we have a connection. We can look at all that with a new eye. One that's a bit more informed."

I leaned back in the chair. It was all presumption and supposition but I felt like he did: that we were closer than we were a week ago.

"Still doesn't explain the DNA," he said, "but we'll run the string along with others in the database. Maybe we'll find a long lost sibling or aunt or something."

"A sister would be cool," Parrish said. "I mean, since you're not my type." She waggled her eyebrows at me playfully.

"She'd have to be gay," I countered with a smile. I felt decidedly better.

She gestured that such a thing wouldn't matter. "Every woman's just a drink away from being gay." She slapped her thighs and hopped off the counter. "Feeling better?" she said. "I'm supposed to bring you shopping. Are you up to it?"

I looked around my shop and realized I did want to shop. I wanted to get out of the store and pretend things were normal for a while. Retail therapy sounded just right. Didn't matter what the reason for it was. A shopping trip was a shopping trip.

She hooked my arm through hers, scooping me out of the chair and hauling me toward the door. "Look after the store, will ya, old man? Spend some time going through all that ephemera you mentioned and make yourself useful," she said over her shoulder to Layne. "We got some things to buy."

She had her hand on the door handle when he stopped her.

"What do you mean you're *supposed* to take Brie shopping?"

She looked at me with alarm in her face. I knew better than to speak up.

"Nothing," she said.

"I know you're lying," he said in a tight voice.

"I know you know," she responded slowly as she turned to face him. "But I don't have to explain anything to you. You're not my alpha."

I couldn't be sure, but I thought she stressed the word alpha a little too emphatically. I wanted to steal a look at Layne over my shoulder to see what effect it had on him, but Parrish pushed open the door and yanked me out with her too fast.

She walked me to her beater of her car, rambling about all the reasons she had to get me out of there before Layne got suspicious. And one of them was the same alpha power she'd indicated he didn't have over her. She was scared she'd give in.

"He and his dad have this thing," she said when we were on the road, swerving in and out of traffic at a speed that would put a cab driver to shame. "Best to keep him in the dark about what we're doing."

I wasn't sure how to formulate my questions to that statement and it took me until we were in front of the lingerie store before I realized her comment meant she was going behind his back—because her real alpha had ordered her to.

"OK," I said as she pulled open the door for me, a most genteel gesture from such a hardened woman. "I went along with this at first out of spite and curiosity. But what in the name of heaven is this really all about?"

She gave me a gentle shove when I didn't move. "Later," she said.

I spun to face her as she stepped in behind me, but the ever eager clerk interjected herself before Parrish could answer.

"Lovely day, ladies," she said. "Perfect for shopping. Is there anything I can help you with?"

The clerk was an older lady, with soft gray curls framing bright green eyes. The wrinkles that formed as she smiled meant it was genuine. I liked her right away, and when she eyed us both up and down, mentally assessing the best way to ingratiate herself with the likes of the clients she saw as money signs, I didn't take offense. I just saw a happy happenstance where I could help her earn a decent commission on some bully's dime.

She took longer with Parrish.

"You need belts and snaps," she said. "Nothing frilly." She was already spinning on her heel and heading to a rack of black lingerie made of leather and feathers, and something that looked like velvet.

Parrish grinned at me. "Gotta hand it to the lady; she knows her stuff."

I followed her to the rack at the back of the shop, where a few vanilla type sex toys were on display. The velvet curtain a few feet to the right indicated there might be more adventurous things beyond, but the clerk didn't so much as glance at it.

She pulled out a onesie cat suit with cutaways in strategic places. It had leather lacing to join the thin strips of material that made up the sides of the outfit to each other as they joined in a wide open gap at the front. The collar of it was made of leather, studded with small metal rings. The whole thing joined in a V beneath the belly button.

A bit risqué but quite beautiful if you paid attention to the suppleness of the leather and the pile of the velvet. She held it up to Parrish who looked down at it with longing.

"Not for me," she said and jerked her chin in my direction.

The clerk's glance trailed over my figure in a millisecond. "You're on the other side of the shop."

Parrish brushed away the onesie. "The other side of the shop is a bit too Victorian. We need something in between."

The clerk nodded briskly and in efficient steps managed to pluck out a beautiful set of purple bra and panties. The satin gleamed in the shop light.

"It's gorgeous." I breathed.

"We can try on?" Parrish asked.

The clerk pulled out several more bra and pantie sets along with several garter belts to match. "We have disposable underwear you can put on underneath. They don't ruin the lines of the product you want to try. There's a stash of them in the dressing rooms." She continued flicking through the racks, sorting and discarding as she went. She paused at a cream colored, gauzy corset with see-through panties and a black garter belt.

"That one," Parrish said. "But we'll try them all."

The clerk gave me one more measuring look and put the garment back in favor of a smaller size, then she hustled us into the dressing room area.

The room was easily as big as the front of the shop with three expensive looking wingback chairs placed strategically in front of 365 mirrors. There was one actual viewing area and I guessed it was because the shop catered to more discerning clients. I imagined men wearing business suits lounging in the chairs as their lovers assessed the way she looked in the mirrors.

But three chairs? Not sure why any man would want others ogling his lover while she paraded in her scanties.

Parrish plopped herself into the middle chair, hanging her leg over the arm and waggled her hand at me. "Go. Change. I'll help you decide."

Chapter Twenty-Three

Heat swam over my chest at the thought of her seeing me in the things we'd picked out. "I'm not sure—"

"Part of the deal," she said. "I was told not to leave until you picked out something suitable."

"I'm sure we can just lie. I mean, I'm not really doing this for either of them. I'm doing it for me."

She sent me a smirk that indicated she thought otherwise, then shook her head. "I know Owen and I know Layne. Whoever you decide to reveal this little ensemble to, you're going to want to make sure it's perfect."

"I think I have an idea what looks good."

The clerk flung back the curtain to the dressing room. Easily as broad as my bedroom, it too was mirrored all the way around. I wouldn't need to come out to look over the results at all. I thought the clerk did it because she could see I was uncomfortable. Seemed I wasn't the only one to read people well.

"If the garments are not for your companion's sake, then it's entirely up to you to decide."

She furrowed her brow at me, and for the first time, I realized she thought Parrish and I were a couple.

Parrish waved her hand. "Up to you, Brie," she said. "But you should know I don't see you that way. I like my partners a bit more...Well, let's just say I like them a bit more."

Meaning she'd already assessed me and decided I wasn't her type, whatever that was. Still. It didn't feel right about modeling for her. I balked, my entire body going rigid.

She sighed. "Look, how many times do you get to peek into a male's sexual fantasies without risking anything? I know what men like because while I might look like a woman, I think like a man. Trust me when I say what you think a man wants and what a man wants are two different things."

She had a point. I grabbed the purple bra and pantie set from the clerk and headed for the curtain.

"Nope," Parrish said.

I looked at her over my shoulder.

"The see through corset for Drake and the leather thong and garters for Layne."

My eyebrows climbed an inch but I took them from the clerk and closed the curtain behind me. The footfalls of the clerk indicated she'd left the room.

I tried on the thong and matching bra first, using the disposable underwear meant for the style as the clerk suggested. I wasn't sure I had the butt for it but the mirrors made me look pretty good. Only a few dimples that were fairly strategically set, I was relieved to see.

"I love these mirrors," I said, projecting my voice over the curtain.

Parrish made a noncommittal noise from her side. "Come out."

I huffed a bracing breath and positioned myself so she'd get a front view, which was more clothed than the back. Then I yanked open the curtain.

She gasped. "Come out. Turn around. If you think those tiny mirrors in there are flattering, you need to see yourself in full light."

I stepped out, subconscious and awkward as I angled so she wouldn't see everything the garments revealed. I took a few mincing steps toward her and caught sight of myself in the mirrors.

"I'd fuck you," she said with a growl in her voice.

I tittered, not sure why I was happy to hear that. She didn't miss it.

"You see what I mean about knowing, really knowing, what will turn someone on?" She pushed herself out of her chair and strode toward me, angling her head this way and that as though she was critiquing what she saw. "You have a good ass for it. Even makes me want to fill my palms with flesh, and I'm not into skinny women." She halted mid-way round me and leaned so I could see her face. She waggled her eyebrows. "You're gorgeous."

I frowned at her assessment of me, mostly because I was way over the line of svelte and my cup size had me growling about petite Chinese seamstresses whenever I bought a bra. "I'm not skinny."

"Skinny is subjective, darlin'." She scanned my form in the mirror that showed my backside, and I got the hint that she liked a fairly large booty as she lingered over the curves. "But for Layne, this is perfect."

I squirmed in the clothes, suddenly feeling more naked than I had a moment earlier. If she noticed my awkwardness, she didn't mention it. Just ordered me perfunctorily to change and toss the thong out so the clerk could wrap it up.

"The see-through corset set too," she said.

I ran my fingers over the material as it lay on the chair inside the dressing room. The gauzy lace would itch against bare skin, especially at the size the clerk had given me.

"Don't I need to make sure it fits?"

"Only if you plan to wear it, honey," Parrish said. "Now hurry up. I got things to do."

I could have hugged her in that moment. She knew exactly what Layne's dad had asked of me, and she'd played along, fully intending to make me buy something Layne would love instead and use the alpha's money to do so. I had no idea if I'd ever get to wear it, if Layne and I would ever get that far or even if I wanted to, but it warmed my heart that she thought enough of a friend to stay loyal despite orders from her alpha.

And all while she'd managed to do exactly what that alpha asked.

Pretty shrewd, really.

When I came out, she was grinning at me and I couldn't help the crazy smile that played across my own lips. "You are one bad ass wolf," I said.

She shrugged. "I'm alright sometimes."

The clerk, who had somehow miraculously appeared without a sound, scooped the garments off the chair where they'd landed when I'd tossed them over the curtain.

"You knew all along I wasn't going along with Layne's father's insinuations."

"You're not like the others," she said.

That there were others didn't surprise me. Owen gave off the vibe of a man who got what he wanted no matter what the desire was. He'd certainly behaved as though he expected me to do his bidding. I felt sorry for the nameless others who had been on the receiving end of his demands.

"So this alpha act and rich coddled father figure works for him?"

"Oh, it works. Women have been known to do some pretty underhanded things to get his attention. He doesn't usually have to do much pursuing. The alpha magic is hard to resist if it turns on you. And he knows how to turn it on."

Indeed, I thought. I'd felt it.

The clerk had bustled us over to the counter and was sorting through the papers in a file folder. She looked up at me as Parrish gave my name.

"Brie Duncan?" she said. "I thought you looked familiar. I knew your mother."

"You did?"

"I certainly did. She was a beautiful woman. Never aged a day that I lived next to her. She kept that gorgeous skin right up till the last. You favor her, you know. It's in the eyes, I think."

It wasn't the first time I'd been told I looked like my mother. I'd heard it a lot as a child, enough that I rankled at the compliment after I'd discovered her secret practices in our basement. I didn't want to look like her. When I emancipated myself, and ended up in foster homes as a result, no one accused me of looking like Kate McAllister because no one cared about her. Just the money they received from the government to care for me.

And in Canada, no one knew her. I'd gone a lot of years without having to hear the comment, and would have been happy to go the rest of my life the same way. Now, with the clerk looking me up and down in a whole different way than she had earlier, I felt more uncomfortable.

"My mother died a few years ago," I said. "I live in her brownstone now." I squinted at her, trying to figure out if I'd caught sight of her on the block. "I don't think I've seen you in the neighborhood."

The clerk packed pink and white striped tissue paper into the boutique bag, making lovely tufts of the tissue. "I didn't know she died," she said. "I moved a month or so after she went missing. Everyone just assumed she died in that apartment of hers. She rarely came out in the last months, and when she did it was just to walk that massive dog of hers. She looked so frail and weak, I felt like all she needed was a bit of good food to set her to rights. I hated seeing her like that. Haunted look in her gorgeous eyes. Sunken cheeks. I left casseroles for her every few days. They disappeared from the step and the dish appeared on my step a few days later empty of food, so I know she appreciated them."

I listened to her as politely as I could, all the while my skin was crawling up my spine in shivers that threatened to peel the skin back all the way up to my neck. Missing, she'd said. Not dead. Missing.

I tried to remain calm, and keep my face impassive when all along I was screaming inside. It took all my energy not to contradict her, to let her finish what she had to say, because she didn't look in the least bit finished.

She took a few seconds to give the bag a critical eye before she pushed it across the counter at me. "A week of her not coming out to walk the dog and the neighbors got worried. Rightly so. She doted on that thing, so it was most peculiar that she didn't walk it. I wouldn't go in, mind you, didn't want to see what might have become of her if she'd just collapsed in the house with no one to feed that huge beast."

My mouth went dry. I couldn't ask a question if I'd been able to form one. Parrish seemed completely oblivious to the tension in my shoulders, the panic that was trying to take over my body. My mother was dead. I'd seen the will. I'd inherited her things. I'd seen her shade.

The clerk was balling up the remnants of the tissue paper that hadn't been good enough to go into the pack when the proper question blazed across my mind.

"What did they find when they went in?" I tried not to clench my fists at my side. I tried very hard to simply lift the bag from the counter and hold it next to my side.

Parrish sent me a quizzical look and I realized I was holding the bag out in front of me as though it was a filthy thing. I lowered my arm and let it hang at my side.

The woman sighed and tossed the tissue into the trash then crossed her arms over her ample bosom. "Police said the place was empty. No dog. No Kate. No sign of struggle. Just looked like she'd walked out the door and never looked back." She set her mouth in a grim line of remorse and regret. "I'm sorry to hear she did pass away after all. I'd carried the hope all these years that she might have just moved on."

I struggled to find the right words because I knew damn well my mother's lawyer had contacted me to arrange for me to collect my mother's things and whatever inheritance she'd left me. That sort of thing didn't happen unless someone died. I expected my voice to be strangled by the confusion and shock I felt, and relieved I sounded normal.

"Thank you," I said when the words came. "Your sympathies mean a lot to me. My mother was lucky to have someone like you to look out for her."

I knew I'd said the right thing when the clerk smiled and reached beneath the counter. She pulled out a black enamel lipstick case and tucked it into my tight grip I had on the handles of the bag. "I liked her," she said. "I'm so pleased to have met you."

I had to wrench my hand from hers but I did it as gently as I could before spinning on my heel and racing for the door. I hoped Parrish would just follow without question. Her footfalls behind me sped up as she realized I wasn't going to wait. All I wanted was to get out of there.

I had my hand on the door when she asked me the question I dreaded. "I thought your mother was dead?"

"She is," I said. "She has to be." I paused a moment to blow out a long breath.

"You didn't ever visit her grave?"

"Why would I?" I said. "Visiting wouldn't change a damn thing."

She leaned in, her hand going to the bag in my hand as though she thought I would drop it. "The dog. That dog that's following you around. That's her dog."

I looked askance at her and I knew when I did that what she saw in my face worried her. It was written all over hers. "I know. Please. Let's let it go for now."

"But this is strange. Don't you think so?" She took the bag from me and planted her other palm on the door, pushing it open for me. "

The lipstick case fell to the floor with a tinkling sound as the door yawned open. I stepped through and Parrish stooped to pick up the lipstick. Her blazing red hair caught the sunlight for a moment before the door started to close on her.

That gleam of sun on her hair was the last thing I saw before darkness and the stink of mold came down around my head.

Chapter Twenty-Four

I WAS PRETTY SURE I heard Parrish growling like a beast at my back. Whoever was shoving me from behind took a slam to the legs because they fell against me hard enough to knock me to my knees. Pain lanced its way up my thighs even as I scrambled to pull the hood from my head. Someone shoved me from behind.

I fell all the way then, with my elbows ramming into concrete. I let go a howl of pain that alerted whoever had yanked the hood over my head that I was unattended. Whoever that was grabbed at my leg. I slid along the concrete. My knees scraped themselves raw on the unyielding sidewalk.

When I howled the next time, it was in panic and rage.

I tried to struggle. With a burst of energy, I twisted in the grip of whoever had me by the ankles. I yelled for Parrish.

What came back at me was a snarl of rage and fury.

Her wolf had her obviously and I was on my own. The hands that had hold of my legs climbed to my thighs and then to my waist. I flailed blindly with my hands, punching, hitting. My blows came to nothing but with my legs freed, I kicked and bucked, determined to get free.

The telltale signs of fighting rose around me. Sirens wailed in the distance. Help, I thought. Help was coming.

I knew without a doubt that help's arrival would be too late.

There were too many of them, I realized. Too many footfalls, too many sounds of grunts and growls, and the occasional shriek that pierced the air had more than one timbre.

Parrish might be tough, but she couldn't take them all. She couldn't. And I think both of us knew it.

I had to fight for my life. I scratched and bit down when a hand came too close to my throat. All I got was a mouthful of musty fabric. It tasted of garlic and onions and a hint of oregano.

I got wrestled into someone's arms. Another snarl came from Parrish's direction, followed by a yelp. I was afraid she'd been hurt but I couldn't do more than call out to her and hope for the best.

Hoisted from the ground, I found awkward footing that got pressed ever forward so fast my feet couldn't keep up. When I got shoved hard from behind and felt the hard coldness of steel, I knew I was being marshaled into the back of a vehicle.

The exhaust leaked up beneath the hood to choke me.

I tumbled into the interior and my hands roamed the surface of cold leather as they sought purchase. Behind me, a snarl that was both pained and agonized and more than a bit frantic tore through the air. My name caught the wind in a rasping half-primal howl. She'd failed, Parrish. She'd tried to defend me but lost.

I just hoped that defense hadn't cost her. In my mind's eye, I saw all those poor victims I'd seen over the last weeks, the ones she had slaved over to bring their lives and their bodily struggle to the police so their killers could be found, and I prayed she'd been spared those same atrocities.

"Tell me she's OK," I pleaded beneath the hood. The fabric stuck in my mouth as I spoke and I had to spit to rid my tongue of dust bunnies. "Tell me you didn't hurt her."

"She'll live," said a voice that sounded familiar. "It might take her a few days to heal, but she'll live, now shut up."

He cuffed me against the side of the head, knocking me in the ear hard enough that it rung.

I shut up. I sat against the back of the seat as the car sped away, trying to memorize the turns and counting the time off but it was no use. Blind, I had no idea which direction the driver was going. The weaving in and out of traffic made my stomach roll.

When we stopped, I was herded from the car down a flight of steps a mere ten paces from the car. The hand on my back was insistent and didn't ease up its pressure until I heard the hollow sounds of my own footsteps on a wooden landing. A door creaked open and I heard in the groaning of gears, a hint of rust.

"I'm going to take off the hood," he said. "I don't want you to try to struggle. Just do what I say and you'll be fine."

I wasn't fooled by the soothing tones but I nodded just the same.

The hood lifted but I couldn't see any better. Whoever had taken me shone a bright light in my face. Dust motes whorled in the beam of light. I coughed as they tickled my palate.

"Sit down," he said.

I presumed something was behind me. Shielding my eyes, I backed up enough to feel the solid weight of an iron bar against my calves. Chains rattled. A bed, I thought, with old fashioned springs. I sank down and was relieved to feel a mattress beneath me. I hadn't been entirely sure I'd have anything soft to catch me when I fell.

"What do you want?" I said, grimacing at the stench of urine that wafted up at me.

"Doesn't matter," he said in a voice that sounded off, like something hard and rough was stuck in his throat. "The waning moon will tell you all you need to know."

"But the wane isn't for another three weeks," I said as he dropped the light and came at me from the shadows. He stank of wet fur and blood. Parrish's blood, I thought. I prayed it wasn't another poor victim's blood, the fluid of a dying innocent.

I held my breath, waiting for my night vision to kick in. I counted time beneath my breath to keep myself from losing myself to panic and adrenaline. If I let all that rush in, I knew my body would start to shut down and I couldn't let that happen.

He hadn't abducted me to question me. He'd done so for some nefarious purpose. Mention of the waning moon hallmarked witchcraft. I knew the goddess of witchcraft, Hecate, was associated with the waning of the moon rather than the waxing or the full. If I doubted before that the killers were Hecate followers and that the followers were the cult of Blackburn, I was sure of it now.

I was in the hands of the black coven.

I thought of all those women who'd died in violence and wondered if they'd been able to reserve any adrenaline for the final fight or if they'd exhausted all they had in fear long before the final blow came.

"You're the killer," I said in a strangled voice that worried me. I couldn't show fear. Predators loved fear. They fed on it. I had to remain calm, or at least sound so.

"People saw you take me. If you let me go, you might still escape the worst."

He laughed and looked up at me. I realized he'd been fussing with something under the bed in the darkness, but now that my eyes were adjusting, I could see him better. He was crouched at my feet and he didn't look human. At least, not fully.

But what parts did look human, I recognized.

"Farrel," I said. "Does Layne know you're the killer?"

"Me?" he said. "I haven't killed anyone. You're here because they wanted you here."

"They?" I asked. "Who are 'they'? Did you try to frame me for the killings to cover their tracks? Was it you who put my amulet at the crime scene?" I didn't need an answer. I knew it was him. Still, I wondered where it was now. It was mine. I wanted it back.

"That's a lot of questions for someone who has no power to get answers." He peered up over the mattress at me. "But sure. I'll play. I was told to put it there. Told to see how you would react. How the amulet would react to you."

I didn't need to ask why. The Cult of Blackburn. They were obviously looking for more wattage. The amulet had drawn their attention weeks ago when they'd killed the shade man. No doubt they wanted to see if I had any powers, and if I did, they needed to know if it was enough to juice them up for whatever they were aiming to do.

The big question wasn't why they tested me. The big question was what they were planning to do with the power they were seeding.

"I know who you're working for," I said. "What are they after?" I said.

He barked out a harsh laugh. "You don't know anything. And I don't ask questions. It's not my place. I just do what I'm told. I was told to fetch you. Here you are." He cracked his neck as he angled his head. I thought he was trying to shift back into his fully human shape, and it was then I realized what he was. Werewolf.

I scrambled backward on the bed and discovered he hadn't so much as tied me to the frame. Wherever we were, he didn't think escape was an issue.

"You were the one in my apartment," I guessed. Layne and Parrish had both said they smelled werewolf. Both of them had brushed it off, presuming it came from the other because it had the scent of pack. They were wrong. It was familiar because they smelled it every day. Probably they didn't even register the difference.

He stood up, more man now than wolf, and angled the light so that it swept across his face as it pointed to the wall. I noted scratches all over his face and neck. A deep gouge ran down his arm and slashed into his wrist. Parrish had got him good. Just not good enough.

He hobbled back into the shadows, that were quickly gathering light from the lamp and becoming less frightening as my eyes adjusted. Even so, I didn't want to be left in complete darkness.

"Please," I said. "Leave the lamp."

He grunted. "I'm not a monster," he said. "You can have the light. I'll bring you water later. For now, it's best you just sleep. It'll make the time go faster."

He headed deeper into the dark and the sound of creaking wood warbled toward me. A slant of light bled down the stairs as he opened the door at the top, then it cut off abruptly.

I was alone. In a basement, it seemed. But everything about the space felt off. I pulled my knees up to my chin and wrapped my arms around them as I peered around the room and tried to work out what bothered me so much about the space.

Fatigue and fear tried to shut my mind down, but I resolutely forced it to keep spinning. I took in everything I could about the cellar. I scrutinized every bit of minutia, from the blacked out windows to the pile of earth I could just make out in the far corner.

I gradually made out the fragrance of sulfur and herbs. I thought the air carried a hint of garlic.

A witch's lair. Or a coven. The area had the sense of space needed for many witches to gather. A flash of the images I'd seen in the flophouse lit through my mind's eye, and panic really tried to shut me down then. I knew the things the coven was capable of. I knew the horror of their magic.

Was this what those murders were all about? An entire coven trying to gather power? But what would a coven need with that much magic that they'd kill so many and so horribly?

And the ritualistic way they did so spoke more of mere spell casting. It was intentional. There was a motive beyond the power. Something they wanted that power to achieve.

The first women had been psychics. In the beginning, I'd thought then the killer was a singular individual just wanted vengeance on frauds and charlatans alike. Not now. Now, I knew they were multiple. They'd hired muscle. They'd thought those women had real gifts and wanted their power. If death magic was a 100 volt battery, then what would killing a woman of power gain them.

My breath started coming in rasps then. My lungs expanded and let go so quickly they weren't pulling in enough air. I had to calm down. I'd been afraid before when I knew I had no real gifts, but now with some strange magic moving through me, what kind of amperage would I offer? The horror of the other murders promised more and worse for me if they discovered I harbored some power.

In the moment, I really cursed my mother and her relics. Without them, I might still be a fraud with nothing to offer a power-hungry black coven.

I bit down on my tongue. Hard. I concentrated on the sounds of floorboards creaking above me. The noise of a television blaring too loudly to be entertaining someone. It was turned up loud enough to drown out the sounds of whatever else was going on upstairs.

The air felt electric, too, the longer I sat there. The tattoos that trailed up my arms and across my chest began to tingle. Even my skin drew tight against my flesh, making me feel as though I was a living lightening rod.

I couldn't just sit there, I knew. I had to try to find a way out.

I dropped my feet down onto the floor, feeling around for anything that might grab me: a trap meant to alert the man above that I was on the move. Nothing fetched up into my foot except the leg of the bed. Emboldened, I stood and took a deep breath. I inhaled more sulfur than was comfortable for my lungs and I coughed. Twice.

My entire body felt like a Christmas tree lit by hundreds of tiny lights. With my hands out in front of me, I started mapping the basement, counting my steps as I went, noting how long it took to move from one end to the other. I shuffled slowly at first then confident, I stepped up the pace.

A furnace of some sort hunkered in one part of the basement. Cold to the touch, I knew it hadn't hummed with life or warmth for some time. Around its base, I thought someone had placed foliage of some kind. I knelt and with tentative fingers sought what my legs had brushed against.

Bushy and dry, the boughs released a distinct scent, even if it was faint. Yew, I thought. One of my foster parents in the Canadian Maritimes had several arranged in a border along their property and I knew the peculiar odor it emitted.

I stood and swung around, better able to see now that I'd traversed most of the room. With careful, measured steps, I cataloged the area in case I had a chance to escape.

One part of the room harbored a stronger scent of sulfur than the rest. In that space, the air felt smothering. I could barely breathe for several steps and then the air whooshed in like a draft through an open window. My tattoos burned. I sucked in a breath against the pain.

Chest heaving, I spun in place and considered the area again. It was just a bit of burning after all. I didn't think I'd done any real harm since the markings across my chest cooled along with the air.

Mind made up, I stepped into the void again and stood there. The longer I held my position, the greater the pain. I grimaced and breathed in quick, shallow inhalations as long as I could stand it. I thought I couldn't bear moment to moment as the pain intensified, but I was determined to remain put. There was power there. Power I might be able to harness the way I'd harnessed the magic of the grimoire. Maybe the damn magic could be a gift and not a curse under the right circumstance.

Just when I thought I couldn't stand one more second, I caught sight of shadows moving along the wall. I sucked in one more breath, my mouth pursed against the scream of pain doing its best to escape my lips. My nostrils whistled as I hauled in air.

And then I saw them. Four of them. All women. All familiar looking.

Here in the basement, they were whole. Their bellies were not sliced open or stuffed with herbs and statues. Their cheeks and foreheads wore no numbers written in their own blood.

They were mournful looking, but otherwise unaccosted. They'd told me weeks ago, when I'd pretended to go into a trance the day Layne and I met, that they were waiting for me.

They waited no longer. All three psychics from the docks and Iris, the psychic who welcomed me when I'd moved home were coming for me.

But it was Iris who stepped from the shadows and reached for me.

Chapter Twenty-Five

A DEAD WOMAN SHOULD not be able to touch the living, but Iris's fingers brushed against my cheek with a solidity that belied the spectral fingers. I shrieked and jumped backward, out of the perimeter of the ring of power.

The other women eddied together as if to defend themselves from some threat, but when I didn't do more than stare at them, they relaxed. I relaxed. Iris looked over her shoulder at them. Their mouths opened and closed, hands moving in time. Talking, I realized.

"What?" I demanded in a whisper. "What's going on? I can't hear you. Please."

Iris swung her gaze to mine and for a second, I did see the empty eye sockets her killers had left her with, then the image was gone and she was just Iris again. She spoke, silent words moving across lips that couldn't form sound. I shook my head. She didn't know I couldn't hear.

"I can't hear you," I said again because I wasn't sure she had caught my comment earlier. "I'm sorry."

She looked sad and confused. I don't know if as a ghost she actually felt the emotions, but she delivered the expressions clearly enough that I got the sense that in the afterlife, she still understood the subtleties of emotive expression.

The hair I knew was always styled in a nice bob moved from some invisible breeze. She tucked it behind her ear so it wouldn't blow in her face but pieces caught in her mouth. I was afraid she'd blow away, a wisp in whatever air currents she lived on.

"Please," I said. "What do you want me to know?"

It felt so ludicrously like the séances I'd faked for years that I bit down on my tongue out of embarrassment. A sharp sob of humiliation and frustration escaped me.

Iris stepped closer. This time she pointed to the floor a few inches in front of her and between us.

I looked down at my feet but saw nothing but the dank cellar floor. There were shadows, of course, the way a gravelly basement might have but I couldn't see anything worth looking at.

"There's nothing there." I spread my arms wide in frustration.

She rushed me then, and I gasped as I felt her go through me. Then a hard push came from behind that I shouldn't have felt moved my feet forward. I stumbled and fell to my hands and knees on the cracked and cold floor.

That was when I saw the blood. It stretched out all around me in dried and crackled markings that extended a few feet around me in every direction. A circle, I thought. And I couldn't see it earlier because the blood was old and black the way it gets when it's oxidized.

I looked up to ask what it meant, but Iris and the others were gone. What they'd wanted me to see, I'd found. They either expected me to comprehend the magnitude of its meaning or they'd simply lost the power to stay with me. I had to be grateful for what I got. It probably cost them much energy to find me here in the place they'd obviously been murdered.

I made myself get to my feet and retrieved the lamp from its wobbly table so I could sweep the floor with its light. In the bald illumination of incandescence, the blood and the breadth of the circle was much clearer.

The diameter had to be three full feet. The thickness of the outline indicated someone had used a brush of some sort to paint the floor with blood. I wasn't foolish enough to think the witch who'd done it would use a household paint brush. She'd have used her own, one made of materials she'd spelled and assembled. Everything would have been done to some black recipe, with nothing left to chance.

In the world of magic, everything had meaning.

Just like the circle itself. It wasn't a plain geometric symbol. Someone had taken great care in drawing a massive Hecate's wheel.

Seeing it made my chest ache. That blood was Iris's or some other psychic I had met. That symbol, my symbol, the one I'd taken as my signature logo and found on the wall in the flophouse was right there at my feet.

I dropped to my knees, thinking to scrub the floor of the blood and clean away the awfulness done to those women. Hair, nails, skin, all those things were important to magic, they bound magic and reality together. What would blood do to a spirit? Surely it was the reason those poor women were still here, bound to this horrible place. I owed them some closure.

At the first touch of my fingers to the blood, my chest burned. Then the tattoos started to sting. Then my entire arms began hurting

A trail of fire lit itself along my arm all the way from my collarbone to my wrists. I might have cried out but I couldn't be sure, because in the next instant, I was standing on the side of the room, watching several women and men chanting around a circle. The air between us felt stagnant and hot. Candles burned everywhere. Black ones melded into white, their flames joining as they died down to stubs of wax and oil. They'd been at it, whatever it was, for a long while.

The air smelled of sulfur. Protective, stinking sulfur, cloaking their spells and their magic from those who would stop them. I held my breath at first, but realized when none of them turned to look at me, that I was cloaked as well from their eyes.

Except they weren't there. Not really. It took me moving from my corner toward them to understand what this was, was a shade of things already done. The room had held onto the memory of the witchcraft the way a body holds onto old hurts. They'd bruised this place with their magic and whatever power I had in me was letting me access that pain.

And it was painful. I felt it in my marrow like a toothache.

They had already done their worst to three women. Their victims lay atop an altar of herbs and flowers. Several dead dogs lay nearby, their throats cut.

I knew at once that the three women were the first I'd seen when Layne had rushed my store. They waited for me here, knowing I'd come. Knowing I'd see this and know the faces of the witches who had harmed them. It would only be later that they'd be strung up on the pier.

I rounded the circle slowly, watching the faces of the witches, studying their features as they murmured their spells. I kept my gaze from the floor and the women laid out as sacrificial lambs for the sake of the things the witches sought.

The living me would have gagged at the sight of the women, but the spectral mnemonic me watched impassively as the coven lifted their hands in the air in unison. They were naked, I noticed for the first time, and the skin of their flesh was riddled with moles and warts that faded and grew as the chanting rose and died and rose again. Skin wrinkled and sagged and renewed itself as the incantations rose. As the crescendo of voices peaked, cloaks and hoods rose from the floor behind them to shroud their naked flesh.

I walked the circle slowly, intent on burning their features into my mind. I'd make them pay for the things they'd done. I took my time and studied each face, each hooded head. I was surprised to discover they weren't all women. At least half were men.

I was at the last figure, a man whose face I could barely make out in the shadows. He kept averting his gaze from the grisly scene at his feet. His incantations weren't as loud as the others. He didn't seem to have memorized the spell quite right, and caught himself now and again the way a fan at a rock concert sings aloud a song they don't know all the words to.

I halted next to him and leaned in. I knew he couldn't feel my presence. He couldn't see me or hear me. I felt safe in my bubble of time. These things had already happened and horrible as they were, I was in no immediate danger.

Just when I thought I might be able to see his face, a noise in the corner behind me caught my attention. I glanced behind me and started at what I saw in the shadows.

Two shrouded figures stood there, weaving side to side as though caught up in the music of their spell. I had a faint glimmer of recognition. The set of shoulders or the turn of head, something fetched up on my memory as though it had stubbed its toe but before I could process it, the figure began to change.

The wolf took his form with painful snapping of bone and popping of sinew and in moments, the largest wolf I'd ever seen lingered at the edge of the circle before it loped for the foot of the stairs.

It disappeared up the treads in a roar. A door broke somewhere above me.

Guarding, I guessed. Guarding the witches who were calling to something dark with their magic.

I turned back to the coven, sensing the casting was coming to a close.

The man I stood next to was looking directly at me.

And I knew him. I knew him because he'd broken into my shop and accused me of being a fraud. He'd tried to yank my amulet off my neck.

I made a sound, and even as it escaped me I tried to reason that he couldn't see me. None of them could see me because this was not happening in real time.

But he reached for me as though he could and when he touched my cheek, I let go a scream.

Everything went to chaos then. As one, the coven turned to look at me. Their eyes glowed red as the blood covering their chests and legs. A clap of thunder rent the room and everything twisted like a bad movie rendition of an acid trip.

I staggered backwards and fell against the stairs. The force of the fall knocked my head against the hard edge of a stair tread and I slid down the risers to the floor and slumped sideways. I couldn't move. No matter how hard I tried to lift a hand or roll over, I couldn't move.

The room shimmied back to darkness overlaid with the weak glow of a dime store lamp. It sat where I'd left it on the floor.

I breathed a sigh of relief. I was back to my time. Back to my present. In a dank and bloody basement, yes, but out of reach of the black coven.

It took several seconds for me to realize I was cold. Colder than I'd been before. And wet. Some sort of fluid was cooling on my skin and sticking to my shirt.

Shock. I thought. I was in shock. It might take a few seconds for my body to begin listening to my mind again, and I'd be patient. I'd have to be. I had a blinding headache and I had no idea if it was from the fall or from the magic.

I was still pondering the question when I felt a bit of movement twitching my fingers. One more thing to be grateful for. I hadn't paralyzed myself with the blow to the head. I lifted my hand, aiming for the back of my skull to see if I'd ended up with a big bump or a bloody weal when my arm caught the light.

It was full of blood. My whole arm. All the way to my chest, I realized when I plucked at my shirt and found it sticking to me.

The marks. They'd bled again. That was why I'd fallen. The magic was too much.

"Shit," I said. What if this kept happening and I kept losing blood. How much could a person lose before it got critical?

"Not long," said a voice from above me.

Panic shot up my spine. I peered up, expecting to see Farrel.

It wasn't the werewolf at all.

It was the shade man. The one from the coven who'd looked at me.

And he was real. And he was holding a very real blade.

"Run," he said.

CHAPTER TWENTY-SIX

THE SHADE STABBED AT me with the blade he held. He missed and the knife glittered for a second in my peripheral vision as it went past my waist. A blithering part of my mind recognized the handle. I'd held it in my hand in the flophouse. I'd dropped it into my pocket and given it to Layne, and yet there it was, impossibly sailing past me in a lucky miss.

I spun on my heel to avoid the strike and I realized the full reason he'd missed. The truth of why he'd commanded me to run.

Farrel stood behind me, arms outstretched to grab me. The detective looked predatory in the mix of light, with yellow eyes that had a sickening shade of neon to them that Layne never showed in his.

It took me a second to realize the shade man had shoved the blade into Farrel's belly. The werewolf howled.

"You," he cried out in accusation as he fell backward against the risers of the staircase. For a heart stopping moment, I stood there, watching him clutch at his stomach. His shirt was black with blood around his fingers. He dropped to his knees and struggled to get back up, all while I stood paralyzed by shock.

"You're dead," Farrel said to the shade over my shoulder.

Dead, the shade man might be but he was perfectly visible. And solid. No ghost I had ever heard of could affect the psychosocial that way. Farrel wasn't the only one who had a hard time believing what he was seeing.

But his words at least freed my legs from their paralysis. I dodged around him, aiming for the stairs. If I could make it to the steps before he got up, I might have a chance at escape.

I thought I might make it for a second, but I'd bolted too late. Farrel's hand snaked out and caught me by the ankle as I streaked by. He yanked hard, and I went down on my hands and knees, striking my cheek against the floor.

I sobbed in pain as I bit my tongue. The coppery taste of blood made my cheeks pucker. Digging my fingers into the floor, I tried to find enough traction to drag myself forward, out of his grip.

"Bitch," he said. "You made him stab me."

The groan he let go made the hair on the back of my neck crawl. When he started to drag me back toward him, I found enough energy to push my face up off the floor. The side of my cheek throbbed and I was sure I'd struck hard enough to break a tooth.

Despite the pain rattling my jaw, I twisted in a frantic move to roll over and out of his grasp before he could yank me all the way back over territory I'd gained. They were only inches of ground, but I refused to give them up.

I couldn't turn. I remained as steadfast in my prone position as his grip remained on my ankle. But at least he wasn't able to move his hand up my leg without letting go of it first. And I waited for that moment. He'd either have to let go his stomach and wound and reach for me with his other hand or he'd have to give up entirely.

Surely, he couldn't hold me indefinitely.

I dug in, throwing out my hand to the steps beside me. My fingers scrabbled over wood. Hot pain bit beneath a nail as a splinter burrowed itself in. I yanked my hand back instinctively.

"Fuck."

I lost another inch of floor to Farrel's grip as I slid backwards. My hands went out ahead of me, seeking purchase. I grabbed for anything. My palms met bare floor.

Seconds might have passed, and no more, and I knew that the only thing saving me from his strength was the wound in his stomach. It was gaining me a bit of power as it drained away his. But I knew it couldn't last.

Even so, I leaned all my torso forward, thrusting as much weight as I could, moving the fulcrum of my body more to my end. Give me just one small bit of advantage.

I was dimly aware that someone had begun to mutter behind me. There were no words that I could recognize and at first, I thought it was Farrel, but when the lyrical sound of chanting met my ears, I knew it wasn't the wolf shifter murmuring in the darkness, but the shade man.

He was casting a spell. Or trying to. I didn't dare look back to confirm it even if there was enough light to prove it. I had to keep moving forward. Forward.

"Let go," Farrel said. "I'm not going to hurt you for fuck's sake. Just let go."

He gave one more hard pull and with a grunt of effort and probably pain, he managed what I feared most. I sailed backwards on my stomach, my shirt riding up. My bare belly scraped along the floor, tearing my skin down to raw tissue. I felt the trickle of blood rise to wet my skin where the cement had scored my skin.

I cried then, helpless and terrified. My hands let go the floor and in one movement, Farrel was able to flip me over. His sticky hand went round my bare waist, partnering the unbloodied one. He leaned over me, straddling my legs.

"Got you," he said with a note of victory in his voice.

He was breathing hard and I noted he'd pulled the blade from his stomach at some point. Where it was now was anyone's guess.

"I'll stay put," I said. "I won't move. Just don't hurt me."

I ran my hand out sideways, searching for the knife. It had to be there. If he'd dropped it anywhere near, it would have to be within reach.

"I swear," I said. "Just don't hurt me."

"I'm not going to hurt you, you stupid bitch," he said. "Whatever they want you for is none of my business. I just do what I'm told."

He leaned back and I saw the depth of the damage the shade man had done to him. He hadn't just stabbed Farrel; he'd sliced across, effectively unzipping a quarter of his stomach.

"I have to change." He panted the words and I realized he knew exactly how critical his wound was. "I need to change now."

I waggled my head as I lay beneath him. "Yes, yes," I said. "I won't move."

"If you do, I'll tear your throat out, orders or not."

It was a threat I believed like a priest believed in the blood of Christ in a gulp of wine. I'd have crossed my heart to show him my sincerity but my hand was still searching for the blade and I knew I was a hair away from finding it.

He slid off me then and sank against the staircase with his back along the stringers. His legs splayed out in front of him. He lifted his chin to the ceiling and howled in agony.

The change began with a snap and crack much like a fire lighting in kindling. There was enough light cast over his form that I could see how much the shift hurt him. I had the feeling it wasn't normally so painful. Something was making it more difficult than he expected. Maybe the wound he'd suffered blocked the magic or maybe it made the change agonizing.

All I knew was I had a few seconds to decide whether my promise was one I should keep. Based on what I saw happening, his change was no less swift than Layne's had been. It just seemed far more painful. If I ran and he healed and caught up with me, I didn't doubt he'd take his vengeance even if he didn't tear my throat out.

I was crabbing my way silently backwards, my eye glued to the form that was now three quarters wolf and one quarter haunted man when the chanting in the shadows took on an entirely different timbre. In all the chaos I'd forgotten the shade man, but he stepped from the shadows once again and dropped to one knee at my waist.

Before I could stop him he splayed his hand over my breastbone. Fire lit itself in my skin. A jolt ran through me powerful enough to make my spine arch upward to meet his hand. I cried out, words in a language I'd never learned erupted from me.

In response, the wolf next to the stairs screamed. It wasn't a wolfish growl or a man's cry. It sounded like a dying rabbit, filled with high pitched terror and pain.

At nearly the same moment, the shade man lifted his hand from my chest and held it toward Farrel. A light plumed around his palm and then shot into the wolf. Farrel screamed again and writhed on the floor. His back dug into the stringers. He begged around a half-formed jowl for mercy.

"He can't change," the shade man murmured. "Your magic has him."

I scrabbled to a sitting position and rolled over to my side, keeping my eye on the shade man. By then, I didn't need much light to see everything that was happening in the basement. I could see as clearly as if it were daylight. I didn't question why. I just thanked the gods I could see.

The shade man looked the same as he had the day he'd burst into my shop, except this time, a Hecate Wheel was carved into his forehead. I was sure it hadn't been there in his lifetime.

"You'll get caught," I said. "All of you. Layne will find you and he will stop you. You'll never murder another woman or poor dog ever again."

His withered smile was more mournful than anything else. "Get up, daughter. Get up and get out while you can."

I stole a look at Farrel who was still writhing in pain, half formed, unable to become either man or wolf. A pang of pity formed in my breast for his suffering. He looked pitiful, not threatening or dangerous in the least. I wavered in my determination to flee, pondering for a second whether I should try to help him.

"I'll hold him here," shade man said. "I have enough of your magic to hold him like this, but not for long. Leave. Leave now before he is able to pull on his pack magic."

With his free hand, he pulled something from his pocket and shoved it between my palm and the floor.

My fingers curled around it. Paper of some sort. Then he stuffed something else in my pocket. I didn't bother to look. I just heaved myself to my feet.

He nodded encouragingly.

"Run," he said.

So I did. I ran up the stairs, not looking behind me. My feet pounded the treads and I threw myself against the door. With it not being shut all the way, I fell through and landed on my knees. My teeth clacked together painfully.

I scanned the area around me and realized I had landed in a long hallway. A table had been set up with a television and an arm chair. The tiles on the floor were industrial green. The walls made of block.

A school, I thought. Or a gymnasium. Didn't matter. I was getting the hell out of there. I staggered to my feet. I was on my way past the desk when I spied a cell phone. My cell phone. I'd know it anywhere from the blue and yellow mandala protective cover.

I grabbed it just as a renewed howl came from the basement. I decided to keep running, my legs of jelly barely capable of beating the path to the broad double doors a hundred yards away. I tucked the phone into my bra as I went so I could pump my arms for speed where strength might fail me.

The windows in the door had shattered in a past life, whether by some design of those who'd broke in or because of neglect. The chains holding them together clung to each other by threads of rust. However Farrel had brought me to this place, however the coven got in to meet, it had not been through these doors. I exhaled a breath of relief when a single shove burst them apart and I stepped out into the exhaust and diesel-fumed air.

Immediately, my phone began beeping and burping and pinging. The night air felt cool against my cheek and I struggled to make sense of the time difference. I'd been taken in full light of afternoon. Had I been gone a day or two? I wasn't sure, couldn't be sure because I'd been denied any sort of time piece and without a window to see the natural light shift, I'd had to guess.

It hadn't felt like two days, so I hoped it had been mere hours. I hoped Parrish had found Layne and the pings and notifications were the result of them searching for me.

I fell against the crumbling block wall, flattening myself against the support because I knew my legs couldn't carry me one more step. I swiped the screen too fast to have it register. I cursed. Tried again. This time, the screen opened up. A dozen notifications.

I didn't dally in opening them. All were from Layne. All terse.

I hit the phone icon and waited for the connection to initiate. The phone rang once before his voice clicked onto the line.

"Where the hell are you?"

I looked around me. The street lamps were dead. The parking lot, nothing but a crumbling bit of asphalt.

"Brie. Where. Are. You?"

"I don't know," I breathed into the phone.

"Doesn't matter," he said. "Turn on your location and send me what it says."

I didn't want to pull the phone away from my ear. I didn't want to lose connection to the only voice I trusted. "Talk to me," I said. "I need to hear your voice."

"It's alright, Brie," he said. "I'm here. I'll come to you. I'm already on my way. You just have to hold on long enough to—"

That was it. His voice cut off even as I hit the location icon. My phone went dead. Whatever battery power had remained in its cells had depleted.

"No," I said. "Not now."

I started to shake as I leaned against the building. I had no idea if it was cold out. I felt numb all over. I looked around me again in confusion, trying to make sense of my surroundings. My shirt clung to me in ways that made me nauseous. I'd bled all over myself, and then Farrel had done the same. I thought I would vomit at the thought of all the blood.

A door thudded open from inside, meters away from the exit where I stood. I reacted as if someone had shot me, startling like a rabbit and dropping to a crouch. Footfalls sounded inside the building, heavy footfalls accompanied by a ferocious growl.

Farrel's wolf had finally come out to play.

Chapter
Twenty-Seven

Farrel was all wolf now, and all I could think of was his last words of warning to me should I run. He'd tear my throat out. And he wasn't joking.

There was no way I could outrun a wolf. No way could I hide in plain sight from the predator's senses either. I considered lying flat on my stomach in the shadows and hoping he'd pass me by, but I knew my blood would be a beacon.

Running would only thrill his inherent drive to give chase to prey.

What I needed was a plan. I had to be smart if I was going to survive this.

Too bad my brain wouldn't cooperate.

The footfalls from inside grew closer. My breathing grew more rapid the longer I hung there trying to formulate the smartest move with a brain so fogged up with fear I was sure it was condensing on my synapses.

It took a roar too close to the door for my comfort to finally free my feet. Brain be damned.

I ran. With the thrust I gained from a sudden sprinter's lunge, I bolted in whatever direction my feet were already aimed in. My arms pin wheeled as I floundered in the first three steps. I nearly fell. I choked and drove myself on until I gained a steady rhythm to my pace.

By then, the wolf in the abandoned gymnasium had reached the double door exit and had come snarling through it. I was several feet away already, but I didn't need to look to confirm it. I heard the doors bang open and strike the block walls on either side.

The growl that erupted from his throat ripped the air behind me. Shivers traveled my spine.

My legs were rubber and I had no idea how I kept going on muscles that fought my every step. Sheer will was all I had. I pulled energy from the kid I once was, fueling myself with the old fear and stubborn will to make my way no matter what happened.

I kept running. Pumped my arms. Threw one foot out in front of me and followed it with another. I kept telling myself I would make it. I wasn't going to die this way. In the middle of a parking lot with nothing but a few dim streetlights and weed peppered asphalt for witness.

I had no idea where I was going I just knew I had to keep moving.

I was halfway across the parking lot when the adrenaline gave out. I dragged in breath after breath, but got no air. Nothing fueled my muscles any longer.

I collapsed before my legs knew they were done running. My body pitched forward as though tossed by some invisible force, and my hands came down on asphalt. Stones bit into my palms. My knees struck the far edge of a pothole.

When the rest of my body landed, I rolled forward on my planted hands, the momentum carrying me further than the place my hands had stopped. My chest slid over my forearms and came to rest on my hands. I sagged onto the pavement and sobbed into the rubble.

I'd given it my all. My all was not good enough. I flattened against the pavement simply because there was no juice left in my body to hold myself up.

When the stink of fur and old sweat wavered over me, I knew he was behind me. Chest trembling, I found enough strength to roll onto my side. With a twist of my neck, I could see the hulking shadow of the wolf above me.

Farrel the wolf was not handsome. He was mangy and long-jawed. Blood still ran from his side from the wound the shade man had given him, and I guessed that whatever the ghost had done to Farrel, it was keeping him from healing the way he should. Garish yellow eyes glared at me from the black mask of his fur.

"Fuck you," I said to him. "You think I was going to just lay there like a docile bitch while you served me up to a black coven?"

He growled in response and I could swear he wagged his tail. He was enjoying this, damn him.

"Maybe you're not the killer, but you're guilty just the same," I said. "Just remember that. You are accomplice to killing half a dozen innocent people."

He advanced, one slow, deliberate step at a time. He was in no rush, despite the blood dripping from his side. He'd caught me but he wasn't going to make his attack quick. I didn't think he would kill me but he would do his best to maim me. Whatever the coven wanted me for, it was clear by my abduction that they did want me. And alive.

If it was just for sacrifice to amplify their own power, he wouldn't flat out kill me. He's save that for the witches.

Gravity rolled me the rest of the way to my back. Let him come, I decided. I wouldn't entertain him any longer with my fear.

There was a moment when I expected him to leap on me, but instead, I heard him snuffling forward. Those precious moments when anything was possible gave me time to think. My brain unglued from all the gelatinous fear that held me in its grip. Now that I had accepted what was coming, now that I knew I wouldn't die—at least not yet—the panic evaporated.

Facts began to leak through the miasma, facts that I'd missed before because I'd been too busy doing, running, and living to see them for what they were.

Inside my prison, the shade man had confessed to using my magic to hold the pack powers at bay and keep Farrel from fully shifting and attacking me.

My magic. Not the coven's.

My magic had shown me Iris, and it had allowed her to communicate with me.

My magic had zapped me silly in my store, when all I'd done was touch the markings that had appeared on my skin the night I'd gone to the flophouse. My magic had brought me to the flophouse in the first place and showed me the murders.

I had magic. As shocking as the truth was, I knew it had to be true. Maybe I'd possessed it all along and circumstances had brought the powers out into the open. Maybe it had been lurking beneath the surface of my consciousness, buried during the times I'd watched my mother sacrifice innocent puppies and stray dogs in our basement.

What had brought about the spontaneous eruption of power had to be connected to the homicides. The specters of the first murdered psychics had visited me the day Layne found their bodies and chased me to the pier. The black dog had appeared the same day. The grimoire, the amulet, the shade man. All those things were connected.

And they tied me somehow to the powers that had brought me to the flophouse and tattooed runes on my skin. Whether innate, inherited or borrowed, magic resided in me. All I had to do was call out to it.

The shade man had known it and he'd accessed the magic through the same runes that had blasted me into a near coma.

It would cost me if I used it, I suspected that much. If I found the courage to use it, the magic would cost me dearly.

But what choice did I have? Dying at my own hand seemed imminently better than at the hands of a coven that would use me to ramp up their own powers. Without hesitation, my hands burrowed up beneath my shirt as I lay on the cold pavement. Before the wolf could come within one more foot, I laid my palms down on my chest and touched down where my skin was already tingling.

At first, nothing happened and I sobbed out loud. I thought I heard the wolf laughing and I rolled sideways, feeling the dig of something in my pocket. The knife.

The blood, I realized. He'd used my blood to access my magic. Each time I'd been able to do the same, the marks had bled.

If it was the ignition I didn't want to chance not having enough to turn the key and ignite the magic. I dug through my pocket and extracted the blade. Even as the wolf prowled closer, I bit down on my lip and forced myself to run the blade over my arm, high up, hoping I missed any critical arteries.

The sting of the blade biting down into my flesh tore a scream from me, but it did more too. The marks seared into me, drilling down into my core. The magic hurtled forward at my bidding. I gasped in pain and my spine arched upward in reflex.

The wolf at my feet paused. It sensed the shift. Maybe it smelled the magic. I knew I smelled it. Filled with sulfur and the pungency of rosemary and thyme, it swelled around me.

A scream erupted from me as something tore from my chest and burst into the air above me. A black shadow bloomed upward and shook itself into the shape I recognized from the back alley of my shop.

I had time to recognize the black dog in the shape that threw itself at the wolf. The snarls that erupted around me, the pained yelps and howls, I didn't try to differentiate from the other.

I didn't have time. The blackness was already taking me.

I sank down into it with relief.

CHAPTER TWENTY-EIGHT

I KNEW NOTHING FOR an indeterminate amount of time.

When I woke again, I started out of reflex even before I realized arms held me pinned against a muscled chest. Then I started struggling in earnest, my arms flailing and feet kicking out at the air.

"Bastard," I said. "Layne will kill you when he finds you."

I wasn't hitting anything and slowly realized that whoever held me was holding me around the waist as we sat together on soft cushions not a stinking mattress, not the cold hardness of pavement.

I leaned into that muscled chest out of primal instinct. It was obvious I'd felt safe enough to let him hold me. He smelled of mint and when his arms tightened around me, his soothing voice caressed the air, I knew who it was.

My entire body went lax as I realized it was Layne who held me. That we were sitting on a sofa of some sort, not out in the night air with a murderous wolf at my heels.

"I might kill the bastard," Layne said, "if I knew who you were talking about."

The disorientation receded, stripping away the residual terror from the basement and later, the abandoned parking lot. The stink of blood and musk and urine evaporated as my senses acclimated to their surroundings instead of memory. The diesel fumes of the old furnace and the exhaust of passing cars was gone.

I tilted my face to his, reveling in the chiseled jaw and day old scruff.

"You came," I said. "You saved me."

I realized how much like a damsel in distress I sounded, but I didn't care. I was so glad he was there, it didn't matter.

His eyes held mine for a long moment but it was Parrish who responded. And she did so with a bitter laugh.

"He wishes he saved you," she said. "You did all that saving shit by your lone self, girlfriend. And I must say: whatever you did back there to save yourself must have been pretty damn impressive. All that blood everywhere." She gestured in a way that indicated that it had been a lot.

I eased away from Layne because his grip had grown too tight for comfort. At first, his arm tightened even more as though he was loathe to let go. Then, it relaxed and I was able to put a breath of air between us. A breath. It was all I wanted. I left my hand on his leg because the contact made me feel human.

I swung my eyes to Parrish.

She sat on an ottoman in front of us, leaning forward with her hands between her knees, her eyes piercing in their regard. I let my gaze roam the area behind her. It wasn't my apartment. Not my shop. The surroundings were too rich looking to be her apartment either.

A bedroom, I realized. A really big one. The sofa I sat on with Layne was on the far side of a sitting area that faced a broad king sized bed with black sheets and a black duvet. The walls were made of rich wood, stained with a hint of red. The flat screen television was large enough to fill half the wall across from the bed.

A desk resided on the other end, with several over-stuffed chairs, a huge bookcase filled with what looked like leather bound volumes.

"What do you mean?" I asked her.

Sitting with her back to all that masculine opulence, and facing us with a glower that would put a marine trainer to shame, she took her time answering. Her gaze flicked to Layne's and she waited, I presumed, for him to give her the go ahead to tell me what she meant by 'all that blood'.

"You are some bad ass chick," she started with and in her voice; the admiration that came through surprised me. "I thought you needed protecting. You're such a frail looking little thing. And believe me: I tried," she said and her voice faltered for a second before she caught herself and pressed on. "I tried to protect you like I promised but it wasn't just one wolf that came for you. It was three. Now, I'm pretty tough one on one, but they were cagey. Hauled you out of that store before I could get to you. Damn lipstick." She spat on the floor at her feet and Layne went rigid beside me.

"What?" she said. "It's your father's bedroom; what do you care? You're too damned uptight Layne." But she got up and pulled a tissue from the box on the table between us and bent to swipe up what looked like blood and not mucous. "I won't apologize about the lipstick, though," she said. "Nothing good ever comes from that shade of red."

"Parrish," Layne said and she shot him a look that made his chest shake. He extracted his arm from my wrist and held his hands up. "I surrender," he said. "Take your time, then."

She swung her gaze to me and I noted that there were scars down her throat that hadn't been there when we'd gone shopping.

"Near killed me," she said. "At first, I thought they were there for me, to be honest. I've made my share of enemies in the pack." She balled the tissue up in her fist. "I thought Layne's old man had finally put the hit out on me. He's certainly threatened it a few times." She chortled as though to take the sting out of the joke but I wasn't entirely sure it was a jest at all. "He'll need more than three damn wolves to take me out."

"Can you get to the blood part?" Layne said.

"You told me I could tell it my way. You'll get your turn," she said. "And then you can tell the rest how you please." She sought and found a trash can next to the television and tossed the wad of tissue at it. When it struck the edge and fell in, she continued.

"Well, since I was thinking they'd come for me, I wasn't paying attention to the bastard who rounded you up like a little filly who needed to be broke. Then I did notice, you see, because I knew the damn bastard and I knew he had a hate on for you. But by then it was too late. But at least I got one, anyway." She plucked a nasty looking knife from her boot. "I hamstrung one of them trying to get to you."

My mouth went dry as I envisioned the scene. "I heard it all," I said. "I'm so sorry."

"Girl, only thing you have to be sorry for is for that poor man's mate. She'll be tending to one cranky wolf until he can purge the silver from his system."

I must have looked bewildered because Layne broke in.

"Parrish keeps a silver blade. A kind of break glass in case of Emergency sort of weapon. Werewolves can't abide silver."

That the man wasn't dead was a strange relief, but it was also confusing. We'd been out in the open. Surely someone would have reported the fight at least. When I said as much, Layne guessed they'd blockaded the immediate area with different cars to prevent being seen by casual passersby.

"So it was preplanned," I said, wondering how they'd known I'd be at the lingerie shop at all. "And it was werewolves. You must know them." I angled my body toward Layne as the thought struck me. His father had known I was going to be at that shop. So did Parrish.

"Your father knew I was going to be in that shop," I said to Layne. I carefully avoided Parrish's eye and didn't quite meet Layne's either. "They couldn't have taken me if they didn't know I'd be there. And there was only three other people who knew. Parrish. The clerk. And your dad."

Parrish made a noise low in her throat. "It's not what you think, Brie. I didn't know those wolves. I knew Farrel well enough but he's not pack. He wasn't even a werewolf a month ago." She looked at Layne for confirmation, and I didn't miss the worried look they exchanged.

"He was human," Layne said with a short nod of agreement. "Someone turned him while I was gone."

I thought of the prick who had never liked me, the one who obviously planted my amulet at the flophouse crime scene in an attempt to frame me. I didn't feel bad for the fact he was no longer entirely human, but I did worry about who might have turned him in the first place. If it wasn't Layne's pack then someone out there wanted me dead enough to entangle a police detective.

"Maybe you can tell something from his body," I suggested and Layne and Parrish exchanged looks.

"What body?" Layne said. "He's gone. Vanished. All that's left of him is the blood you left on the pavement in the parking lot. Somehow I doubt he'll be coming in to work in the morning."

"It was my magic," I said. "I called to the dog and it came. I think it killed him."

Parrish shook her head. "Werewolves don't disappear like vampires," she said. "We leave a corpse."

"There's vampires?" I asked feeling pretty nauseous at the thought there was something else out there to worry about.

"Figure of speech," Layne said. "What she means is there was no corpse. So he had to have survived."

"Or my dog ate him," I suggested, feeling even sicker now.

"Maybe," Layne said. "But I doubt. There would be some residual evidence. And there was a blood trail leading back to the gym's basement. But he wasn't there." His fists clenched next to his sides.

"We'll get him," Parrish said. "I have his scent up my nose like bad B.O. I won't soon forget it."

"So he's still out there somewhere," I said. "Ready to pounce again."

"Him and those other three," Parrish said. "The same someone who turned Farrel would have turned them too," she mused aloud. "My guess is someone wants disposable lackeys to do their dirty work. Create a little distance between him and the crime."

"Him," I said. "You're thinking the real perpetrator is a man and not a woman."

She shrugged. "There are no alpha females running a pack."

I leaned back against the sofa, feeling spent. Farrel had said he'd been under orders, so it was clear he had to obey whoever his alpha was.

"That means there's another pack in the city?"

"Seems so." Layne didn't look pleased about the thought. "I'm not sure why a pack would be helping a coven, if this is what you say it is, Brie. A single individual has motives. Greed, lust, rage. That sort of thing. But a whole pack? Incomprehensible."

"It is one wolf, though, if you think about it." Parrish said. "Those lackeys were new but they are not individuals anymore. They are an extension of the alpha." The way she said it, I knew she was thinking about her own alpha, Layne's dad and having to take his orders.

Layne nodded. "That makes sense, I suppose."

"There's another possibility," I said, as I mused through the information. "The clerk. She knew I was there."

At the comment, Parrish bolted to her feet and prowled the room. "The bitch. She had me completely fooled."

Layne held up his hand and she stopped pacing. "Did she smell like wolf?" he asked her and she shook her head.

"Doesn't mean she didn't get paid," she growled at his patronizing look. "I'd say it's your first place to start."

I hugged myself. A place to start. It was more than we had a day ago.

"You start there," I said to Layne. "And I'll go to the shop and do some more digging. I have a task I need to finish anyway, and all this has given me some unexpected insight."

I got up, fully intending to head home, but Layne stopped me. I was glad of his hand on my waist to be honest, because getting up so quickly made my vision pool with black. I waited for the specks to disintegrate before I looked at him.

"Where are you going?" he asked.

"Where do you think?"

"Considering you've been here all night and it's not nearly 5 a.m., I don't think you'll be going to the shop right now. Your bandages will need to be changed in a few hours."

I looked down the gauze wrapped around my forearm. A small circle of red showed through.

"Fair enough. Then I need to head home to shower." I stretched. "The shop doesn't run itself and I'm not about to let you and Parrish do all the leg work. This is personal now."

Parrish shuffled in her spot, toeing the carpet with her combat boot.

"What?" I asked. She wasn't one to look all chagrined. Something was up. "Tell me."

She waited for Layne to nod at her before she approached me and passed me a piece of paper.

"Since it's personal, I think you should know we found this in your pocket."

I recognized the paper the shade man had stuffed into my fist in the basement. I took it from her and uncrumpled it.

Dizziness swam over my vision as I looked down at the face of my mother.

Chapter Twenty-Nine

THE PHOTO OF MY mother was edged in a brownish stain that looked like old blood. In the photo, she stood with three other people. The shade man was on her left. Two other women stood on her right. I recognized them from the basement and from the picture of the shade man that I'd shown Sherry.

They were the same women murdered at the flophouse.

Until that moment, I hadn't processed the faces I'd seen in the abandoned basement. I'd just seared the features into my memory. With the stress and shock and fear, my mind was working on other things, but here and now, I knew without a doubt that the coven had murdered three of their own.

"My mother knew these people," I said, catching his eye.

"Your mother knew the women Parrish has at her morgue." It wasn't a question. He and Parrish had obviously already discussed the picture while I was unconscious. They knew exactly who was in the picture. They just needed me to confirm one of them was my mother.

I swallowed nervously. "I've seen them before. They are part of the coven."

"How?" Layne asked. "How do you know? Where did you see them? When? Details, Brie."

I presumed he thought I'd seen them sometime when I was a kid but this picture was older than that.

"The visions." I closed my eyes as the scenes began working their way through my mind's eye. "I saw them in the ritual sacrifice of the three psychics when I was in the basement. They are members of the coven."

A movement that sent a waft of air over my faces made me open them, and I discovered I was looking directly into Layne's eyes. He had closed the distance between us and had his hand on the wall beside me, hemming me in.

"That photo is from at least the thirties. How could your mother be that old?"

Parrish sucked the back of her teeth. "And those women I examined were not old crones. Each of them had the skin of a thirty year old."

"I don't know," I murmured. "But that is her. And those with her are in the coven. I know what I saw." I angled the photo so it caught the light better. "My mother is no older in this photo than she was when I was a kid."

"Maybe that's what they're doing with their magic," Parrish said. "Fountain of youth. Sacrificing to some witchy god to stay young." She huffed. "Maybe someone should turn them. They might find werewolf hood less illegal."

"I doubt my mother was trying to stay young. She barely wanted to comb her hair after my dad died."

Parrish took the photo from me and looked at it. "Didn't that clerk at the lingerie shop say something about your mother? Didn't she call her a shut-in?"

"Never aged a day, is what she said," I responded thoughtfully. "Though I'm not sure about the shut-in thing. She was quite outgoing when my dad was alive. Full of life. Laughed a lot. I mean, she changed when he died, but I can't think of any reason she'd lock herself up in the house unless she was afraid of something."

"Maybe you were right, Brie." Layne started pacing the room with Parrish on his heels before she outpaced him. "It makes sense with all you've said that she was involved in the coven. Maybe she was afraid of them."

Parrish stopped short to yawn and Layne stepped on her heel. She swung at him with closed fist. He feinted. She growled. They both laughed. Uneasily, but the laugher still sounded good. Normal.

I thought about the possibility that my mother was afraid of the coven. I recalled the faces of the women and men from the abandoned basement and the way the shade man had been able to catch my eye, hold it, and then find a way to gain corporeality long enough to help me.

Daughter, he'd called me, but I knew he wasn't my father. Why he'd help me was as much as mystery as why he'd attacked me in the first place.

They had power, that was for sure. Perhaps the ritualistic sacrifices gained them all that power, but I didn't think it was all of them who had that sort of magic. It was only the shade man, a dead man, who was able to step out from the residue of an event that had already happened to gain enough physicality to affect his surroundings. The rest of them acted as they should—ignorant of my witness—because the event had already happened. It was, as Scrooge's ghost indicated, but a mere shade of things that had been.

Maybe the power, the true magic, and the real potency was with the shade man.

"You know, I can't be sure they're all bad." I paused and caught Layne's eye. "The ghost of the man you saw at my shop, the shade man. He helped me. He didn't try to hurt me. He did everything he could to keep Farrel from harming me."

It took several moments, but I filled him and Parrish in on all the things that had happened in the basement, complete with the fear I'd suffered when I caught the shade man's eye during the ritual. As I stuffed the gaps with information that made both of them fall into the nearest chair and perch there with rigid postures, I started to put together some things that I'd not been able to figure out until I spoke them aloud.

"What if some members of the coven were plants. Defectors. Spies. Something like that. What if they were trying to stop the other witches?"

Layne rocked back on his heels. "We'd have to figure out what they're after if that was the case." he said. "I can't imagine what sort of goal they'd have to kill their own. Most murders have simple motives. The killer is greedy, power hungry, enraged, or just plain insane.""

"Sacrifice," I corrected. "They sacrificed their own. And they killed the psychics, remember. Innocent people have died because of them. Your pack left a coven of witches who turned to black magic. Don't you think it plausible that some members found the magic too dark as well?"

Parrish groaned. "Oh how I long for a good old fashioned psychopath. This is getting too freaky even for me."

Layne took the photo from me and stuffed it into his shirt pocket with a heavy sigh. "Brie is right," he said.

"We have to at least start with what we know. If she says these women were in the coven, I have to believe her." He turned to Parrish who was chewing her lip thoughtfully.

"Do you have names for the victims?" he asked her.

She shrugged. "Janes and John Doe," she said. "No one claimed them."

"If they were as old as this picture indicates, maybe there is no one to claim them." He patted his pocket. "I'll go question the clerk at the lingerie shop," he said. "If she says she moved away a month or so after your mother disappeared, I'd say that's a bit too convenient."

"That bitch," Parrish said. "And to think I liked her."

I pulled to mind the faces I'd seen in the basement and couldn't find the clerk's face among them. Even so, it was prudent to check and even I knew that. I nodded, not wanting to believe it of the kind lady but not wanting to leave any stone unturned.

"I feel as though we've finally got something to work with," I said.

"They're the best leads we've had in a while." Layne smiled at me.

"I feel like it too," I said. "I'll dig through all that stuff my mom left me again tomorrow. With a fresh perspective, I might find something new."

I started looking around for my cell phone, intending to call a cab and head home so I could collapse in bed and sleep for a hundred hours.

Layne prodded me with a finger. "I think you should stay here in the guest suite until we get this all sorted. I don't think I could take another night like we just had. You need to be where I know you're safe."

All I heard in the long diatribe was that this was a guest suite. It seemed like an entire apartment to me.

Still, I wasn't about to argue. I didn't have the heart for it. And after what I'd just gone through, I was more than ready to feel safe. I nodded tiredly.

"I don't even want to argue," I said. "But someone will need to go to my apartment and pick up a few things."

"Parrish will do it," Layne said. "I'm not sure you want me picking around your unmentionables."

He didn't even try to tease me. That had to indicate the gravity of the situation. Under regular circumstances, I was sure he'd waggle his eyebrows and to suggest he was the perfect person for the job.

The kindness wasn't lost on me. I gave him a grateful smile as I sank down onto the bed. "I don't think I even have it in me to open the shop in a few hours."

The exhaustion was taking me and I thought he knew it. He bent to tug off my shoes and lifted my legs onto the bed.

"I'm sure things can wait a few hours." He signaled at Parrish over my stomach and I heard her rustling toward the door with the comment that she had the lingerie bags in her car and would bring them with her in the morning.

"Think you can sleep in one of my T-shirts for now?" Layne said. "I don't think the coven will be in a rush to do anything tonight."

"Not for weeks, actually," I said. "They cast on the waning moon." I stared up at the ceiling, bringing everything I thought I knew to mind.

I ticked one finger up over my stomach and aimed it at the ceiling. "My Hecate's Wheel amulet. The dog. The numbers on the victims. The crossroads. Her statues. The waning moon. It all ties to Hecate. How can you doubt it now? It has to be the Blackburn Cult doing all this. They are alive and well and repeating a cycle they began decades ago."

"Shit," said Parrish from the doorway. "Once again, I long for a good old fashioned psychopath."

I twisted my head to look at her. She'd gone and come back, obviously, and held onto the lingerie bag I'd dropped when I'd been abducted. I found I couldn't look at it.

"Who says they aren't psychopaths?" I said. "If they are killing as sacrificial rites to Hecate, there has to be something missing inside for sure, especially if they think they can raise someone from the dead."

Parrish rounded the sofa and leaned on the back. "Let's hope it's Prince they're trying to bring back. I miss that fucker's music. He'd be about the only person worth all this shit."

She tossed the lingerie bag onto the bed and turned to leave but Layne stopped her.

"I have one question before you go, Parrish," he said and she paused with her hand on the door knob.

He looked at me. "You said something a while ago, and I let it slide because we were busy with other things. But now I want to know. Why did you say my father knew you were at the lingerie shop?"

He stood very still, his gaze holding mine with a yellow tinge that warned me he had a good idea how I was going to explain myself.

Parrish swept past him, grabbing for his sleeve as she went by. "You already know why, Layne. Don't press it. You'll just get hurt." She clapped him on the shoulder and held his gaze for a long moment before she murmured something that sounded very motherly. I didn't catch it, but I did understand the sag that weighed his shoulders down.

His look of betrayal was absolute and I found I couldn't hold his eye any longer. It didn't matter that I'd given into his dad's suggestions out of spite for his sense of superiority. It was a betrayal and I knew it.

Parrish tugged on Layne's arm. "Come on. We have things to do today."

He blinked but swung on his heel to follow her and I was left alone in the guest suite with my own conscience and a feeling of guilt that dogged my every step.

CHAPTER THIRTY

GUILT IS A TERRIBLE thing. I suffered it in spades when I called the government on my mother after multiple attempts at running away got me nowhere. I'd learned to live with it, and it was part of the trauma I'd started seeing a therapist for in my new adulthood.

This time, this guilt, I knew I'd carry for a while until I could find a way to explain to myself why I'd let Layne's dad tempt me into buying lingerie I knew I had no plans to wear for him.

I'd ruined any chance I had with Layne because of it. But it wasn't the fact that I'd blown it with him that bothered me the most. It was the look of betrayal in his eyes when he caught mine.

That gaze kept me from sleeping after they'd left me alone in the room. No matter how exhausted I was, my brain was on overdrive, like a limb that had been sat on for too long and was prickling itself awake. The synapses were on fire.

I figured I might as well put the activity to use.

It took some doing with being so sore from the attack and then my calling to the magic. The wounds I sustained made it difficult to move smoothly or not wince when I forgot about the bandages, but I eventually shoved on my jeans under the t-shirt Layne had left me to sleep in and I scooped my shoes from the floor.

I tiptoed to the guest door and slipped out into the early dawn with my cell in my pocket, careful to keep my jacket pulled up over my chest and closed tight.

I hailed a cab at the end of the long driveway that twisted out of reach of the city streets and unfurled itself around a huge manse nestled into a copse of old growth trees that had probably been there since before the city rose up around it.

I'd had much to think about in the basement of the gym, and I'd put together a few things with the insights I'd gained in talking about the case with Layne and Parrish. Farrel had taken hair and nail clippings from my trash when he'd broken into my apartment. He wasn't a witch by any stretch, so he had to have collected them for the coven. They still had them. That meant they could and probably would weave some pretty dark magic around me.

That was a disturbing notion that ate at me, but I'd have to set it aside for the moment. No sense agonizing over something I couldn't control.

But the thought of the hair sparked another thought, and it had to do with an old lady who had come to me with a plea and a few thousand dollars and who was due to check in on me the next day to see my progress.

Before I became a victim to black magic, I had to find a way to divest her of the dark magic that was wound around her so she could take her property home with her.

I unlocked my store and crossed straight away to the death mask. It lay where I'd left it. I snapped on the overhead light behind the counter and added the little table lamp to the illumination with a snap of its on switch as well.

The mask stared at me in the golden glow with vacant sockets. The burls of the counter I loved so much showed through the holes.

"You, my lovely," I said to the mask as I lifted it from the counter. "You are chock full of magic. I should have realized it before."

It wasn't a mere haunting Maureen was suffering. There were times she felt oddly comforted by the mask, the same as I'd been during the time I'd connected with its magic while Layne and I tested it.

The old lady hadn't indicated she was a witch or that her mother was, but someone in her family certainly had power. And they'd used that power to cast a spell on the mask.

I slipped her business card out from the cash register and held it between my fingers as I one-fingered the text, telling her to come to the shop as soon as it opened.

Then I lifted the mask in both hands, holding it carefully so I wouldn't drop it. I flipped the object over and angled it toward the light. Sure enough, the filament of hair that I'd noticed the first day was still there. Like the first time, I had an incredible urge to run my finger along the strand as it showed through the plaster. I'd wanted to dig it out then, but resisted because I didn't want to ruin her treasure.

This time, I did run my finger along the shaft, and I felt several other strands beneath the surface that weren't immediately visible.

Without knowing exactly whose they were or even if they were from the same person, I was loathe to dig the strands out. I wasn't even sure if exhuming them from the plaster would be all it took to cleanse the mask of its bad juju. It was entirely possible that doing so would have effects I didn't understand. The truth was, I didn't know enough about magic to understand the consequences.

But I did know that whatever my own magic did, however it worked, it allowed me to connect with the dead. I'd seen my mother. I'd seen Sherry's father. I'd seen the shade man, and I'd seen something in this mask.

Maybe, just maybe, this one fraud could use real power to make a difference for a woman who really needed some peace.

I set the mask down on the counter again and regarded it with a thoughtful eye.

"Just you and me here," I said to the mask. "No one to help either one of us if this goes awry, and I'm sore as blazes, so be good, alright? You don't want to crack and I don't want to have to break you."

The mask kept its counsel and I sighed most theatrically as I shook my hands out. I yelped when a jolt of pain ran down my side but, determined to press on, I bit down on it.

"Bitch, bring it," I said to the plaster as I propped it up against the register, facing out. "But you are not going to catch me off guard this time."

I took great care in the preparations. Now that I knew what the runes were capable of, I was careful to treat them with respect. I put out a bowl of water to collect any wayward energies. The grimoire, I hefted in both hands, careful to hold it from the bottom, touching the cover only so I didn't accidentally set off some ingrained spell like I had before.

I brought a wet towel and a needle with me to the most comfortable wing back chair in the shop. I'd had to cut myself in the parking lot to initiate the power; it made sense that I'd have to draw blood now to use it.

Then I dragged it closer to the counter, facing the mask.

I'd already locked the door behind me since I wouldn't be open for business for another two hours.

I couldn't remember how long I'd been out before each time I'd accessed the runes, and each time seemed to be different. I hoped a few minutes at most, but I was prepared for a couple of hours.

I settled deep into the chair in case I passed out, which if history was an indication, would no doubt happen.

"Remember," I said to it. "I can break you. Now show me who you are."

I jabbed my finger with the needle and waited. Nothing happened. Safe so far. With a sharp bracing intake of breath, I shoved my hand down the collar of Layne's T-shirt, seeking the tattooed runes.

Nothing.

No wash of dizziness. No blackouts. No sizzling of magic.

I just blinked at the mask as I sat there.

"Damn," I said. I so thought I had it figured out. It was a letdown of epic proportions. I sighed in exasperation and picked up the grimoire, fully intending to heave myself to my feet and hurl the thing back on the shelf I'd taken it from.

But the moment my fingers went round the edging, all the horrible tingle of magic swept over me. I bit back a groan and had the presence of mind to burrow back into my shirt for the runes.

I no sooner touched down on them when the room went black.

This time, the mask came with me wherever the magic took me. The smell of formaldehyde and old blood wafted up my nose and then evaporated in favor of lilacs and the smell of summer air. I caught sight of a curtain of ginger hair on grass. Calico fabric spread across a soft plaid blanket. The sound of laughter rang around me. I smelled hair pomade and the aroma of expensive cigars.

Abruptly, the laughter cut off and sounded strangled. I strained to see through the haze of magic that kept me from seeing events clearly instead of shrouded in shadows. I worked to focus the power, the way I might have angled the old fashioned bunny ear antennae my grandmother kept on top of her television set.

The young girl had started to plead with her companion. The pomade smeared over young skin in a film that I was sure couldn't be seen except for here in this space. The scent intensified, overtaking the fragrance of grass and summer air.

I knew what was happening even though I wasn't really present in the moment. All I had was the filmy image and shadowed movements, but I didn't need more to understand what was going on.

I didn't register the assault on Maureen's mother the way senses normally process things. I didn't see it. I didn't hear it. I wasn't there, but I *saw* it. Felt it.

I came back to the shop with a gasp. The mask blinked at me, those beautiful amber eyes looking out with a mournful expression, I knew to be Maureen's mother.

I was vaguely aware that the sun had made thin fingers of inroads into the shop, caressing the floor while I had sat there, unmoving for what must have been a couple of hours but felt like a few moments.

Maybe I'd come back to the shop within moments from wherever the magic had taken me but I'd only just come back to my own consciousness. There really was no telling. The only other time I'd done this on my own, I'd ended up fugue walking to the flophouse.

This time, I'd done it on my own terms. No forcing of the magic. I'd given it some respect. I hoped that had made a difference.

I held my breath as I looked down at my hands, praying I wouldn't see what I suspected I'd see. My eyes closed of their own volition when I saw the blood pooled in my upturned palms. The trail started beneath the cuffs of Layne's T-shirt and I felt the dribbling of it between my breasts.

The price of the magic, I knew. I understood that now. Parrish and Layne might not believe the blood was mine, and maybe it wasn't, but someone was paying the piper. If I was suffering the first, awful sting of the price, someone else was enduring the rest of the payment while I blacked out.

But I was conscious, and the blood wasn't mine, so I knew when the dizziness and the vertigo evaporated, I could find the strength to get up and cross my shop to wash up. I waited, patiently, for those things to happen, and when they did, I sucked in a breath and did exactly that.

The water was running red beneath the tap someone knocked on the door to the shop. Maureen, I knew. I finished rubbing the water over my arms and sopped up the wet with a towel. One quick check in the mirror and I knew I'd have to pinch some life back into my cheeks.

I was peaked and sick looking but there was also a hint of victory in my eyes. I'd done it. I'd used real power the way a true witch might. A true woman of power.

Maureen looked much the same as she had the first time I'd seen her. Her perfectly coiffed bob of silver hair framed bright eyes and set off the royal purple sweater she'd pulled on over a cream colored blouse.

"I didn't expect to hear from you so soon," she said as she swept into the shop. She carefully avoided the bowl of water I'd placed on the floor as well as the bloody towel draped over the rim. I took her elbow and aimed her away from the worst of it toward the counter where the mask waited.

"I had a bit of a break through," I said and gave her a warm smile that she returned.

"You exorcised it, then?" she said.

I waggled my hand back and forth in a motion meant to say, sort of. "I'm not sure you'll want me to when you know what it's doing?"

I explained, as best I could, about her grandfather's assault of her mother. I told her how I felt her fear and inevitable surrender. It was difficult to watch her expression register all the emotions I knew were spiraling through her mind, but I kept up the recitation.

"I know why he did it," I said. "Not that it makes it any easier. Do you know much about your heritage at all? I mean, did he ever talk about his family?"

She hoisted her name brand purse higher on her elbow as she sank into one of the chairs nearest the register. She perched there and I crouched in front of her. I wanted her to understand, the way I did, about his guilt and shame, and his desperation. She'd loved the old man, I knew, and I didn't want to take that away from her.

"He came from a noble line of witches that skipped the women and went only to the third son every other generation," I told her. My thighs quaked with the effort of supporting myself under the strain of exhaustion, but I was too stubborn to sit on the floor. "I believe he was desperate. He was old as you know by the time your mother was a teen. His own wife dead in childbirth, the same as your mother."

She nodded. "I know this. I hope I didn't pay you to tell me things I already know."

"Right," I said. "But what you don't know is he felt he had very little time left to him. Without a son, he took the last, desperate step that he could think of to save his lineage. "

She harrumphed and glared at the mask as though it was her grandfather staring back at her. It was, in a way.

"He hated himself for what he'd done to her," I said. "He ached with guilt and shame every time he looked at her afterwards. Her age left her confused and afraid and ashamed. And when he avoided her out of guilt, whatever faith in herself that had begun to bloom in her withered.

"But you changed him. You, the unfortunate girl-child instead of the son who could carry the powers of his DNA, you changed the old warlock. You brought out a softer man, one who came to believe his powers should die with him because they had made him do vile things in order to keep them. He believed that any magic that required such a revolting sacrifice should be left to wither."

She dug a tissue from her purse and dabbed delicately at the corners of her eyes. "So the mask?" she said. "It's him? If it is, I want it destroyed."

There was anger in her voice and I didn't blame her. I nodded in understanding.

"It is him," I said. "And it isn't. He couldn't part with the daughter he loved so much, the one he killed with his own fears. The innocent girl whose childhood he'd stolen. He wanted her to have the chance to live on. He thought he owed it to her to watch you grow to a woman. It was the least he could do."

I told her then how I'd watched him craft the spell as he mixed the plaster for the mask. He burned sulfur to protect the weaving while he tugged several strands from his daughter's gingered head.

"He found a dog wandering his property," I told her, in a sign that he was doing the right thing after all, using his magic for a good thing, a labor of love in the end. He tempted the poor thing with deer meat for two whole days to his doorstep. The mangy thing was on its last legs, and the last meal he offered it was a compassionate offering. He was convinced it was meant to be.

"You were born two days before a waning moon," I said although I didn't expect her to be able to confirm it. "He saw that too, as fortuitous. He sacrificed the poor beast on an earthen altar he built at the end of his driveway just outside the gardening shed, creating a makeshift crossroads of sorts to intensify the magic. Then he called to the goddess Hecate to bind the spirit of his daughter to the mask as he smoothed the plaster over her face."

"So it's my mother?" she said, this time her expression softening as her gaze flicked back to the mask. "The eyes watching me are my mom's?" she hugged herself and the purse fell sideways against the arm of the chair.

"It's her and it's him," I said. "Some of his own hair got caught up in the spell. He didn't plan it. It just happened."

She nodded. "That explains a lot."

"Do you want me to exorcise it? You could just break it, I think. That should effectively separate the mask from the soul, but I'm not so sure what will happen to them without proper transference. You might need a spell for that. I can keep working if you like, and do that for you."

She shook her head. "No." She sighed and pushed herself to her feet and crossed the room to place both hands on the mask, splaying her fingers along the cheeks. "I will keep it as is. It's a comfort to think it's my mother watching me. I think she must enjoy seeing me live." She swung around to face me, the mask left on the counter. "I would, however, like to will the mask to you if you don't mind."

"Will it to me?"

"Yes. I'd hate to think of my mother trapped here indefinitely when I'm gone, with no reason to stay. I don't think my son will be interested in such a thing, and though she might want to watch her own grandchildren, I couldn't be sure of her safety in clumsy hands."

She didn't have to explain she thought clumsy hands meant unbelieving hands.

I ran my hand along the counter, holding her eye so she'd see I was sincere. "I accept. And I'll find a way to release him and her both when the time comes."

She barked out a harsh laugh. "Him? I don't care what happens to that old bastard. Release my mother. That's all I ask." She dug into her purse and pulled out another wad of bills, the same as the last.

"I will leave payment for the final spell with the lawyer."

"You've already paid me more than enough," I said and she held up a softly veined hand.

"It may take you months or years to accomplish that," she said. "It's important to me. I want it done."

She waited for a moment, hesitant, it seemed to be done with it all. But then, with a sigh, she lifted the mask again and held it cradled against her chest. "Damn good thing it got stored so long and didn't get broken." She smiled broadly, showing unusually white teeth for her age.

She refused my offer of a bag to keep it safe as she traveled, and with a slip of a smile, left the shop with a tinkle of the bells above.

I stood there for a long moment, watching the door, knowing that I'd done something good with the magic. Not all magic had to be bad, I realized. It didn't have to hurt or harm. The magnificence of it possessed its own sort of power, tied it to a voltage the black coven would never know because their notion of power was built on negative force. It was selfish and shadowed.

I thought of my own mother as I stood there. She'd been a good mother once. Kind. Loving. Her transformation to a witch obsessed with death was proof that black magic robbed power not granted it.

I wasn't convinced anymore that she was a grief-crazed woman trying to raise her dead lover from the grave and traumatizing her daughter because of it. This new image of my mother, of her being a possible hero trying to stop a black coven from doing unmentionable things to innocent people soothed the restless child within. My therapists would be proud of the progress.

But while the inheritance my mother left me, of magic and relics and familiars might have given me a new perspective on a woman I wanted to love and forgive, it put me in that same black coven's line of fire.

And if the witch who possessed it all wasn't able to stop the Cult of Blackburn, how in the world would a reformed charlatan?

-the end for now-

***

Don't stop now. You'll miss the best parts. Get your copy of Ritual Magic

Have you got your free ebook yet?

Be sure to visit http://theaatkinson.com to get your freebie.

WHAT'S NEXT?

Not sure where to go from here?
Check out these series for more action-packed,
kick-ass chicks fiction in any of these series:

THE IRON KING'S ASSASSIN

ISABELLA HUSH SERIES

COUNTERFEIT PSYCHIC

WITCHES OF ETLANTUM

VAMPIRE ADDICTIONS

REAPERS REDEMPTION

GRAVES FILES

ROGUE HUNTRESS

THETA WAVES

QUEEN OF SKY AND SHADOW

About Author

Thea is a NEW YORK TIMES and USA TODAY Bestselling Author. She used to have a black lab at her feet when she wrote, warming up the calves. It can be cold in rural Nova Scotia. Now it's just a cuppa tea keeping her warm.

Whether she's finding ways to lure Isabella Hush into the Shadow Bazaar or throwing the switch on a new monster, her urban fantasy pulses with dark themes and action-packed intrigue. Her characters are always deeply wounded creatures struggling for redemption. The romance is slow-burn but worth it, and the humor just might have a touch of Canadiana.

As a fan of Dannika Dark and Patricia Briggs, she hopes you enjoy slipping into the skin of her characters as much as she enjoy theirs.

Hang out with her on the socials like Instagram, Tik-Tok, and Facebook

Author Thanks

Several loyal readers have special places in my writer's heart. Some of them, like Caroline Jenkins and Denise Sherman always take the time to find my little oopsies and sometimes my big ones. An author needs readers like that.

Then there's readers like Crystal Crystal Amason, who isn't just a reader, she's a sponsor, and you don't get more loyal than that. She is the first reader to make me feel like my tales were worth reading. Thank you, Crystal. I hope I can continue to write stories you enjoy.

To my other patrons who prefer to remain anonymous, I thank you. You know who you are.

I really appreciate you all.

-thea-

9 780099 214 8935